"It's Time for us to Talk,"

Kirk said.

"There's nothing to talk about."

"Oh, yes, there is. There's a great deal. I demand to know what possessed you to run away from our home, Lilly."

"I don't know why it matters so much to you." Her voice was brittle.

"Don't be childish. Of course it matters to me."

"Oh, yes. I suppose it would in the sense of your swollen ego losing a prize possession, such as one of your race horses running off."

"That's a callous thing to say."

"No more callous than you marrying me when you didn't love me!"

PATTI BECKMAN
and her husband, Charles, have enjoyed playing jazz together since the time they met. Patti has drawn from her own experiences and enthusiasm to describe the Bourbon Street scenes in *Tender Deception*. One of Silhouette's most popular writers, this is Patti's second Special Edition.

Dear Reader,

Silhouette Special Editions are an exciting new line of contemporary romances from Silhouette Books. Special Editions are written specifically for our readers who want a story with heightened romantic tension.

Special Editions have all the elements you've enjoyed in Silhouette Romances and *more*. These stories concentrate on romance in a longer, more realistic and sophisticated way, and they feature greater sensual detail.

I hope you enjoy this book and all the wonderful romances from Silhouette. We welcome any suggestions or comments and invite you to write to us at the address below.

Karen Solem
Editor-in-Chief
Silhouette Books
P.O. Box 769
New York, N. Y. 10019

PATTI BECKMAN
Tender Deception

Silhouette Special Edition

Published by Silhouette Books New York
America's Publisher of Contemporary Romance

SILHOUETTE BOOKS, a Simon & Schuster Division of
GULF & WESTERN CORPORATION
1230 Avenue of the Americas, New York, N.Y. 10020

Distributed by Pocket Books

ISBN: 0-671-53561-7

First Silhouette Books printing December, 1982

10 9 8 7 6 5 4 3 2 1

Map by Ray Lundgren

SILHOUETTE, SILHOUETTE SPECIAL EDITION
and colophon are trademarks of Simon & Schuster.

America's Publisher of Contemporary Romance

Printed in the U.S.A.

Other Silhouette Books by Patti Beckman

NEW ORLEANS AND VICINITY

MISSISSIPPI

LAKE PONTCHARTRAIN

MISSISSIPPI SOUND

New Orleans

LOUISIANA

N
W E
S

GULF OF MEXICO

Chapter One

The desert at midday had become a boiling cauldron. The lone figure stumbling in the vast expanse of barren sand and scrubby cactus amounted to no more than a crippled insect in a hostile world.

Blonde hair that had once been lank and silky was matted with blood. Delicate features had been smashed and bruised beyond recognition. Nothing remained to hint that the battered creature had once been a beautiful woman—or even a woman at all. It was a scarecrow, a bloody caricature of a human being.

Pain that had raged agonizingly through her body had been numbed by impulses released by a brain that had passed the point of endurance. Blankness now stilled the mind. Only a faint animal instinct of survival, glimmering like a half extinguished spark in the primeval brain stem kept her rubbery legs moving in their swaying, tottering motion.

She fell, sprawling as she had fallen countless times before in the past twenty-four hours, grinding sand into raw wounds. She lay utterly motionless. Above, in the cloudless blue sky, buzzards wheeled in a graceful ballet of death. They circled ever lower until the loathsome creatures settled on the sand with a rustle of black wings.

The natural harmony of the primitive setting was disturbed by a discordant note from the twentieth century. A rusty pickup truck appeared over a distant rise.

Henry Brownfeather gripped the steering wheel with work worn hands; the flesh had long ago hardened into horn-like calluses. He was pursuing a line of thin, faint tracks that snaked across the desert toward a mesa in the hazy distance. He slammed a heavy, booted foot on the clutch and rammed the floor shift from gear to gear with a rasping screech of metal to jockey the bouncing truck through arroyos and over sand dunes.

A day's hard work doctoring his cattle had left a film of sweat and dust on his lined, bronze face. He was on his way home to the pueblo high atop the mesa. His mind was not on his day's work or his driving. His thoughts wrestled with the problems of his family—his daughter, Raven, and his son, Luke, both of them grown now, and causing him sleepless nights.

When he thought about his children these days it was not so much with feelings of concern as bafflement. Especially the girl, Raven. She brought mixed feelings to his heart, ranging from pride to disappointment. Like so many of the young people these days, she had turned from the old ways to the white man's culture. She dressed like the people in the city and spoke of things he didn't understand. The change had come over her since she had gone to college in Albuquerque. At first he had been proud that one of his children would get a higher education, but it had made them strangers.

He preferred to remember when she was one of the brown urchins in the pueblo, chasing the dogs, playing the children's games in a high, carefree voice, climbing on his lap when he came home from a hard day's work. Now they had become self-conscious and awkward with each other. He felt a sullen resentment at the change, believing that she had grown to secretly scoff at the old ways of her people.

Luke, his son, was different. Luke made him angry sometimes, chasing around with his friends, driving the truck into town on Saturday nights to dance and drink beer. But Luke, he could understand. He could remember the wildness of his own youth. Luke did not have the complex, white man's kind of thinking that had entered Raven's mind. In time, if he didn't break his fool young neck, Luke would settle down, marry, and be content to take his rightful place in the tribe.

Henry's thoughts were interrupted when he caught sight of the buzzards. His truck bouncing by frightened them, and they took to the air with an awkward flutter of black shadows. He hated buzzards. He was certain they carried the spirit of death from the underworld.

He glanced briefly at the figure beside the dirt tracks, the dead or near-dead thing that had attracted the buzzards. It could be a neighbor's calf down. His heavy foot hit the brake, causing the rusty old truck to come to a slow, shuddering halt.

He swung out of the cab, slamming the door behind him with a metallic bang. A frown crossed his stolid features. He crouched beside the prone figure, thoughtfully coming to grips with an unexpected situation that had been thrust upon him.

The creature sprawled before him was unrecognizable as an individual. But he could determine that it was a woman—a white woman. And that raised serious concerns. What was a white woman, so badly injured, doing alone out here in a remote desert area of an Indian reservation?

He contemplated the unconscious woman for several moments, his mind proceeding in a characteristically careful, plodding manner, laying out the situation like sticks in a row. His keen-eyed gaze left the unconscious woman and surveyed the area carefully. On one horizon rested the hazy outline of a far-distant mountain range, the sacred place where the ancient gods of his tribe's ancestors lived. On another horizon was the flat-topped mesa, the home of his Pueblo tribe that had lived there in the adobe city high in the sky for centuries, even before Coronado had come with his clanking Spanish armor in quest of the seven cities of gold.

Except for the buzzards circling above and a brown lizard scurrying across the hot sand, there was no other sign of life. A dust devil whipped across the land, sucking up its funnel of dust and then faded away, leaving only an eerie stillness.

Henry Brownfeather stared at the woman again. He saw the gleam of gold and diamonds on her wristwatch, and on one swollen finger was a ring set with a large diamond. So, she was a person of wealth. And she was not the victim of a robbery.

Too much puzzling about a thing made Henry Brownfeather weary. He was a man of action. There was only one thing to do. He could not leave the woman out here to die.

Reality came back to her in snatches, like shadowy glimpses through a dense fog. She was aware of brown, solemn faces looking down at her, then they dissolved. Another time she realized she was looking up at a ceiling the color of the earth. A touch of color, the red and brown zigzag pattern of a blanket on a wall beside her bed caught her eye, then faded away as the fog closed in.

Pain came back in acid waves that caused her teeth to grind. She would be freezing cold, shivering with a chill that shook the bed, and she would feel heavy blankets piled on her. Then, she would thrust the blankets away as fever raged through her body.

When the fever came, the grotesque figures and shapes of delirious hallucinations danced around her, taunting her.

Sometimes a different kind of face looked down at her through the fog—a white man's face, his eyes thoughtful and compassionate. She came to associate the man's face with a respite from pain. When he was there, something would prick her arm, and she became drowsy and comfortable, sinking into a deep, dreamless sleep from which she had no desire to return, but return she would, eventually.

Other times, she would look up to see the face of a lovely young woman who had hair and eyes as dark as midnight and hands that touched her gently, bathing her bruised body with tender care.

"How do you feel today, Lilly?"

The voice penetrated the fog, dispersing it. The kind face of the white man was in sharper focus. The beautiful dark-haired girl stood behind him, also looking at her.

"Well, I do believe you are with us today, Lilly," the man smiled. "Your eyes are much clearer this morning. Do you think you can answer me?"

Her tongue touched her swollen lips. She made an attempt to speak and heard a croak. She swallowed hard and tried again. A strange, rasping whisper totally unfamilar to her came from her lips. "Why do you call me 'Lilly'?"

"Isn't that your name? We found a gold locket on you with your picture. The locket is engraved, 'To Lilly With Love,' and the letter 'J.' We assumed that must be your name."

The man held the heart-shaped locket for her to see. It brought a curious rush of emotion to her throat. A tear trickled from her eyes. She didn't know why the locket made her want to cry. Her mind felt stuffed with cotton. She was becoming very weary. She didn't want to think anymore. She closed her eyes and drifted back to sleep.

Once, she awoke and there was no one else in the room. She gazed around, her befuddled mind trying to find some familiar object. She saw a square window, and through it distant sunset behind a mountain range. The room was small, plain, bare. The walls appeared to be made of earth or clay. Except for her bed, there were some rustic, hide-bottom chairs with ladder backs and a table. On the wall was the blanket with the curious zigzag pattern. On the windowsill was a yellow flower in a pot that was decorated with a similar zigzag design along with other strange symbols. Nothing about the place was familiar to her; she was in an alien world.

Painfully, she reached up to touch her face and encountered gauze. Except for her eyes and mouth, her face was swathed in bandages.

A figure entered the room through the low doorway. It was the dark-haired young woman.

"Where is this place?" the injured woman asked in her hoarse whisper.

The dark-haired girl drew one of the chairs closer and sat beside the bed, her hands folded in her lap, her eyes intense and searching. "This is an Indian pueblo village, Lilly. You are in the home of the Brownfeather family. My father found you unconscious out in the desert over a week ago. My name is Raven."

"A *week* ago?" She looked at the young Indian woman with a feeling of consternation.

"Yes. You've been in a coma part of the time, and delirious. But you do seem to be coming out of it now. Your fever is gone and you look much better. Do you feel like talking?"

"I—I think so."

"Don't tire yourself. If you start feeling tired, just close your eyes and go back to sleep. The doctor says you must rest a lot."

"Doctor?"

"Yes, Dr. Glenn Marshall. He's been taking care of you. He lives in town, but he comes to the village to take care of sick people when we need him. By the way, 'Lilly' is your name, isn't it? That's what we've been calling you."

The injured woman frowned, struggling with her own confusion. "I—I'm not sure. It does sound kind of familiar."

Raven looked at her curiously. "You're not sure?"

"I—I feel kind of dazed."

"That's understandable. You were more dead than alive when Dad found you. Dr. Marshall said you were suffering from exhaustion and exposure, not to mention sunburn, shock and countless bruises. Do you remember what happened to you?"

The woman shook her head.

"Maybe you can tell me your last name. If you have a family, I'm sure they should be notified."

The woman could only look at her with a helpless expression, tears gathering in her blue eyes.

Raven patted her hand. She adjusted the blanket. "Well, don't worry about it now. Dr. Glenn said it will all come back to you. For now, we'll call you Lilly and let it go at that. Okay?"

She nodded, repeating the name to herself, knowing that it must be her name yet finding no clear link between it and conscious memory. "Lilly," she thought. "I am Lilly. But 'Lilly' who? A terrifying loneliness crept through her. It was as if she had awakened on a foreign planet with no knowledge of how she got here.

She slept restlessly that night, tormented by nightmares. Grotesque forms and faces, creatures from the dark underworld of her subconscious, leered at her in a procession of nightmarish episodes.

Dawn came at last. Raven brought her a breakfast of tea, toast and warm gruel. Then Dr. Glenn Marshall appeared in the doorway, black bag in hand. For the first time, she saw him clearly. He was a tall man who had to stoop to get through the doorway. He had large hands, a gangling frame that had never entirely lost its adolescent awkwardness, a thick, rumpled mass of sandy hair and brown eyes that radiated kindness. She held onto his gaze, drawing courage from it.

"Well, Lilly, Raven tells me you and she had quite a conversation late yesterday," he smiled. "That's very encouraging." He pulled one of the ladder-back chairs closer, turning it around to sit astride it, folding his arms on the back and resting his chin on his forearm as he studied her with a professional scrutiny.

"But something is very wrong with me," Lilly whispered, tears rushing to her eyes. "I—I can't remember anything about myself, not even my name."

The doctor's eyes looked serious and thoughtful.

"What's wrong with me?" she demanded.

"Well, a lot has been wrong with you, Lilly. You were badly banged up when Henry Brownfeather brought you home. You were covered with first degree burns and bruises. I'd guess that you had been wandering around in the desert for at least twenty-four hours, getting blistered by the sun during the day and half freezing at night. Among other things, you were suffering from a mild concussion and possible internal injuries. It's not surprising that you're dazed and confused. You see, there is a mechanism in the mind that rejects memories that pass a certain pain threshold of tolerance. It's a defense mechanism. Perhaps the ordeal you've been through was so frightening and painful, your mind refuses to remember anything until the healing process is more complete."

"When will that be?"

"That's hard to say," he murmured, spreading his large hands in a gesture of uncertainty. "My guess is that it will be a gradual process. Slowly, as your body heals and your strength returns, you'll begin regaining bits of memories. It will be like putting a jigsaw puzzle together. A piece one day, another the next. Eventually, the whole picture will be complete. But I can't predict how soon that will be. It could be a matter of weeks. It could take six months or more."

Lilly's eyes filled with fresh consternation. "If I have a family somewhere, they'll be frantic."

The doctor rubbed his chin thoughtfully. "You have no idea what happened to you, no memory at all of being in some kind of accident, or being beaten up?"

She shook her head. "Nothing." Then she asked, "Didn't I have any kind of identification?"

"All we found on you was the jewelry you were

15

wearing. We showed you the gold locket. You also had on an expensive wristwatch, a dinner ring, a diamond and a wedding band."

"Wedding band!" she gasped. It was the key word that set off a tumult of emotions. She tried to sit up, but the doctor and Raven quickly held her back.

"Hey," Doctor Marshall grinned. "Not so fast. You need to take it easy a few more days."

"But if I was wearing a wedding band, I must have a husband somewhere—perhaps children. I have to get word to them."

Then a fresh horror assailed her. "What if we were together in some kind of accident out on the desert. What if my family is lying out there, injured, needing help—"

The doctor's large, strong hands held hers, trying to soothe her. "Lilly, as soon as we found you, we notified the state department of public safety. They searched the desert where you were picked up and found no one else. Whatever happened to you, happened to you alone."

But she was not reassured. Perhaps no one else related to her had been involved in whatever unimaginable catastrophe had befallen her. But nevertheless, her wedding band was a mute link with her forgotten past. Somewhere she must have a husband. How could she get word to him if she couldn't even remember her name?

Seeing the fresh consternation in her eyes, Dr. Marshall squeezed her hands again. "Lilly, you won't accomplish anything by worrying yourself into a state of emotional exhaustion. Right now you need to relax and rest so you can regain your strength."

The warm comfort in his grip soothed her, calming her panic. Gradually, she relaxed. Then another concern flashed through her mind. She touched the gauze on her face. "All these bandages. My face must be a mess. . . ."

"You've had some injuries there," he admitted, rising from his chair. "But we're not going to worry about that, either, at this point. The human body has an amazing ability to heal itself. Now, you're in good hands here with the Brownfeather family, Lilly. And Raven is an excellent nurse. I'll drop by in a few days and check on you again, although I'd say from now on it's simply going to be a matter of convalescence."

After he left, Raven brought some items tied up in a silk bandanna. She untied a knot and laid out several pieces of glittering jewelry on the bed. "These were all we found on you besides the clothes you were wearing. I thought you'd like to have them now."

Lilly looked at the diamond encrusted wristwatch, the rings and the locket. She felt Raven's searching gaze as she touched the objects one by one. She thought that the young Indian woman was watching her, hoping the jewelry would open the door to her locked memory. But it was as if she were looking at these personal items for the first time in her life.

Raven said cheerfully, "Well, I have some chores to take care of. If you need anything, you can call me with this." She placed a small, silver bell within easy reach and left the room.

Lilly welcomed some time to be alone. A painful lump filled her throat as she gazed at the small pile of jewelry. If only these things could speak. They could tell her who she was. But they mocked her with glittering silence.

She held up the wristwatch, studying it. A shaft of sunlight struck the diamonds and sprinkled a shower of light on her pillow. The watch must have cost a fortune.

Then she looked at the diamond engagement ring and thought it was worth a ransom.

She was moved by the honesty of the simple pueblo family who had taken her in. How easy it would have been for Raven's father to have put all the jewelry in his pocket and then claimed someone else had stripped the valuable items from her before he found her!

The jewelry couldn't speak to her in words, but it did tell her one thing very clearly. She must have lived in wealthy circumstances. The man who gave her the engagement ring must be a successful person. It was difficult to use the words "my husband" in her mind. No matter what kind of life they had shared before, no matter how intimate they had been, how their days and nights had been entwined, her husband was now a stranger to her. That was a shocking and desolate truth not easy to face.

She examined a dinner ring heavy with stones that made it every bit as costly as the engagement ring. Finally, she came to the gold locket. The instant she touched it, a flood of emotions swept over her. It was as if the pendant were a talisman, linking her with an event out of the past that reached deeply into her heart. She could tell at a glance that it was not nearly so expensive as the rings and watch. It was merely gold-filled. The inexpensive gold coating was worn thin on the chain, indicating that she had worn it constantly for many years.

It was a simple, heart-shaped design, an item that could have been purchased from a discount jewelry chain store. Yet it must have meant a great deal to her.

She turned it over and read the engraving, "To Lilly With Love. J."

She stared at the letter "J" for long, painful moments, groping in the shadows for this person who had been so important in her life. Finally, she snapped the locket open. Two small photographs were contained in the heart-shaped enclosure. One was a young woman with a cloud of blonde hair and deep blue eyes. She looked at the picture seeing a stranger, yet seeing herself. Yes, the picture was of her. She couldn't understand why she knew this, but she *knew*. She might have forgotten everything else about herself, but she recognized her own face. The picture told her that she had above-average good looks with a facial structure that had delicate bones, a slender nose, wide mouth. She appeared happy and carefree in the photograph. Her eyes were alight with joy. The woman in the photograph had long eyelashes and well-defined eyebrows under a smooth, broad forehead. Her cheekbones were etched above shadowed cheeks, her jawline clean, her chin slightly cleft. She appeared quite young in the photograph, but it might have been taken several years ago; it was somewhat faded.

It gave her an eerie feeling to be staring at her own likeness, yet seeing the face of a stranger.

What was she like? What kind of person had she been? Did she have good morals—or bad? Was she religious? Had she been wicked? Did she like outdoor sports, or prefer a more sedate life? What kind of education did she have? What were her friends like? Was she an optimist, or did she worry a great deal? Was she healthy, filled with energy, or did she have medical problems? Was she gregarious, shy, extroverted or a private person? Did she skip breakfast, read the comic strips, have a favorite color, drive a car, have bad dreams, sing off-key?

The questions rose in a sudden, engulfing tide that overwhelmed her. Her heart pounded. Her eyes burned with unshed tears of frustration and bewilderment. She felt very confused. Her thoughts were so jumbled, so chaotic.

Then she turned her attention to the other photograph in the locket. It was the picture of a young man with brown eyes, unruly blond hair that tumbled over his forehead, and a broad, infectious grin.

Seeing the two young, smiling faces made her think of the phrase "Our hearts were young and gay."

But the locket was worn and the pictures were faded.

"Who are you, 'J'?" she asked the young man's picture through her tears. "I think I must have loved you a great deal. What part did you play in my life? Are you someone I loved and lost? Did we have a happy love story together, or did it have a sad ending?"

Was "J" her husband?

Somehow, she didn't think so. The man who gave her the costly watch and the expensive rings would not have given her such a modest little locket.

Staring at the locket brought no answers. It only made her feel sad.

She turned her attention again to the rings. The swelling in her fingers had gone down so she was able to slip them on. She spread out her left hand, gazing at the engagement and wedding rings. What was her husband like? Did he love her? Did she love him? Was he still living . . . or was she a widow?

Only questions. No answers.

More questions. She had avoided asking herself this question because of the pain involved, but she could not hide from it forever. Did she have children? They would be heartbroken, missing their mother, perhaps by now thinking her dead.

She was overwhelmed by the multitude of agonizing questions. Her tired brain refused to cope with them any longer. A feeling of indescribable weariness spread through her. She closed her eyes and fell into a deep sleep of mental exhaustion.

Later that day, she met the other members of the Brownfeather family. Raven's parents, Dawn and Henry Brownfeather, were shy, dignified people. Their bronze faces were stoic, but their brown eyes showed a kindness and concern for her. She made what seemed a totally inadequate attempt to thank Henry Brownfeather for rescuing her from a horrible death out on the desert, but he gruffly waved aside her thanks. "I did nothin'—just threw you in the truck and brought you home," he muttered.

Both Raven's mother and father spoke with a heavy accent. Raven, however, spoke perfect English.

Her brother, Luke, who appeared to be a few years younger than Raven, was a handsome, happy-go-lucky young man who grinned and kidded a lot. His eyes sparkled with mischievous highlights. Lilly suspected that he must be the target of many coquettish glances from the young women in the village.

Lilly found her appetite returning. When Raven brought her supper tray, her mouth watered at the delicious fragrances wafting her way from the bowls.

"Doctor Glenn said it's time to take you off mush and gruel and serve you some good, hearty Indian food," Raven grinned.

"It smells heavenly," Lilly said.

Raven helped her sit up, propping extra pillows behind her, then placed the tray on her lap.

"There's garbanzo stew, green chili, Pueblo bread and rice pudding," Raven explained. "Be careful with the chili. It has chili peppers. I told Mother to go easy with them, but she's used to cooking her own way."

"Umm. This bread is delicious," Lilly murmured after her first bite.

"Yes. We still bake it outdoors in the *hornos*, the adobe ovens. It just doesn't taste the same if you make it in a modern stove. I tried baking some in my oven in my apartment in Albuquerque. It was a disaster," she laughed.

Lilly gave the dark-haired girl a curious look. Raven seemed at ease in her simple cloth dress and moccasins, and yet at the same time, out of place in these surroundings.

"You live in Albuquerque?" Lilly asked.

"Yes. I'm a nurse at a hospital there. I went to college in Albuquerque. Right now, I'm home for a vacation."

"Some vacation," Lilly murmured ruefully. "Having to spend your time nursing me."

"But I like taking care of sick people. I have hopes of maybe becoming a doctor some day. So, you see, it's really been a pleasure being able to help you. I'm just glad I was home when Dad found you."

They fell silent for a few moments, then Raven asked, "Have you been able to remember anything about yourself?"

Lilly shook her head despondently. "Nothing. When I try hard to remember, it's as if my brain just shuts itself off."

"Try not to brood too much. I've been reading some of my medical books about amnesia. Like Dr. Glenn told you, severe stress, a trauma, an ordeal like the one you've been through can cause the memory and personality to become temporarily separated from one another."

"Are you sure the books say 'temporary'?" Lilly asked, tears filling her eyes.

"Sure," Raven insisted, giving Lilly's hand a reassuring squeeze. "Your mind is going to heal just as your body will. Give yourself time."

"There isn't much else I can do," Lilly said sadly. Then she asked, "Why is my voice so hoarse? I don't think it was always like this. It sounds strange to me."

"You had a neck injury, bruises all around your throat. Dr. Glenn thinks your vocal chords sustained injuries. He thinks that will improve too, though your voice may have a permanent huskiness." Then Raven smiled, "I wouldn't worry about that, though. It will have a seductive quality that a lot of women will envy. I often wished my voice were more of a contralto rather than up in the soprano range where it is."

Lilly didn't feel like continuing the conversation. The heavy mantle of weariness was spreading over her again.

Lilly spent the next few days sleeping much of the time. Rest, nourishing food and the vitamin injections Raven administered daily slowly brought back her strength. By the end of the week, she was able to spend her time in a chair by the window instead of in bed, and she ventured on a slow journey through the rooms of the small pueblo home, holding Raven's arm for support.

Her body was healing faster than her facial injuries. At least, it seemed so to her. The soreness when she moved about was almost gone. But still the bandages remained on her face. When the doctor visited her, he treated her facial injuries with medications, then replaced the bandages. Her face continued to hurt and the flesh pulled when she talked or ate. "I had to take some stitches when I first saw you," Dr. Marshall explained. "You were pretty badly cut up. It will feel better when the stitches come out."

He refused to listen to her request to survey the damage herself. "Leave the bandages on," he ordered sternly. "Wait until things heal up a bit more."

But as her strength returned, so did her normal feminine concern for her appearance. Somewhere she had a husband to whom she would return when she got her memory back. She didn't want to go back to him looking like a freak.

One evening when she was in her room alone, she searched through a chest of drawers and found a small mirror. With trembling fingers, she pulled adhesive tape free and removed the bandages that swathed her face. She held up the mirror. Her eyes went wide with horror. She heard her own hoarse, choked cry and she crumpled into a sobbing heap on the floor. . . .

Chapter Two

"Lilly, I'm really exasperated with you for disobeying my orders," Dr. Glenn Marshall said severely. "If you had only waited another week before taking those bandages off, some of the swelling and discoloration would have faded away and things wouldn't have seemed so bad."

Lilly heard the words, but they didn't register. Since the shock of confronting the disfiguring injuries to her face the night before last, she had sunk into a deep depression. She sat beside the window, staring into space in an almost catatonic state of despair.

How much kinder it would have been, she now believed, if she had been left to die out in the desert. She now hated Henry Brownfeather for saving her. Perhaps it had been intended for her to die, and this was her punishment for thwarting the fates. At times the gloomy thought assailed her that she *had* died and this was a kind of purgatory where she could remember nothing of her past life and had been made ugly beyond description.

She had no desire to eat. Any movement, even so much as lifting a hand, was too much of an effort to bother with. She didn't feel like talking to anyone. She just wanted to be left alone.

When she had first regained consciousness and realized the problem she was facing—the loss of memory—she'd had the motivation to fight back. She had been eager to get well, to recover her memory, to find her past life and her family.

But she no longer had the desire. It would be better for all concerned if she never remembered the past. If she did, how could she go back with a face that was burned and scarred beyond recognition? How could she return to a husband or to the smiling young man in the locket whom she must have loved very much, only to see the horror and revulsion in their eyes when they beheld the grotesque wreckage of her face?

She sat beside the window with the gold locket clutched in her hand and grieved for the pretty, blue-eyed young woman who smiled innocently from the picture. That young woman had died out on the desert. All that was left was a disfigured robot, a broken doll who had no more purpose in life.

It was all too much for her. She felt totally overwhelmed. Life was no more than a monstrous joke with no point or purpose, a foolish journey that had no meaning, ending in death and the grave.

She knew that Raven and Dr. Marshall were talking, but the words meant nothing to her. She shut them out, wanting to hide in the safe, secret corner within herself, closed away from the world.

Dr. Marshall sighed as he turned to Raven, whose dark eyes were strained with worry. "She's been like that ever since night before last," Raven said. "I can't get her to eat. She won't talk to us."

Marshall nodded. "She's in a bad state of depression. There's no getting through to her."

"I feel so guilty. I should have watched her more carefully to see that she didn't take those bandages off."

"Don't go blaming yourself, Raven. She had to find out sooner or later. I was just hoping it would be later, after she'd gotten stronger and the wounds didn't look so bad. It has been too much of a shock, right on top of everything else she's been through."

Marshall turned to Lilly again. He drew a chair closer to the window, took Lilly's hands in his and spoke to her again, patiently, gently. "Now I want you to listen to me, Lilly. Yes, your face is pretty much of a mess right now. It's the truth. You were burned and there are some deep gashes. But it doesn't mean you're going to be permanently scarred or disfigured. I have a friend in Albuquerque who is an excellent plastic surgeon. I've seen him do miracles with facial injuries that were much worse than yours."

For the first time that morning, Lilly allowed herself to pay attention to her surroundings. She found herself listening to Dr. Marshall's words, permitting them to pass the barricades she had erected in her mind. She frowned and gazed at him suspiciously. "You're saying that to make me feel better," she whispered.

He shook his head. "No, I'm simply telling you the truth. You're going to need plastic surgery, yes. But the injuries to your face can be repaired, and I can tell you that flatly with no equivocation. Believe me, Lilly. The kind of injuries you have can be repaired by a good plastic surgeon so you won't have a scar left."

Tears began to fill Lilly's eyes. "If I could be

sure . . . if I could really believe you," she murmured, a glimmer of light flickering in the darkness. But then a fresh wave of despair engulfed her. "But plastic surgery is terribly expensive. And I have no money. Perhaps my husband could afford it, if I could remember my past life. Judging by my engagement ring, he must be a successful man. But I don't know when I'll be able to remember . . . my mind still feels so confused. And even if I could remember, I couldn't go to him looking the way I do now—"

Marshall leaned back in his chair, rubbing his chin thoughtfully. "I'm sure my friend would allow you to pay for the surgery later, either after you find your husband or if you get well and can get a job. But there would be hospital expenses, the operating room, medication. I was wondering if you would consider selling your jewelry. The watch alone would bring quite a bit, and the rings appear to be worth a great deal of money. I'm no judge of such things, but we could have them appraised."

"I'd forgotten about the jewelry!" Lilly exclaimed. "Certainly I'd be willing to sell it. Everything except— except the little gold locket. I don't think that would bring much anyway. And I'd want to keep my wedding band. But the watch and the diamond and the dinner ring, I would sell them in a minute. What good are they to me now? Do you think your friend would be able to help me? It would take a miracle."

"Plastic surgeons perform miracles every day," Dr. Marshall said confidently. "But first you must get your strength and health back. No more of this sinking into fits of despair and giving up. You must eat and begin to exercise, Lilly. I'm going to prescribe one of the new anti-depressant medications that can help you fight off the depression. But you must get back some of your own fighting spirit, too. There's a limit to what we doctors can do."

"Well," Raven Brownfeather exclaimed, "today is the big day!" She stood just inside the doorway of the hospital room in her crisp, white nurse's uniform, holding a huge bouquet of flowers.

For the moment, Lilly's chaotic thoughts became centered as her gaze focused on the cluster of bloodred chrysanthemums in Raven's arms. Her heart filled with warmth at the devotion and kindness Raven had shown her in the past weeks. "They're beautiful!" she murmured. "But, Raven, you shouldn't have gone to such an expense."

"They're from the whole Pueblo tribe," Raven explained. She crossed the room, her crepe soled white shoes whispering on the tile floor. "They've made you my adopted sister." She arranged the flowers in a vase on a table near the window, then turned, smiling. "An occasion like this calls for a celebration with flowers and wine." She winked mischievously. "I sneaked a bottle of champagne up to this floor. The head nurse is a buddy of mine. She's cooling it in the refrigerator." She giggled.

Lilly had been resting on the hospital bed. Now she sat up. She had awakened early this morning, bathed and dressed in a light cotton dress Raven had lent her. For the past hour, she had been listening to the muted sounds of the hospital, the murmur of nurses passing in the hall, the voice on the hospital intercom calling a doctor's name, the rattle of breakfast trays. The hopes and fears of the past weeks were culminating in this morning's drama.

She could feel the chill in her body, the trembling of her fingers. "Raven, I'm scared—"

"Sure you are," the Indian girl nodded sympathetically. She moved to the side of the bed and clasped Lilly's hand. "After all, it isn't every day a woman gets to see her new face."

Lilly looked down at the hospital identification band on her wrist. The name "Lilly Smith" had been placed there by the staff. It was a made-up name. Everything she had was borrowed, the dress she was wearing, even her last name. Tears blurred her vision. If only she could think clearly!

Her mind was spinning with thoughts of all that had happened since Dr. Marshall had brought her to Albuquerque from the Indian village. He had checked her into this hospital. The sale of her jewelry had been enough to cover hospital expenses. She had been introduced to Dr. Edmund Graves, the plastic surgeon. He had given her a careful examination. He assured her the damage to her face could be repaired, but there would have to be a series of painful operations, then a period of convalescence. She had readily agreed to the operations. By then, pain was nothing new to her.

Pain killers and tranquilizers had kept her mind so hazy that those weeks seemed like a dream. After the surgery, Raven had moved her to her apartment in the city to convalesce. Her mind had been in a fog during that time.

"I'd rather you didn't look at your face without the bandages," Dr. Marshall had told her. "I'd hate for you to be thrown into another spell of depression."

"Yes," Dr. Graves had agreed. "Until things start to heal, plastic surgery can make matters look even worse. Your face will be swollen and bruised and, for a while, the incisions will be obvious. In time, all that will fade away."

This time, she'd needed no doctor's orders to keep

her away from mirrors. She was too afraid to look, afraid that the hope the doctors expressed would turn out to be empty words, afraid that she was condemned to spend the rest of her life a pitiful freak.

Whenever her groggy mind could grasp a rational thought, it tried to reassure her. Every time the surgeon had examined her, he had expressed satisfaction with the way the surgery was healing. Raven had applied prescribed medications to her face every day, and each time had assured Lilly that everything was progressing as it should.

Nevertheless, Raven had discreetly removed all the mirrors from the apartment and kept a light gauze mask on Lilly's face so she wouldn't see her reflection in a window pane or bit of shiny metal. Lilly preferred to spend her days in the apartment with the shades drawn like a sick animal hiding from the world. Daily headaches continued to torture her.

Raven had brought her back to the hospital the day before for a final examination. She had spent the day having various blood tests and X rays made. Now she was waiting half with anxiety, half with terror for the arrival of the doctors on their morning rounds.

What would their final verdict be? Was she going to be condemmed to a life of hiding away from the world? Would her face be better, but still a mass of scars? Or would it be halfway normal again?

Now that the moment of truth had arrived, she didn't think she had the courage to face it. A wave of panic made her want to escape to Raven's apartment and hide there with the shades drawn. Her head throbbed painfully.

She moved from the side of the bed to the window and gazed out across the hospital lawn. She could see nurses striding briskly up the walk, their uniforms shimmering white in the bright sunlight. Cars were passing in the street. A lawn sprinkler was turning. A gardener was clipping a hedge. Outside the hospital life was going on in its daily routine, oblivious to the crisis of a patient with the name "Lilly Smith" on her identification wristband.

Except for the persistent, chronic headaches, her general physical condition had greatly improved. Her strength had returned. Her body no longer throbbed from painful bruises. But her memory was still a blank. Sometimes she had fleeting dreams that taunted her with jumbles of half-familiar scenes. Other times fragments of her past seemed on the very threshold of her consciousness, but when she eagerly reached for them they flew away like scraps of paper in a whirlwind.

"Don't struggle with it now," Dr. Marshall had told her. "The worry and trauma you're going through with this plastic surgery is keeping your mind fuzzy. And, in addition, all the medication you're taking has you pretty well sedated and confused. Just be patient, Lilly. I feel sure when you're recovered from this surgery, when we can take you off so much medication and your life settles into a normal routine, your mind will clear and your memory will come back."

Lilly turned from the window and looked at Raven, who was waiting beside the bed. The young nurse had been a rock during this dreadful ordeal. Without her friendship, Lilly could never have endured the past weeks. Now she suddenly said, "Raven, I want to say something to you before the doctor gets here. No matter how this surgery to my face turns out, I can never begin to thank you for all you've done for me."

Raven made an attempt to interrupt, but Lilly stopped her with a gesture. "No, let me finish. You've taken me into your heart and your life. You've let me live in your apartment. I know taking care of me has added to your living expenses and robbed you of a lot of your free time. And you don't know a thing about me. I could be a criminal . . . a murderess for all you know."

Raven laughed. "Whatever happened in your past, Lilly, I seriously doubt you murdered anybody. I've come to care a great deal for you as a friend. I want to see you well again; we all do. I told you—you're my adopted sister. So, we're going to have to think up a good Indian name for you."

"How about Lilly Don't-Know-Who-I-Am?" Lilly murmured bitterly.

Their conversation was interrupted by the doctor's voice in the hall. "Oh, Raven, hold my hand," Lilly gasped, a fresh wave of panic seizing her.

Dr. Edmund Graves, a tall man with a head of bushy gray hair, strode into the room, followed by a nurse. He was leafing through a sheaf of papers on a clipboard."I've been looking over the results of your tests, Lilly. Everything looks just fine. Now, let's have a look at the face."

The nurse had Lilly sit in a straight-back chair beside the table. On the table was a gooseneck lamp which she adjusted so the light would fall directly on Lilly's face. Dr. Graves sat on the side of the table, leaned forward and removed the light gauze mask from Lilly's face. He studied her face critically, turning her from side to side. Then he sat back, clasping his hands on his knee. "Not half bad, if I say so myself. Not half bad."

"Not . . . bad?" Lilly asked weakly.

He smiled. "I think it's time you see for yourself. But first I want to explain some things to you. You're going to see a number of thin, pink scars. Those are going to be with you for a while, possibly six months or so, but they're going to gradually fade until you will no longer be aware of them. But that really won't be a problem. They can easily be covered with makeup. As for the swelling and discoloration, I'm glad to say that has gone completely. I do want to prepare you for something else, though. You're going to have to get used to looking like a different person. A lot of the bone structure in your nose and face was damaged and crushed. In addition to the skin grafts to repair the burns, we had to do some bone restructuring. That has changed your appearance considerably." Then he turned to the nurse. "Could we have a mirror, Miss Alexander? I expect our patient would like to have a look at our handiwork."

The nurse left the room, and returned shortly with a hand mirror. Lilly clasped the mirror with fingers that were bits of ice. For a long moment, the silence in the room was tense.

She looked at the faces around her, the doctor, the nurse, Raven. Her Indian friend smiled and nodded encouragement.

I can't, she thought desperately. *I can't make myself look.* . . .

She drew a painful breath. She felt foolish. All the weeks of suspense and hope pressed down on her like a smothering blanket. Now all she had to do was hold the mirror up and look into it. Either her prayers would be answered or her worst fears realized. The answer was here in her hands, the mirror that was waiting to mock her cruelly or flood her with relief. Which would it be? How could she find the courage to face the truth?

As if sensing the dreadful struggle going on in her,

Raven quietly stepped forward, took Lilly's hand which held the mirror and guided it up so the mirror was before her eyes.

Again, a long silence settled over the room. Lilly's breath was suspended. With wide eyes, she gazed at the stranger's face which looked back at her from the mirror. The blue eyes and golden hair were still the same as in the picture in the locket. But there the identity ended. Her face was no longer the same. Would anyone who had known her before recognize her? She doubted it. The face in the locket belonged to another person. It had been replaced with different features.

But as her first shock subsided, it was replaced by a wave of utmost relief. True, as the doctor warned, quite a few pink scars were still visible. But she had a human face again. Not as beautiful as before, perhaps, but reasonably attractive and, most important, no longer disfigured.

Tears began trickling down her cheeks. She looked up at the surgeon. "Dr. Marshall was right," she choked. "He said you could work miracles. I didn't think I would ever look human again. How can I ever thank you?"

He smiled, looking pleased with himself. "Things are going to look even better," he predicted, "in a few months, when those scars fade away."

At that point, another white-coated figure entered the room. Dr. Glenn Marshall was wearing a broad grin. "I see I'm late for the big moment, but everyone seems pretty happy."

"The important thing is that the patient is happy," Raven told him.

"Yes, happy . . . and very, very grateful," Lilly exclaimed. A sudden impulse seized her. She hugged Dr. Marshall and kissed his cheek, which appeared to both embarrass and please him.

"Hey, I'm the one who did the operating," Dr. Graves protested.

"Yes, you too!" Lilly cried, and hugged and kissed him.

Dr. Marshall held up a bottle by its neck. "Raven, I understand you are responsible for this bottle of champagne being in the hospital refrigerator. Strictly against regulations, you know."

"Well, I thought . . . under the circumstances—" Raven stammered.

"As I see it," Glenn Marshall scowled, "the only way to keep you out of trouble over this matter, is for us to drink up the evidence. Sorry, though, Lilly. Considering the medication you're on, the patient will have to stick to ice water."

They toasted the success of the plastic surgery. Then Glenn Marshall said, "This calls for more of a celebration. Would you two ladies allow a lonely bachelor doctor to take you out to dinner this evening?"

Raven's dark eyes sparkled. "That would be nice. How about it, Lilly?"

Lilly felt a mixed response. It would be the first time since Henry Brownfeather had discovered her half dead out on the desert that she would go out in public. She felt nervous about doing it, yet knew that she would have to start making the adjustment to normal life sooner or later. "Yes . . . all right."

"Good," Glenn Marshall grinned. "How about it, Dr. Graves? Can you and your wife join us?"

"Thanks, but Mrs. Graves has me scheduled for dinner with friends tonight. I approve of your plans, though. In fact, I prescribe an evening out on the town for our patient. It will be good for you to start living a normal life again, Lilly."

"It won't be normal," she said sadly, "until I know who I am and how I got here."

Would she ever know? Why couldn't she reach through the veil that separated her from the other life . . . the life that had ended out on the desert? What dreadful tragedy had befallen her? What terrible event had torn her from her friends, from her lover, from her husband, to leave her wandering half dead in that barren wilderness?

She was released from the hospital and she returned to Raven's apartment. Raven had taken all her mirrors out of hiding. Lilly spent the afternoon becoming acquainted with her new face, gazing at herself from every possible angle. She was especially intrigued by the new shape of her eyes which, because of the skin grafts, now had an exotic, oriental shape. And she had a new voice to go with the face. Dr. Marshall had told her that the huskiness would be permanent.

She spent some time experimenting with makeup and found a combination that skillfully hid the remaining scars.

When it was time to dress for their dinner date, Lilly exclaimed, "It hasn't been enough that you have taken me into your home and nursed me back to health. Now I'm having to borrow your clothes. I'm beginning to feel like a parasite."

"Nonsense," Raven said. "It's just fortunate that we're the same size. Anyway, that dress looks much better on you than it ever did on me. It's designed for a blonde, not a brunette."

The dress was a dramatic black and white, a perfect foil for her golden blond hair that tumbled in soft, natural waves to her shoulders. The pullover dress had extended shoulders with tucking and a white bodice. The elastic waist was accentuated by a cord belt with a mock shell. The black skirt was a fluid swirl of pleats, and a short bolero jacket, also black, featured soft shirring beneath the shoulder yoke, a curved front and long sleeves.

"Somewhere," Lilly murmured, "I have a rich husband, and when I remember who he is, I'm going to see to it that he buys you a whole new wardrobe."

"Okay," Raven laughed, "but in the meantime, you're more than welcome to anything in my closet."

Presently, there was a knock at the door. Raven greeted Dr. Glenn Marshall, who stooped out of habit as he walked across the threshold. He was wearing a dark suit, which, though neatly pressed, was somewhat at odds with his tall, gangling frame.

When he saw Lilly, he froze and his eyes widened. For a moment he was speechless. She was acutely aware of his penetrating gaze, which, for the first time, revealed more masculine than professional interest. It swept her from head to feet, and she experienced a flush of warm pleasure racing through her with a tingling sensation. He was giving her what she needed most—a look that made her feel like a woman again for the first time since this nightmare had begun.

He found his voice and exclaimed, "You're ravishing, Lilly! I'm going to have to send Dr. Graves more patients."

She blushed with pleasure. "It's just that you're seeing me in something besides hospital gowns for a change," she murmured.

"Whatever it is, all I can say is, 'Wow!'" Then he said, "I was so overcome, I almost forgot these." He presented a small, square cardboard box to each young woman. Lilly lifted the lid of her box and gasped as she saw an orchid corsage.

"It's lovely, Dr. Glenn," Raven cried, holding her corsage to her shoulder.

Lilly's eyes filled with tears. All that had happened today was overwhelming her. She was afraid if she tried to speak, she'd break down.

"Permit me," Glenn Marshall said. Clumsily, his big hands fumbled with the delicate flower and somehow got it pinned to her shoulder.

"Thank you, Dr. Marshall," Lilly whispered, touching his hand.

For a moment, their eyes met and held. His direct, brown-eyed gaze brought a confused wave of emotions that Lilly couldn't define.

"Starting tonight, let's be less formal and just make it 'Glenn,' okay?" he smiled. Then he said briskly, "Well, this is going to be quite an evening. I'm going out with a lovely young woman on each arm, a blonde and a brunette. All the other bachelors in Albuquerque are going to hate me tonight!" With a grin and a flourish, he held out his arms. Raven tucked her hand in his right arm and Lilly held his left as they walked to his car.

Lilly's mind was still in a state of confusion, partly from the heavy medication she'd been under. There was a sense of unreality about the evening. Raven chatted gaily and Glenn Marshall was in an expansive, happy mood. But Lilly was quiet, trying to assimilate the confused medley of sights and sounds that bombarded her senses.

Everything was strange, yet somehow familiar. She felt painfully self-conscious when they entered the restaurant. Yet she found herself doing the correct things, knowing which fork to use, but not understanding why she knew all this. There were too many people, too many voices. Later, the flashes of lights, the bright signs, the passing cars, when they were on the street, frightened her.

Still later that evening, they were in another place where there were small tables. People sipped drinks and conversed quietly. The lights were dim here. She liked this place better than the restaurant.

Glenn Marshall spoke to a waitress and she brought a tray of drinks. "A soda for you, Lilly," he smiled. "No strong alcohol while you're still on medication."

Lilly barely heard him. Her attention was drawn to, and focused on, a man playing a piano behind a small bar. She couldn't tear her eyes away from the instrument. The music affected her in a disturbing way, like a voice telling her something, calling to her. She seemed to know every melody the man played, hearing it in her mind, knowing what melodic phrase would come next. She fell into a hypnotic trance. She heard Raven and Glenn Marshall talking, but couldn't make out their words. Only the music was real to her.

The man left the piano. The sounds in the room were muted now, the soft clink of glasses, the hum of conversation. Lilly felt an aching void for the music. She wanted desperately for the man to come back and continue playing.

In the grip of the curious spell, she rose from the small table. Like a sleepwalker, she moved to the piano and, in the same trance, sat before the keyboard. She gazed down at her fingers. They were touching the piano keys with a loving caress of welcome to a beloved old friend. Then she began playing. There was no conscious volition on her part. Her fingers simply moved of their own accord, knowing just what to do. Suddenly, she felt as if a great, empty void in her was being filled. It was as if a vital part of her being had been starved, and she had discovered the food it had so badly needed. Hungrily now, her hands flew over the keyboard. Rich harmonies flooded her senses. One melody after another sang under her fingers.

She was dimly aware that Raven and Dr. Marshall were standing beside the piano bar, wide-eyed with amazement . . . that other people in the room had come over to listen to her. But she was shut away from them in a world of her own, a world filled only with her music and the melodies that had been locked in her heart for so many weeks.

She felt a need to sing, and somehow knew the words of many songs. But when she tried, her voice, with its new husky quality, was entirely strange to her.

Then she became aware of the man who had been playing the piano earlier standing at her side, staring at her curiously. Suddenly she felt embarrassed and self-conscious. She wondered with a sense of horror what had possessed her to act like this. "I'm—so sorry," she mumbled, making an attempt to rise from the piano bench.

But the male pianist touched her shoulder. "Hey, lady, don't stop. Where are you from, anyway? I thought I knew all the pros working around town."

"Pros?" she echoed blankly.

He chuckled, "Lady, don't try to fool an old ivory man. You're no amateur. You got one heck of a repertoire. You were playing tunes I haven't heard in years. Hey . . . have you ever played in New Orleans?

"N—no," she stammered, wondering if she had.

"Funny. I once heard a young woman down there who had a style just like yours. She was playing with a dixieland traditional jazz band. Kind of unusual, seeing a lady pianist with a group like that. I'm trying to think of the name of the band. It was led by a young trumpet player. His name is on the tip of my tongue—"

Lilly's head suddenly felt as if it would split open. The room swam before her eyes. She had trouble breathing.

"Ex—excuse me," she mumbled and fled to the rest room. There, she opened her purse with trembling fingers and groped blindly for her medication. She gulped a pain killer and a tranquilizer. Then she sat on a couch, covering her eyes with her hands.

Raven found her there. "Lilly, have you become ill?" she asked anxiously, sitting beside her.

"It's just one of my headaches," she stammered. "I'll be all right in a few minutes, Raven."

"I can hardly blame you for being upset."

"You mean, discovering that I can play the piano—"

"Yes, that must have come as quite a shock. And what that man said about New Orleans. Do you think you were ever there, Lilly?"

She pressed her palm against her throbbing temples. "I just don't know, Raven. It certainly got me shook up when that man started talking about it."

"Why would it upset you unless he touched a vital spot?"

"I don't know. Raven, it's so bewildering to be confused like this. I feel like I'm beating my fists against a closed door in my head!"

Later, physically and emotionally exhausted, Lilly slumped in the car between Raven and Glenn Marshall.

Her two friends were chattering excitedly over tonight's surprising development. "I'd say tonight we've come very close to the real identity of Lilly Smith," Marshall exclaimed.

"I can't get over how well you play," Raven added

with a mingled note of surprise and awe. "You're a superb musician."

"Did playing the piano awaken any other memories?" Marshall asked.

Lilly shook her head numbly. The experience had left her more depressed and confused than ever.

Raven was on duty at the hospital that night. They stopped at the apartment so she could change into her nurse's uniform, then drove her to the hospital.

Marshall then took Lilly back home. "Are you all right, Lilly? You look pale."

"I—I think so," she mumbled.

But as he was seeing her to the door, a blinding pain suddenly squeezed her head in a vise. She gasped and stumbled against the doctor.

With a muffled exclamation, he scooped her up in his strong arms, carried her into the apartment and gently placed her on the bed. He left her for a few moments to hurry out to his car for his medical bag. Lilly was moaning with pain, her trembling fingers pressed against her throbbing head.

She felt the prick of a hypodermic needle. Then Marshall sat beside her, holding her hand. Gradually the excruciating pain in her head eased.

"That was a bad one," she whispered, feeling shaky and weak now.

"Feeling better?"

"Yes. The pain has eased up." She gazed at him tearfully. "Why do I keep having these headaches? That was the worse one so far."

"Seems to be a kind of migraine," the doctor said, looking at her thoughtfully. "Though, to be perfectly frank, we're not entirely certain. It could be a part of the trauma, the confused mental state you've been in.

Apparently the experience you had tonight upset you and brought on this attack."

"Yes. It—it was a scary feeling, as if I were some kind of programmed robot automatically carrying out someone else's command. I seemed to have no control over what I was doing. I certainly made no conscious effort to play; I was as surprised as you were that I knew anything about music. I just sat there and the music came out."

"But obviously you are a musician, and a darn good one. Evidently, the knowledge and skills were coming from your subconscious where all the other memories are locked. If you ask me, it's a positive sign. It may be the beginning of your remembering other things."

Slowly, Lilly said, "I was so eager to get my mind straight again, to know who I was and where I came from. But I'm beginning to wonder if I really want to open those doors. I'm suddenly becoming frightened. What kind of dreadful things will I find out about myself? It's all becoming scary to me. Something about the music tonight stirred unpleasant emotions. In a way, I felt good about playing. Touching the piano keys was like coming back to an old friend. But at the same time, there was an element of fear, too, as if part of me was about to start down a dark, lonely road, and the rest of me didn't want to go."

They sat together, talking, until the medication made her eyelids grow heavy.

Glenn Marshall's deep voice and the strength in his broad hands gave her a feeling of security that dispelled some of the dark, haunting terrors. She could feel the power of his character strength emanating from him, enveloping her in a protective warm cloak of kindness and caring.

Her thinking grew fuzzy as the sedative effect of the

medication took over. Vaguely, she was aware of him picking her up and carrying her to the bed in the next room.

With surprising gentleness for such a big, awkward man, he laid her down, removed her shoes, and drew a cover up around the lower portion of her body.

She was vaguely aware of him sitting on the edge of the bed, gazing down at her in the dim light filtering through the doorway from the other room. She heard him murmur her name softly. Then he bent and kissed her.

A warm, sweet emotion suffused her. She knew without thinking about it that she had come to care for Glenn Marshall a lot. She seemed to be existing between two worlds: her unknown past and a future equally unknown and uncertain. In her present world she had come to depend on this kind, awkward man who had just kissed her with such tenderness and caring.

His presence gave her a feeling of security. She slipped into a deep, peaceful sleep.

Toward morning, Lilly woke with a start. Raven was sitting on the edge of her bed, gently shaking her and calling her name. Streaks of dawn came through the windows.

She sat up, trembling violently.

"You must have been having a bad dream," Raven said. "I heard you cry out. I just came back from the hospital."

"Jimmy. . . ." Lilly whispered tearfully.

Raven gazed at her with a mixture of concern and curiosity. "What do you mean, Lilly? 'Jimmy' who?"

"The face in my locket! The young man . . . his name is Jimmy!"

"Jimmy? Are you sure, Lilly?"

"I've never been more certain of anything. I saw him as clearly in my dream as I'm seeing you right now. We were walking across a field together. It was spring and there were wild flowers all around us. He was holding my hand. I said his name, 'Jimmy,' and he looked at me and smiled. But then he let go of my hand and walked away from me. I was running after him, calling, but he kept walking away, faster and faster. I called for him to wait. . . ."

Lilly began crying. Raven held her, murmuring sympathetically. "Do you remember anything else about the dream?"

Lilly frowned. Another word flashed across her mind. "Millerdale!" she cried. "I saw the name on a railroad station. It's—it's kind of jumbled up. The field we were in was on the outskirts of a small town and I seemed to catch a glimpse of the railroad station—one of those small brown and yellow buildings on a railroad siding that you see in little rural towns."

"Those two names must mean a great deal to you . . . the name of the man in your locket and the name of the town. They may hold the secret of who you are, Lilly!"

"I'm sure they do! Tonight that man in the lounge said he'd heard a woman like me playing with a jazz group in New Orleans. He said the leader of the group was a young trumpet player. Raven, it's all beginning to fit together. That's why I became so upset. He must have been close to my past life, and it caused me to have the dream tonight which brought some things to the surface."

"Do you think you really were the woman he heard playing in New Orleans?"

"Yes, I think so. And I think the leader of the jazz

group was the boy I dreamed about. In the dream, we were both very young, like teen-agers. Maybe the part about New Orleans happened later."

"It sounds as if you might have the key you've been searching for," Raven nodded gravely. "You'd better talk all this over with Glenn Marshall."

When Lilly phoned Dr. Marshall after breakfast, he asked her to hurry over to his office.

They sat together on a couch. He held her hand in a warm, firm grip as she told him about the dream. A strange expression filled his eyes. "Lilly, these past weeks, I guess you know I've come to care a great deal for you. From a selfish standpoint I've found myself half wishing that you could just go on being Lilly Smith, and I could keep you with me. But in reality, I know it's vital to your health and to your whole future to regain your memory. When you know your past, we'll know what the future holds for us." His smile was rueful. "I'll just have to take my chances. . . ."

Impulsively, Lilly moved into the circle of his arms. She clung to him for a moment, needing the security she found there. "Glenn, I have to go to the town I dreamed about. I'm sure I'll find my identity there."

"Let's see if we can locate the place," Glenn said. He phoned the research division of the public library and found there was a town named Millerdale in Louisiana.

"I'm sure that's the place!" Lilly cried.

"Okay. It's certainly worth checking into. Just be prepared for a disappointment if it turns out to be a blind alley."

There were no flight connections directly to Millerdale; the town was too small. Lilly flew to the nearest large city in Louisiana and there rented a car.

As she drove into the city limits of Millerdale, Lilly felt her heart begin to pound. Breathing became difficult. Her hands felt clammy as she turned down the short main street. The buildings were like figures emerging from a fog, slowly recognizable—Thompson's Drugs, the J. C. Penney store, Fred Boudreaux's Hardware, Marcie Alenon's Dress Shop. . . .

She picked out each name, whispering it aloud, reaching deeply into her confused thoughts to grasp the familiar thread.

"Turn down this street!" she suddenly exclaimed aloud, not knowing why.

It was a neighborhood of modest houses. Her attention was drawn to a small, white frame home. She stopped before the house. The front porch had a weary sag. The house had long needed a coat of paint. A window screen was torn.

A child's battered tricycle had rolled near the curb. Lilly got out, retrieved the toy and put it in the front yard among the weeds. She gazed at the house through a mist of tears.

She knew who she was.

She had been born in this house.

Her name was Lilly Parker.

Chapter Three

The flood of memory that began as a trickle now became a torrent that totally engulfed her.

There was no turning back now. She had to remember it all, the joyous moments of falling in love with Jimmy LaCross, her childhood sweetheart; the high points when her heart was swept heavenward, and the dark parts, when she was crushed to earth; and Kirk Remington. A shiver ran through her as his presence swept through her mind, shoving aside the other memories. Through her tears she looked down at her wedding band that now seemed to burn her finger. Yes it was all there—her childhood, her music, the men in her life. She had to face it and accept it; it added up to the person she was.

Much of Lilly Parker was the music that had played such a vital part in her life and had eventually taken her from this bleak little town to her life's drama in distant cities.

Her parents had been Martha and William Parker. She remembered them vividly, seeing them before her mind's eye, hearing again the sound of their voices. William had been a child of the Great Depression and never seemed to outgrow its trauma. He worked at various jobs in the small community, doing the best a man could who had but a sketchy grammar school education and a minimal amount of ambition.

The strongest influence in Lilly's young life had been her Uncle Daniel Webster LeDeaux, a fiery backwoods evangelist preacher. Lilly remembered him vividly too—a huge, towering man who wore a broad-brimmed hat and black coat and spoke in a thunderous voice. Himself childless, he had taken a great interest in his niece, Lilly, who was his sister's only child. He had discovered that the child had a sweet, pure singing voice. He had taken her with him on his crusades through the rural South, standing her on the platform in his tattered rivival tent. She captivated the congregations with her singing while her uncle pumped away lustily at his wheezing, portable organ.

She had barely been five when her uncle had made an astounding discovery about the extent of her natural talent. When not on one of his traveling crusades, he preached in a small frame tabernacle on the outskirts of town. The tabernacle boasted a real piano. Uncle LeDeaux made it his mission to give Lilly an education in music, teaching her the notes out of a frayed hymn book and guiding her chubby little fingers over the black and white keys.

One day he was plunking on the piano and pointing to the corresponding notes in the hymnal, asking her to identify them. It suddenly dawned on him that she was devoting all her attention to a rag doll on her lap and none to the hymn book or piano but still calling out the notes correctly.

He stared at the child with an expression of astonishment that bordered on fright. Cautiously, he touched a note on the piano. "Lilly, honey, what note was that I just played?"

Lilly, busily adjusting the dress on her Raggedy Ann doll said, "D."

"And this?"

"F sharp. Same as G flat."

The Reverend Daniel LeDeaux fell on his knees crying "Praise the Lord!" He have his niece a mighty hug. "The Lord has richly blessed you with a rare gift, child. He's given you perfect pitch. Do you understand what that means?"

Lilly shook her head.

"Why, child, it means you have a perfect musical ear. You can hear any sound and tell right off what the pitch is without looking at the notes or the instrument. Not one person in ten thousand has such a perfect musical ear. The Lord has destined you to go far with your talent."

Remembering those childhood scenes flooded her with emotion. Lilly bowed her head and wept.

Several sources had fed her growing knowledge of music when she was a child. Her uncle, the Reverend LeDeaux, had given her what he could from his limited, self-taught knowledge of music. He had given her a basic understanding of the keyboard and musical notes. Later, a dedicated public school teacher, Miss Wilma Andrews, coached her singing voice and increased her understanding of the classics.

Another influence had come from a black family who lived on the street behind the Parkers, the Willard

Washingtons. Lilly grew up playing with the Washington kids. Their father, Willard, was a blues singer of some reputation in the area. Lilly often sat entranced in the evenings, listening to Willard as he sat on his front porch in a rickety old hide-bottom chair tipped back against the wall and wrung wailing blues melodies from his battered acoustic guitar, sliding a bottle neck lovingly across the strings.

Willard, who had grown up in New Orleans, remembered hearing in person many of the great New Orleans musicians—Bunk Johnson, Alphonse Picou, Louis Armstrong, Barney Bigard. He had an extensive record library. Lilly listened by the hour to the classic blues singers—Blind Lemon Jefferson, Huddie "Leadbelly" Ledbetter, T-Bone Walker and B. B. King . . . and, above all, the great Bessie Smith. The jazz library included early recordings of Jelly Roll Morton, King Oliver, Louis Armstrong, Bix Beiderbecke and Duke Ellington.

Willard Washington's love of the blues and his jazz records had a lasting influence on Lilly. She loved the music. She memorized all of Bessie Smith's blues vocals and tried to imitate that great singer. When her uncle wasn't around to catch her, she experimented with jazz improvisations on the tabernacle piano.

As Lilly grew older and could earn spending money from baby sitting, she accumulated a modest record library of her own of jazz pianists—Art Tatum, Earl "Fatha" Hines, Jess Stacy, Oscar Peterson.

The school choir director, Miss Andrews, discovered Lilly's talent when she entered junior high and took over her musical education where Uncle LeDeaux had left off. Because of her singing and playing talent, Lilly was often called on to perform for school and community functions.

Her first year in high school was the great turning point in her young life, and her life would never be the same afterward. That was the year she fell in love with Jimmy LaCross. Tall, broadshouldered, with a reckless grin and a mop of blond hair that he'd push back from his forehead with a habitual, careless gesture, Jimmy was the most handsome boy in Millerdale High. He was a senior and as unattainable as a Hollywood movie star. Realistically, Lilly expected no more of life than to be allowed to worship him from a humble distance.

But the magic alchemy of music that was so strongly shaping her life intervened to bring them together. Jimmy, too, had been blessed with musical talent. His young life revolved around his souped up Chevy convertible and his golden trumpet; one supported the other. His parents were no better off financially than Lilly's. But he had been playing for Saturday night dances, the *fais-dodo* of the lusty bayou Cajun people, since he was in junior high and whatever money he earned from blowing his horn went into his beloved car. A common sight in Millerdale was Jimmy LaCrosse speeding down main street in his convertible filled with adoring high school girls.

Jimmy's brilliant, flashing trumpet was the pride of the Millerdale High band. He was also the hope of the music department that would send him to the state competition, hoping to win first place in the solo trumpet division with his flawless performance of *The Carnival of Venice*.

When the band director cast about for a pianist to accompany the trumpet solo, Lilly's name immediately came up. Her heart almost forgot to beat when the choir director, Miss Andrews, called her out of English class to tell her, "Lilly, Mr. Clemmons, our band director, asked if I'd speak to you. As you know,

Jimmy LaCross is going to the state music meet in Baton Rouge. He's going to need a piano accompanist when he plays his trumpet solo. Would you be interested in doing that? You're certainly the best pianist in this school, probably the best in town. Both Mr. Clemmons and I will be going along as chaperones. Of course, it would mean spending some time practicing with Jimmy before the meet."

Lilly found it hard to breathe. Speaking was out of the question. She had just been offered a place in heaven. The best she could manage by way of reply was to gulp and nod.

In that moment, Lilly uttered a silent, fervent prayer of thanks for the long hours she had spent practicing. All the years she was growing up, the piano had been her friend and companion. She'd loved it more than playing games with other children. Somewhat shy and introverted, she hadn't made friends easily. But the piano never teased her or played cruel tricks the way children often did. The times she was happiest were the hours she spent at the keyboard.

Her father promised each year that he was going, somehow, to buy her a piano, but he never succeeded. Fortunately, she had the tabernacle piano to use when she was little, and once she was going to school, the music department allowed her to play on the school piano in the auditorium after classes.

The day Miss Andrews told her the breathtaking news about being chosen to accompany Jimmy LaCross, Lilly was to meet him after school in the auditorium for their first practice session. She arrived fifteen minutes before the appointed time. Her stomach was a nesting place for butterflies. Her hands were icy.

To get her mind off her nervousness, Lilly ran her

hands over the keyboard. She played through some classical études to limber her fingers. Then, becoming relaxed, she allowed her left hand to move idly over a boogie-woogie, eight-to-the-bar bass pattern. Compelled by the rhythm, her right hand touched the keys lightly, improvising jazz phrases.

She became so engrossed with the music that she forgot her surroundings. Her fingers, long and supple for a girl, found rich chords while the rhythm of her left hand matched a primitive racial heartbeat deep within her soul. Her eyes were closed; her shoulders moved to the beat. She ended with her musical signature, a complex thirteenth chord.

Only then did she become aware that she was not alone. Hearing a clapping of hands behind her, she spun around. There stood Jimmy LaCross, grinning and handsome, trumpet under one arm as he applauded. "Very cool. Very groovy. You blow up a storm on that box, little girl."

Lilly shriveled up with self-consciousness, her tongue again paralyzed. She could only stare at her beloved first love with wide and timid eyes, and think, *I'm not a little girl, Jimmy; I'm fourteen, and as much in love with you as a grown woman.*

But he was eighteen, a staggering age difference in the teen-age world. To her fourteen-year-old eyes, he was worldly, sophisticated, self-assured. He'd "been around." He "knew the score." He was a man. And she was awed in his presence.

"I've heard you played a lot of piano," Jimmy went on. "I didn't believe a girl could play jazz like that, but you're really good. How did you learn to play that way?"

Lilly clutched the crumbs of praise to her heart, wanting to remember every word forever. She tried desperately to think of a reply that would sound cool. But her mind had turned to mush. She mumbled a reply so stupid that she wished she would forever be struck dumb. She said, "At the tabernacle."

Jimmy gave her a lopsided grin that wrenched at her heart. "At the tabernacle? Do they play that kind of music there? I'm going to have to start going to church."

"N—no," she stammered, wanting to drop dead on the spot. "I m—meant I practiced there. My uncle is the pastor. I—I learned about jazz by listening to records."

Jimmy wiped his trumpet mouthpiece on his sleeve, raised the instrument to his lips and blew a mellow warm-up phrase that sent a shiver down Lilly's spine.

"Well," Jimmy said, "from the way you were playing, I'd say you've been listening to the right records. We'll have to get together sometime. I've got some pretty good disks too. Not many guys my age dig good jazz. Maybe you and I speak the same language, kid."

She was willing to forgive his calling her "kid" in exchange for this incredible possibility he had offered her—that he might want to spend some time with her, that they shared something special, an understanding and love of the same kind of music, which the glamorous senior pep squad leaders who rode around with him in his convertible did not.

"Well, I guess we'd better run over this solo," he said then, placing before her on the piano the score she was to play.

They spent the next half hour concentrating on the solo he would play at the state music competition. But then he grew tired of that. He rattled the keys of his trumpet, blowing water from the spit valve, then played a casual jazz riff.

"Bet you don't know *Indiana,*" he challenged.

"Bet I do," Lilly grinned, beginning to feel more relaxed with him. "What tempo?"

He tapped the rhythm with a toe. Lilly picked up the beat and played a four bar introduction. Jimmy stuck close to the melody the first time around, but improvised on the second chorus. Lilly backed up his riffs with harmonic and rhythmic figurations. It was the most thrilling experience of her young life up to that moment. She and Jimmy were speaking the same language, elevated to a creative plane of consciousness where they exchanged ideas and inspirations. The mundane world around them was forgotten. Together, they were exploring a different kind of world of pure feeling and ideas.

Lilly did not know how to exchange the glib small talk that Jimmy's teen-age crowd batted back and forth so easily. She felt tongue-tied and painfully self-conscious in his presence. But now she had found a way of communicating with him that was as easy and natural to her as breathing.

In later years, she would reminisce about that impromptu jam session in the high school auditorium that afternoon when she was fourteen and Jimmy was eighteen, and realize how far they were from sounding truly polished. She would smile, remembering the rough spots, the gaps in technique, the times they reached for heights and missed. But at the time, the music they played was the sound of angels. It would echo in her heart forever.

They finished in a rousing climax. Jimmy reached for a high C, missed, and put his horn down with a laugh. Lilly laughed with him. Then Jimmy caught her up in a rib-crackling hug. "Hey, you're okay, kid! When I first saw you, with your pigtails, freckles and flat shoes, I thought, 'Boy, what a little square.' But you're a bunch of fun. I like you, kid.''

Lilly gazed at him, wide-eyed and breathless, and she wanted to tell him how desperately she loved him. But that was not a thing a girl could dare tell a boy, and she could only blink back the tears and try not to say something terribly dumb.

That last year, when Jimmy was eighteen and still in school before he went off to New Orleans, was a gem that sparkled in Lilly's otherwise drab childhood in the dismal little town. Her music and being in love with Jimmy LaCross were the magic that transformed her life.

After that first encounter in the high school auditorium, Jimmy became her friend. He treated her with a kind of amused kindness, like a big brother, and always called her "kid." They went to the state meet and Jimmy won first place in the solo trumpet division, and they celebrated with hamburgers and milkshakes afterward.

There were other times when they played together, sometimes after school or Saturday mornings when they could use the school piano. Jimmy had decided that Lilly was the only person he knew in their small home town who could play the piano with the same understanding and feeling for jazz that he had. According to Jimmy, all the other pianists in town were "little old ladies who played for Sunday School."

Lilly told herself that Jimmy LaCross had no personal interest in her, that his only reason for spending any time with her was their mutual interest in music. But she was grateful for even those crumbs. She hated the senior girls with their long legs and flirty eyes who went out with Jimmy. She felt sick with jealousy when she saw one of them walking across the campus holding possessively onto Jimmy's arm.

But the times she and Jimmy had their private little jam sessions, he belonged to her. When he took off on one of his inspired jazz solos, a driving, smoking explosion of creative expression, Lilly's heart would pound with excitement. Other times, he would be in a sentimental mood and play the rich, gutsy style of Bunny Berrigan's *I Can't Get Started With You,* and bring a rush of tears to Lilly's eyes.

Sometimes, when he wasn't occupied with tinkering over his car or dating the pep squad leaders, he'd pick up Lilly and they'd listen to records together, discussing and analyzing the jazz styles of the artists. The "discussion" mainly consisted of Jimmy doing the talking while Lilly hung on every word.

Once, driving her home after they'd played for a while in the auditorium, Jimmy turned out of town on a narrow farm road. It was a balmy day in early spring. The top of his convertible was down. The wind blew Lilly's hair and the sun was warm on her face. She didn't ask where they were going, or care. She was just grateful for the time to be with him.

He came to a spot where a grove of trees bordered the road, and parked there. "C'mon, kid," he said, "let's take a walk down to the creek."

They followed a path through a field down to a stream where the clear water rushed over stones with a soft murmur. They lay on a grassy bank with wildflowers all around them. Lilly stretched out on her stomach and plucked a blade of grass and chewed on it as she gazed at Jimmy. He was on his back, arms folded behind his head, looking up at the clouds.

It was one of those special moments in growing up

that stays with an individual the rest of his life. Lilly knew it would always live in her heart. All of her senses were sharpened. The purple, red and green colors of the wildflowers were almost painfully vivid. Sounds were intensified. She could hear the rustle of squirrels playing in the giant oak trees that fringed the creek, and the song of a bird far downstream. She could almost hear the grass growing. The perfume of the wildflowers was intoxicating. Mingled with it were the special smells that clung to Jimmy, the faint scent of his hair dressing, the mingling of school chalk, grease from his car, and shaving lotion. The blade of grass she was chewing tasted sweet.

She felt like pinching herself to believe she was actually in this secluded, romantic spot, alone with Jimmy. If it were a dream, she hoped it would never, never end.

"I used to ride down here on my bike, when I was a kid," Jimmy said, "and catch crawdads in the creek there. Once, a buddy and I dammed it up and made a little lake and sailed toy boats on it."

He rolled over on his stomach, propping himself on his elbows. His shirt sleeves were rolled up, revealing the swell of biceps in his tanned arms. He grinned. "Want to go wading?"

"Sure."

She kicked off her loafers. They ran down the bank, laughing. Jimmy took off his shoes and socks and rolled up his trouser legs. Lilly raised the hem of her dress and ventured into the water. It curled around her toes and ankles, tickling her.

Jimmy splashed into the water behind her. She waded into the middle of the small stream. She turned and then became aware with a warm flush that Jimmy was looking at her legs. She was holding her dress above her knees, revealing her thighs.

Jimmy was grinning, but his voice sounded a trifle thick as he said, "You're developing a nice set of legs, kid. You're going to have a great figure in a couple more years."

Her heart began beating swiftly. A strange, sweet yearning filled her. Emotions she had never felt before stirred deep within her. The way he was looking at her awoke a feeling of forbidden excitement. She was partly embarrassed, partly glad that he was looking at her bare legs that way. For once he wasn't treating her like a child.

She felt a bit frightened. Instinctively, she sensed that glimpsing her bare legs had aroused his male desire. What would she do if he reached out to touch her here in this secluded place? Her knowledge of the details of sex were still somewhat vague. Yet, she was more afraid of her own ignorance and of the unknown than she was of Jimmy.

But the moment suddenly passed. As if reminding himself how young she was, Jimmy picked up a flat stone from the creek bed, skimmed it across the water, then said gruffly, "C'mon, kid, let's go back up on the bank."

When they had settled back on the carpet of grass and wildflowers again, Jimmy said, "Well, I'll be graduating next month and I guess after that I won't be seeing you anymore."

The joy of the day was suddenly dispelled in the cold wind. "What—what do you mean?" she asked in a small voice.

Jimmy shrugged. "I'm blowing this burg. You know, I never have gotten along very well with my folks. My old man and I have been at each other's throats since I can remember. He's a mean old coot, and dumb as they make 'em. He's always hated my music. Thinks it's a waste of time. Just because he never got past being a grease monkey at Joe Simm's garage, he thinks I think I'm better than he is because I want to do something else. My brother, Kirk, hated the old man even more than I did. I guess because he was Kirk's stepfather."

"I didn't know you had a brother."

"Half brother. My mother was married once before and had Kirk. Her first husband, Kirk's father, died, and then she married Dad. Kirk was ten years old when I was born. He hung around until I was about six years old, then he split. Went to work in the oil fields. Did all right for himself, too."

Jimmy laughed, chewing on a blade of grass and gazing up at the clouds. "I worshipped Kirk when I was a little squirt. 'Listen, kid,' Kirk used to tell me, 'as soon as you're big enough to buy a bus ticket, get out of this lousy town. You'll never amount to anything here.' I still get a letter from him now and then, offering me a job in his company. But I've got other ideas. I've been saving my money. The day after I graduate, I'm getting in my car and heading for New Orleans. I'm going to get a card in the musician's union, and get a job playing in a jazz band. I've got big plans. One day I'm going to have my own band, and we're going to play Bourbon Street. I'm going to make records and I'll be famous, like Al Hirt or Pete Fountain."

Lilly fought back her tears. "I—I guess I'm going to miss you," she choked.

"Yeah," he said casually. "We had some fun, didn't we? You're a real little swinger. You've got a lot of talent, Lilly. Don't get stuck in this miserable town. Do something with your talent when you finish high school."

"I don't know what I'd do—"

"What do you mean, you don't know? You wouldn't want to wind up a lonely old maid, playing for local weddings and the church choir would you?"

She shuddered. "No, I guess not."

"Well, that's what will happen to you if you stick around here," he warned. "This town will suck the life out of you. It will leave you like a dried up prune with all the spark gone. Heck, with your talent, there's no telling how far you could go."

Then, remembering something, he reached in his pocket and took out a small package. "Hey, I wanted to give you a little something to show I appreciate the times you've helped me practice."

Lilly turned the package over in her trembling fingers, looking at it through a mist of tears. "You—you didn't have to give me anything. I liked it very much, when we played together. . . ."

She fumbled at the wrapping. There was a small box, and inside, nested on a bed of cotton, was a small gold locket.

Lilly's face was pale. She was struggling valiantly to hold back a flood of tears. Finally, she managed to whisper, "Thank you so much, Jimmy. I'll always treasure it." She bit her lip, then gathered the courage to say, "I—I wonder if you have an extra one of your school pictures. The small ones. I'd like to put it in the locket."

"Sure," he shrugged. "I think I've got some extra ones in my locker. Remind me at school sometime, okay?"

And that was how his picture came to be in the locket

that she would wear around her neck from that day on. Later, she'd put her own picture in the other side of the locket.

True to his word, Jimmy LaCross left Millerdale shortly after school ended that term. He didn't tell Lilly good-bye. The day after his graduation, Lilly saw him driving downtown with one of the senior pep squad leaders snuggled close beside him. Then she didn't see him anymore. She heard from the small town grapevine that he had gone.

Lilly wore the inexpensive locket Jimmy had given her all through high school. She knew she would never forget Jimmy LaCross. He was her first, her only, love, she thought, and he had left a void in her heart that no one else could fill.

She was a quiet, studious girl during her high school days in Millerdale. She had few friends and hardly any dates. Her friend was the piano and its music. She didn't know how to make light, meaningless chatter so important in school social interaction, and had no desire to flirt with boys. She made top grades. The choir director continued to take a special interest in her. On graduation night, Lilly was the valedictorian of her class.

With the help of Miss Andrews and the school principal, she had earned a scholarship to a college with a fine music department. A college education was more than William Parker had ever, in his wildest dreams, imagined within the realm of possibility for his daughter.

Lilly would never forget the sight of her father and mother, standing in the bus station the day she went off to college. Her father was a gray, faded little man with stooped shoulders. He was indelibly stamped with a look of a life that had amounted to nothing. But that day, there was a look of pride in his otherwise defeated eyes that Lilly would remember and treasure. Her mother, plump, a little bewildered, dabbed at her eyes with a balled handkerchief, and waved good-bye to a daughter she had never understood.

Her parents would both be dead by the time she'd earned her college degree. Her father was the first to go, the victim of an accident at the paper mill where he was working on the last of a string of dreary, meaningless jobs. Less than a year later, her mother succumbed to complications of a diabetic condition that had plagued her most of her life.

Lilly went back to Millerdale for the funerals. After her mother's death, she stood beside the grave in the small town cemetery, and knew there would be no reason for her to return to the town after college. Except for a few personal items, her parents had left her nothing. Even the delapidated frame house where she'd lived all her life, had been rented.

Lilly had another plan for her life. It had formed in her heart that spring day so long ago, when she and Jimmy LaCross had laid in the wildflowers on the creek bank, and Jimmy had talked about his dreams.

Seven years had passed since then. Lilly was grown up now, twenty-one years of age. Life on the big city college campus had polished some of the rough edges of her small town awkwardness. She felt more sure of herself and more confident than ever of her musical ability. The college training had added a great deal of technical knowledge about music theory to her great natural talent.

During those seven years, she'd had no direct contact with Jimmy LaCross. He hadn't written her a letter, nor had she ever expected that. Probably, he would be hard pressed to even remember the skinny little fourteen-year-old pianist he had known back in high school. From people she'd talked with in her home town the times she had gone back for her father's funeral and to visit her mother during her final illness, she'd heard that Jimmy had, indeed, gone to New Orleans and was making a name for himself in music circles.

Lilly had a small amount of money when she finished college, a bit of insurance money her father had carried with his company on his last job, plus some she had earned playing at night spots on weekends and scoring musical arrangements for local groups.

With her funds, she bought a bus ticket to New Orleans.

She had gotten her degree at midterm. It was a blustery winter day when she boarded the bus for New Orleans. She settled in her seat and gazed out the window, a tiny smile playing across her lips. For seven years, she had carried a secret goal in her heart. And now it was going to be realized. She was going to see Jimmy LaCross again. . . .

Chapter Four

They gave Tiny Smith a real New Orleans funeral. Jimmy LaCross led the band through the narrow streets in the cold, drizzling rain. Musicians, bartenders, bookies, show girls and jazz fans formed the second line, walking in measured steps behind the band, timing their pace to the sad funeral dirge.

After the grave-side services, the procession wound its way between the slick, wet marble vaults out to the streets again. The band, carrying out the tradition all the way, swung out with happy, two-beat jazz, the way New Orleans funeral bands had done since they gave birth to that kind of music in another age.

They were expressing their joy that Tiny's worldly troubles were over now and he was in heaven. They played, *Let The Tailgate Down*, *Rampart Street Parade*, and *Muskrat Ramble*.

Tiny had had a lot of friends along Bourbon Street,

and that night a lot of glasses were raised in tribute to the departed. Bourbon Street was not one to mourn for long. It had a lot of jazz to play and absinthe to drink and pretty girls to watch.

The rain was still coming down slowly, steadily. Cobblestone streets in the French Quarter and ancient wrought-iron grillwork gleamed darkly. Ghosts of Creole ladies, Napoleonic soldiers and swarthy pirates· hovered in the dripping shadows of courtyards and behind shuttered windows.

Later, Jimmy LaCross described that night to Lilly.

Tiny had been more than his band's pianist. He had been Jimmy's close friend since Jimmy quit playing as a side man and formed his own band four years ago. The place was not going to be the same without Tiny's round, smiling face.

A musician's life was a hard one—irregular hours, too many cigarettes, too much booze. The doctor had warned Tiny to get out of it before his heart stopped ticking one night. But Tiny had grinned in his characteristic manner and shrugged, "Live fast, die young—make a good-looking corpse." And he'd made his exit the way he would have chosen, bouncing on his piano bench in the middle of a hot chorus of *Panama*. And now there was an emptiness in Jimmy's heart to match the vacant place in the band. The personnel in a jazz band changes rapidly. Tiny had been the last original member of the band Jimmy formed four years ago.

Jimmy had spent the afternoon when they came back from the funeral drinking steadily, but the alcohol had little effect on him today. Now he lit a cigarette and flipped his match into a running gutter. He walked slowly toward the Sho-Time Bar in the next block Around him, Bourbon Street was coming awake for the evening. The rhythm of jazz music floated out of the bars. Neon tubes glowed around provocative, life-size photographs of bare-legged dancing girls.

Six nights a week, from ten in the evening until four the next morning, Jimmy led his band at the Sho-Time bar. Tonight would be no different. Tiny would have been sad if it were otherwise. There would be a substitute pianist, but the music would go on.

The crowd filled the place tonight to drink and listen as usual. Jimmy tapped off the beat of the opening number and raised his golden horn to his lips. Tonight, he played with a special inspiration.

He made up the improvisation, big and mellow, out of the shadows of smoke and dripping rain and fog on the Mississippi, out of the licorice taste of absinthe and the smell of close-packed bodies and marble vaults wet and cold in the night rain. He made it up and blew it out of his horn, and it made the people laugh and clap, and sometimes it made them shiver.

They played *Bourbon Street Parade* good and solid, the way it had been played here in the French Quarter, the Vieux Carré for years. He put himself in it—a message for Tiny, a message for the world that he was Jimmy LaCross, and he had something to say with his horn.

As he was playing, he opened his eyes a little and saw the young woman through the fog of smoke. She had just come in. Beads of rain glistened in her blonde hair like diamonds and on her cheeks like tears.

She moved through the crowd. The Sho-Time Bar was a long, narrow room with padded, wine-colored walls, sparkling chandeliers over the bar and a dais behind the bar for the band. The customers sat around the walls at miniature tables or on stools at the bar and watched the musicians perform. She edged her way to a vacant stool at the far end of the bar, and sat there alone, listening intently to the music.

Something about the young woman disturbed Jimmy. It wasn't the first time he had seen her. She had been visiting his place nightly for the past week. She always came alone. She usually came about midnight and stayed as long as the band played, carefully nursing along a single drink, much to the scowling displeasure of Alex, the bartender.

The thing that bothered Jimmy was that there was something vaguely familiar about the blonde. He tried to fit her into the parade of attractive young women who had moved through his life, but he couldn't place her. Yet the feeling was there that he knew who she was. He'd been planning to speak to her, but at every intermission he'd been cornered by fans wanting his autograph or by the bartender with some new crisis. Jimmy hired bartenders with the understanding that they would handle the operation of the club while Jimmy ran the band. But it never quite worked out that way. Not the least of the problems was the fact that the last bartender he'd hired had stolen him blind.

So far this week, by the time the problems were solved, the fans were off his back, and the band had played its final tune for the evening and instruments were packed away, the girl had gone. But tonight, at last, he got off the stand after the final number before the young woman left. "Hi," he said, pausing at her spot near the end of the bar.

"Hello," she said quietly, looking directly at him with large, violet-blue eyes.

"You must like music," he smiled. "I've seen you come in for several nights now."

"Yes. You've really gotten good since I last heard you, Jimmy."

He gazed at her with a puzzled frown. "Do I know you from someplace?"

She smiled quietly. "Yes, but you don't remember, do you? I didn't expect you would."

His frown deepened. "Here in New Orleans? That time we played in Baton Rouge? On the riverboat? No?"

She shook her head. "Much, much further back than that, Jimmy. . . ."

Each night, Lilly had tried to find the courage to go up to him. But, whenever he stepped down from the bandstand, other people had claimed his attention. Tonight, when she saw him coming directly toward her, she had felt a thudding in her chest. Her hands had grown cold. She had dreamed about this moment for seven years. Now she found it hard to believe it was actually happening.

The years had changed Jimmy LaCross, though probably not as much as they had changed her. He seemed taller than she remembered, and a bit heavier, and there were tiny crow's feet around his eyes. He was more handsome than ever, with the slightly dissipated look of a professional musician. Her heart had wrenched at the sight of him, and she wished she could reach up and push back the hair that still tumbled carelessly over his forehead.

Whatever changes time had wrought in both of them, it had not disappointed her. She had often wondered if, when she saw Jimmy again, it would turn out to be a sad illusion. She would see him and realize the dream she had carried in her heart for so many years was only

71

that, just a dream, with no claim on reality. The Jimmy LaCross she'd pictured had only been a childhood fantasy, a teen-age crush that had turned an ordinary boy into a romantic hero.

But, no. Jimmy stood before her now, very much flesh and blood. And she was not disappointed. The boy she had loved all these years was very much a real person. And what she felt was no illusion.

There was one important difference. She was no longer a naïve fourteen year old, so overwhelmed by him that she couldn't find her tongue. She still felt some natural shyness. But she could meet him more on his own terms now.

She challenged him with a look and a smile. "Perhaps if I give you a clue, Jimmy, you'll remember."

He followed her curiously as she moved off the stool, around the bar to the band dais. She wondered at her own brashness. But the importance of the moment gave her courage. She had not waited seven years and come all this distance to let inhibitions get in the way. Besides, she felt more confident when she was seated at a piano.

Now, on the bandstand, she ran her fingers lightly over the piano keys. She made herself comfortable on the bench, and began playing one of the traditional New Orleans tunes that the band had played tonight, *The Bucket's Got a Hole In It*.

She sensed Jimmy's presence at her left shoulder, watching her intently. She swung into a stride rhythm with her left hand. Nature had blessed her with a large reach for a woman. She played tenths with ease. She improvised a chorus with the joy and excitement she felt. When she had finished, she swung around on the bench. "Now do you remember me, Jimmy?" she asked.

He wore an expression of stunned surprise. "I've only heard one female in my life play that kind of jazz piano," he exclaimed. "A little girl back in my home town—"

"Do you remember her name?" Lilly asked, raising an eyebrow.

"Uh—"

"Try Lilly."

He snapped his fingers. "Lilly Parker! You're Lilly Parker. My Lord, I can't believe it. Little Lilly Parker, all grown up!"

He lifted her from the piano stool and gave her a mighty hug. "Why in the devil didn't you come up the first night and tell me who you were?" he demanded.

Joy and excitement bubbled inside her. She felt warm all over from his hug. "You're a popular guy," she said breathlessly. "I never could get close to you. Anyway, it was kind of fun to just sneak in and listen to you and see if you'd remember me."

"Tell me all about Millerdale," he exclaimed. "How are the kids we went to school with? Is old Jeff Singleton still the town constable? He used to be on my back all the time about the way I'd race down Main Street!" Jimmy laughed.

Lilly shook her head. "I don't know, Jimmy. I've been gone for several years getting my music degree."

"No kidding! You went on to college? How did you swing that? Your folks weren't any better off than mine."

"Music scholarships . . . government loans. And I worked part-time—"

"Well, that's great, kid. I'm glad you didn't let that small town smother you. You have too much talent." Then he asked, "What the heck are you doing in New Orleans?"

She hesitated. She couldn't tell him the truth, that she'd quietly been carrying a torch for him all these years and coming here to see him again was the realization of a dream that had lived in her heart for so long.

Instead, she murmured, "Just a whim, I guess. I graduated at midterm. I had saved a little money. I thought I'd like to see New Orleans. You know, a kind of pilgrimage to the place where our kind of music got started."

"This is the place," he nodded. "Louis Armstrong got his start playing at Lulu White's joint in the old Storyville section. Just down the street is the place where Jack Teagarden was playing his last engagement when he died—"

He interrupted himself, "Come on, Lilly. I'll buy you a cup of coffee." He motioned to the bartender.

He led her to a private booth at the rear of the place. The bartender brought them steaming mugs of coffee. Jimmy sipped the black Louisiana brew with its sharp chicory flavor. He leaned back against the booth seat, smiling at her.

His smile brought a flood of emotion to her heart. She wanted to grasp this moment, to distill every bit of feeling from it, to memorize the sound of his voice, the touch of his gaze. She had waited so long.

"You've—you've gotten really good on that horn, Jimmy. I remember how good you sounded back in high school, but you're even better now. Your tone is bigger. Your technique is improved. And you have some wonderful ideas—"

"Yeah, well, there's something about this old city that inspires you to play good jazz," he said. His eyes half closed and he seemed to gaze past her, at scenes in another time and place. Dreamily, he said, "So much of it happened right here, back in the early days when it all got started. King Oliver, marching with a brass band down these very streets. The riverboats with their jazz bands coming down the Mississippi, docking at the levee. The funeral bands playing *Didn't He Ramble*. You kind of feel it in the air." He looked directly at her again and grinned. "Y'know, sometimes I have the feeling that the ghosts of those legendary old horn men—Buddy Bolden, Freddie Keppard, Bunk Johnson —are still around and some nights they come in out of the fog and mist and put their fingers on my keys when I'm playing, showing me things I never thought of on my own."

Lilly felt a shiver run down her spine, but she nodded. "I think I know what you mean. I have a feeling kind of like that, walking down the narrow street of the old French Quarter. You feel so close to the past, you can almost reach out and touch it."

Then, as if suddenly embarrassed at the direction their conversation was taking them, Jimmy said, "Well, tell me, kid, what are your plans now that you've seen New Orleans?"

"I—I really don't know," she admitted. "I don't guess I have any. I suppose I'll spend a few more days here until my money starts running out. Then I'll have to go somewhere and find a job. I have several teaching possibilities—"

"Teaching? That sounds like a drag. You're too good to waste your time teaching, kid." He fell silent, a slight frown shadowing his brow as if he was wrestling with an idea. Finally he said in a slow, thoughtful manner, "Hey, would you be interested in a temporary job playing in a jazz band?"

Her heart turned a sudden flip. "What do you mean?"

"I guess you know my regular piano player, Tiny Smith, died suddenly this week. The substitute I hired for tonight is a dog. You heard how badly he plays. The guy's all thumbs. I was just thinking that putting you on the band might spark things up. Tiny's death has got all of us down. The band's in a slump. You're young and full of fresh ideas. You've got a good style and a solid left hand. Some women are terrific jazz pianists— Norma Teagarden, Lil Hardin, Hazel Scott. . . ."

Lilly's heart was racing furiously.

"How about it, kid? Think you'd be interested?"

Lilly couldn't trust her voice. She could only nod.

"The job only pays scale and it's kinda rough, from ten at night till four in the morning."

"That's all right," she said breathlessly.

"I think I can work it out okay with the union. But I want you to understand it's just a temporary job. Y'see, I'm not completely my own boss here." He hesitated, then asked, "Did I ever tell you I have an older brother?"

She nodded. "I think you talked about him one time."

"His name's Kirk. Kirk Remington."

"Remington?"

"Yes. He's my half brother. We have the same mother. Kirk kept his real father's name. That's why our last names are different. Anyway, to make a long story short, Kirk is involved in this place. He'd have to approve of anyone I put on the band. Right now, he's out of the country. I can only promise you a place on the band until he gets back in a couple of weeks. Then we'll have to see how he feels about it."

"Well, that's all right, Jimmy. I'm just happy to have the opportunity to play with you for a while. Maybe your brother will like the way I play, too."

"Maybe," Jimmy said doubtfully. "You never can tell about Kirk."

"What's he like? Is he like you?"

Jimmy laughed. "Not at all." He glanced at his wristwatch. "Tell you what, Lilly. I'm starved. Let's go get a real New Orleans breakfast of eggs and *café au lait*. We can talk some more there."

They left the club and strolled arm in arm down the narrow streets of the old city. Streaks of dawn were touching the Mississippi as they crossed Jackson Square.

In the small, crowded cafe, Lilly sipped her mug of coffee and milk while Jimmy devoured a hearty breakfast. Then he pushed his empty plate back, lit a cigarette, and began telling Lilly about his brother.

"You wouldn't remember Kirk, of course. He left our home town when I was six years old. You were still in rompers. He and my father didn't get along at all. Kirk went to work in the oil fields as a roughneck. He's a hard-working son of a gun and smart as a whip. A lot smarter than me where business is concerned," Jimmy said with a laugh. "Kirk learned the oil business from the bottom up. Then he invented some kind of improved drilling tool. I don't understand exactly what it does. But what it did do for him was make him rich. Now he's got his own business and flies all over the world on big oil deals.

"When Kirk found out I'd left home and was in New Orleans pursuing a musical career, he became very interested. He flew down, heard me play, said I had a lot of talent, and offered to lease a club here on Bourbon Street so I could have my own place.

"Y'see, Kirk is very interested in music. He's actually a frustrated musician, himself. That's one reason he and my old man couldn't get along. Kirk pestered him for guitar lessons when he was a kid and the old man said it was a waste of money. It would have been the same for me, but I got some lucky breaks. The school band director took me under his wing and got me my first horn through the school. I think in spite of all his money, Kirk envies me. He'd give about anything to be able to get up in front of a band and blow a horn the way I do. Since that isn't possible, he does the next best thing by promoting my music and having a hand in running my band."

"How do you feel about that, Jimmy?" Lilly asked.

Jimmy shrugged. "It's a big break for me and the band, I guess, but you know how relatives and business don't mix very well. We get into some pretty big arguments. Kirk is supposed to be a silent partner, but he thinks I don't know anything about business. He's probably right about that. The trouble is, he also thinks he knows a lot about music, and that's where we get into some fights. I admire old Kirk in a lot of ways, but he has an infuriating way of ordering people around that sometimes burns me up."

"And you're not really sure he'd approve of your hiring me for the band," she concluded.

Jimmy nodded. "Yes. It makes me sore, Lilly, but that's the way it is."

She reached across the table and squeezed his hand. "Don't feel bad, Jimmy. I understand. I don't want to cause trouble between you and your brother. We'll just see how things work out. I'll play the best I can and maybe he'll like my style."

"Well, he's bound to like your playing. It's having a woman on the band that may not sit too well with Kirk. Right now he's kind of soured on females. He just got his heart broken by one. Have you ever heard of Marie Algretto?"

"The opera singer? Of course I have. She's one of the world's most beautiful women. To say nothing of her magnificent voice." Suddenly Lilly's eyes widened. "Don't tell me your brother was involved with her!"

Jimmy nodded.

"But she's an international celebrity!" Lilly gasped.

"That's the kind of people old brother Kirk runs around with. When I said he's rich, I meant jet-set rich. The kind of rich that plays roulette in Monte Carlo and has dates with movie stars and countesses. Kirk chased Marie Algretto around Europe for a year. They had a torrid romance going. Kirk was all set to marry her. Then she broke it off, and broke his heart. I really felt sorry for Kirk," Jimmy admitted. "He took it hard. I don't think he's gotten over her yet."

"I can see why," Lilly agreed. "I heard her sing Carmen once at a performance in the city where I went to college. She's the most gorgeous redhead I've ever laid eyes on. And she has a magnificent voice."

Jimmy nodded. "It was the perfect combination for Kirk: style, beauty and musical talent. Kirk seems to fall for women with talent. Before Marie Algretto, he was involved with a lady concert violinist, though not as desperately as he was with Marie."

"Sounds like he's quite a lady's man." Then she teased, "It must run in the family. I seem to remember a certain young trumpet player back home riding up and down Main Street with a convertible full of cheer leaders."

Jimmy chuckled. "There's a difference. I'm just out to have a good time. Kirk is very intense."

Lilly searched Jimmy's eyes for a deeper understanding of his words. Was he warning her when he said, "I'm just out to have a good time"? Or would there be a difference now that he was older and she was a grown woman? Whatever chance she might be taking, she intended to play the game, win or lose, even if it meant heartbreak for her, too. She had carried her dream of Jimmy LaCross in her heart for too many years to turn coward now.

The next night, she arrived at the club early. She had shopped that afternoon, investing a sizable portion of her limited funds on a black cocktail dress. It was form-fitting enough to underscore her femininity, but not too revealing. Jimmy whistled with approval. She warmed all over at his gaze. "You sure have filled out in all the right places from the skinny kid I remember back in school," he grinned.

She remembered the time he had stared at her bare legs when they went wading in the brook and felt again the same undercurrent of sensual excitement.

As the other members of the band assembled for the evening, Jimmy introduced them to Lilly. The drummer was Cemetery Wilson, a good-natured, ruddy faced individual. The banjo was played by Skinny Lang, a tall, emaciated fellow with a chronic, hacking cough. The front line, besides Jimmy, included the clarinet player, Charlie Neal, a slender, intense individual who kept a bottle of Maalox on the band stand to comfort his ulcer. The third member of the front line was the trombonist, a happy, rotund, hard-drinking Irishman named Ted Riley. Riley bounced around the stand as he played, a bundle of exuberant energy.

The musicians were polite to Lilly, but reserved. It was obvious they missed Tiny Smith and resented a newcomer trying to take his place. Besides, they were all tough pros and no doubt viewed her as an inexperienced amateur who was going to foul up the band. They were noticeably cool to Jimmy, probably wondering what had possessed him to hire a naïve girl from the sticks to play in a New Orleans jazz band.

They took their places grimly. Nothing could ruin a band like a bad pianist. Lilly sensed they were bracing themselves against an evening of musical disaster. Charlie Neal took an extra large gulp of Maalox.

Jimmy called the first tune, *Jazz Me Blues,* raised his horn, and tapped off the beat. An electric charge raced through Lilly. All her life, she'd dreamed of playing with a bunch like this. The group was tight and sure. They played with a fierce drive.

Cemetery's drumbeat was a solid rock. His snare rolls were crisp and clean. Jimmy's golden horn punched out the lead with hot, smoking notes as Charlie Neal's clarinet hemstitched a counter melody around it. Ted Riley bounced around, working his slide in a swinging tailgate style.

Lilly knew what a band like this expected from its pianist—a good, solid pattern of rhythmic chords and not too much butterflying around when she wasn't taking a solo. She gave them what they wanted. When the soloists improvised, she backed them with a clear line of chord progressions, occasionally punctuating one of their licks with an answer from her right hand. When Jimmy nodded toward her, she took her own solo chorus, more inspired than she'd ever been before in her life. She was in a state of euphoria, an ecstatic high. Creative ideas raced to her fingertips, electrifying them.

The number ended with a drum break and a wild, eight-bar tag. She realized all the members of the band were staring at her. She turned numb. Had she done something terribly wrong?

But Cemetery Wilson put his sticks down and said, with a note of awe, "Hot damn!" Ted Riley did a happy little shuffle. Charlie Neal scowled at her and said, "What is the chick trying to do—get on steady?"

Jimmy grinned at her proudly. He winked and nodded. "Kid you're really bad," which in musician lingo meant she was terrific.

Lilly's spirits soared. Before the first break, the band had fallen in love with her, and she was in love with every one of them. They played *King Porter Stomp, Back O' Town Blues, That's-a-Plenty* and *High Society*.

Jimmy tried Lilly on a vocal. She belted out one of her Bessie Smith blues numbers and the audience applauded wildly. From then on, Jimmy featured her songs several times each evening.

During the next two weeks, Lilly threw herself into the job with every ounce of her being. She slept until noon, then spent her afternoons writing arrangements. Timidly, she showed them to Jimmy one night.

He leafed through the sheets of music manuscript paper with muttered exclamations. *"Chime Blues, Mabel's Dream, Snake Rag . . .* Hey, these are some terrific old King Oliver tunes. Where on earth did you get them, kid?"

"Off old records. That's the only way you can find some of those classic jazz tunes. You know I have perfect pitch. I can hear a record and write it down the way most people write a letter."

"I know, but these aren't just melody lines. They're great arrangements. How did you learn to score a band like this?"

"I studied arranging and orchestration when I was getting my music degree. I earned some of my tuition arranging for groups around the area where I was going to school."

Jimmy shook his head. "You're something else, kid. You play knocked-out jazz piano, sing a mean blues, and then come up with these terrific arrangements. It was a lucky night for the band when you came walking in here!"

Lilly devoured his words of praise. But she longed for much more—some sign that he was beginning to think of her in other ways than as a competent musician and a valuable addition to his band. Each night, she prayed for a different look in his eyes, a sudden contact in his touch. But, much to her despair, he continued to treat her with a kind of amused affection, like an older brother, just as he had when they were in school together.

She had become so absorbed with those nights spent close to Jimmy and the band that she forgot she was Cinderella at a ball; in two weeks the clock was going to strike "midnight" and her coach was going to turn back into a pumpkin.

The night came without warning. Jimmy had not told her that Kirk Remington was back in town. Later, she discovered that Jimmy hadn't expected him that night. Remington had returned to New Orleans, and simply showed up at the club without warning.

The first hint Lilly got was a sudden tenseness in the band. She noticed a serious look on Jimmy's face. The clowning that normally went on among the musicians became subdued.

Lilly glanced out at the audience in the club. Her gaze was drawn to a tall, swarthy man standing in the doorway. His eyes had a smoldering, brooding expression. She had never seen eyes quite like that—dark, fierce, compelling. The other patrons in the bar seemed to fade into a vague mist as the dark-eyed man's presence dominated the place. Electromagnetic waves emanated from him, a charge of powerful energy that collided with everything in its path.

His brooding eyes swept over the bandstand and settled on her. She felt a strange weakness in her knees, a fluttering in her stomach. A chill raced down her spine. The man's look unnerved her in a way she had never before experienced. His gaze rudely stripped the clothes from her body, leaving her sitting at the piano under his raw inspection.

She had just come face to face with Kirk Remington.

Chapter Five

*K*irk, Lilly went to school with me back in Miller-dale. She came down to New Orleans a couple of weeks ago, right after Tiny died. I hired her to fill in until you got back."

The band was on its first break of the evening. Jimmy, Kirk and Lilly were in the nightclub's back office where Jimmy introduced Lilly to his brother.

Kirk shook her hand, his dark eyes gazing steadily into hers, sending a warm shiver through her body.

She gazed at him curiously, looking for a family resemblance between the two brothers, but finding them as different in appearance as in temperament. Kirk was dark where Jimmy was fair. Kirk's body was as lean and sinewy as a whip. His olive complexion, strong, dark eyebrows and beautiful eyes reminded her of the movie actor Tyrone Power. Only around the mouth did she notice a resemblance, a kind of sensitivity common to both the brothers.

Kirk wore all the badges of a successful man. An expensive suit was hand tailored to drape smoothly over his broad shoulders, the hard-woven dark wool material strained against the rippling muscles of his thighs. Gold cuff links gleamed in the sleeves of his blue, monogrammed shirt. A heavy platinum wristwatch circled his left wrist.

Lilly sensed that the difference between the personalities of Jimmy LaCross and Kirk Remington was even more striking than their appearance. Where Jimmy was happy-go-lucky, Kirk possessed a brooding intensity.

"Lilly, I'm very glad to know you," Kirk said in a rich, softly modulated voice that sent a fresh shiver down her spine. "So you're from our old home town."

Lilly nodded, finding herself strangely at a loss for words.

Kirk laughed, flashing even, white teeth. "Millerdale is a great place to be *from*."

Lilly found her tongue. "I take it you don't think any more of the town than Jimmy does."

"Oh, I really don't have anything against it. I suppose I have bad associations from a not very happy childhood there. I'll have to give the town credit for producing young people with remarkable musical talent. You play very well."

"Thank you," Lilly murmured, her heart leaping with hope. She *had* impressed him. He was going to let her stay in the band!

But his next words dashed her hopes. "I hope you'll understand that it's no reflection on your playing if we can't give you a permanent job."

Lilly's shoulder's slumped. She looked from Kirk to Jimmy, fighting back a rush of tears.

Jimmy was scowling. "Kirk, dammit, what kind of attitude is that? Lilly plays up a storm. You heard her.

She's sparked the whole band. I want to keep her with us."

The brothers locked gazes that were like steel striking flint and giving off the sulfurous odor of flying sparks. "We'll discuss it at another time," Kirk said calmly.

"Another time, heck!" Jimmy cried. "I'm tired of you all the time throwing your weight around. I wish you'd leave running the band up to somebody who knows something about music."

Again, Lilly was made aware of a difference in the two men. Jimmy, for all his happy-go-lucky nature, could be hot tempered. Kirk met his younger brother's outburst with a look of cool disdain.

Then he turned to Lilly with an apologetic smile. "Just a little family argument, Lilly. The fact is that I know quite a bit more about music than Jimmy gives me credit for. Jazz music happens to be a great passion in my life. While I'm not a musician myself, I do know a lot about music. I probably own one of the most extensive libraries of jazz records in the world. The way I relax from the pressures of business is to come down here when I'm in New Orleans, settle at a table near the bandstand, and listen to Jimmy's band. I think he and his boys have a great future and I'm willing to gamble money on promoting them. That's why I'm so concerned with their future and Jimmy's choice of the band's personnel."

"If you're all that concerned about our future, maybe you'd better think twice before letting Lilly get away from us," Jimmy exclaimed. "Here, look at some of the arrangements she's written since she's been with us." He thrust a bundle of music into his brother's hands.

Kirk raised his eyebrows in surprise. "You're an arranger, too?" he asked her.

"A darn good one," Jimmy said.

Kirk glanced through the pages, then gave Lilly a look of new respect. "These do look good. Some of these tunes are quite rare and hard to come by. They certainly would be a valuable addition to the repertoire of any band that plays traditional jazz."

"Wait until you hear the band play them," Jimmy exclaimed.

"Okay. I do want to hear them. If they're really good, maybe we could keep you on as an arranger, Lilly. But I just don't think it would work out to have a woman playing in the band. Sorry."

With that, he walked out of the room.

Lilly was fuming.

"See what I mean?" Jimmy growled.

"He can be infuriating," she agreed. "I'd like to leave right now. I don't want to give him the satisfaction of firing me!"

Jimmy's face clouded. "You really wouldn't do that, would you, Lilly? It would put the band in a tough spot. We've got a big crowd tonight. And you'd have the union on your back something fierce for walking off a bandstand without notice."

Lilly's bright-eyed look of anger softened. "No, Jimmy, of course I wouldn't do that to you."

He hugged her, grinning down at her. "That's my girl." He kissed her lightly and whatever anger was left in her melted in a rush of emotion.

Jimmy said, "No matter what Kirk says, I can't kick you off the stand without notice. Let's go play the heck out of those new arrangements. I know when Kirk hears them, he's going to hire you as a full-time arranger."

"All right," Lilly said reluctantly. "But, Jimmy, I do think it's unfair for Kirk to tell you how to run your band. I think you're right—he's jealous because you're the one with all the talent."

Jimmy shrugged. "Maybe so. Anyway, at this point we're all pretty dependent on Kirk's money. Jazz has never been a very commerical product. Right now it's the rock groups and the country western stars who are raking in the big money and making the million dollar record sales. Some of the greatest jazz musicians died broke, forgotten and alone in some charity ward. So, I guess we're lucky having someone like Kirk with his money and influence behind us. I keep reminding myself of that. With Kirk, we might make it big some day—records, jazz festivals, European tours."

"I'll keep that in mind when I'm around Kirk. I'll smile sweetly and bite my tongue—for your sake."

Jimmy kissed her again. "Thanks, sweetheart. Now let's go out there and blow old Kirk out of the joint with those great arrangements of yours."

Intoxicated by Jimmy's kisses, Lilly returned to the bandstand and played as she had never played before.

Lilly was under a strain for the rest of that week. She dreaded looking over the crowd in the small nightclub; she knew she would see Kirk Remington. He was there every night at a private table in the shadows against a wall. He appeared immobile, lost in comtemplation, his attention never wavering from the band.

Lilly took out her frustration and anger at the ruthless man by throwing her energy at the piano. She played jazz solos with thundering chords that made the instrument shake. Jimmy grinned at her after one of her onslaughts at the keyboard. "Don't break it, honey. It ain't paid for."

She sang her Bessie Smith type blues numbers with all her soul, belting them out from the tips of her toes.

She sang *Gimme a Pig's Foot and a Bottle of Beer* with a powerful delivery that didn't seem possible from such a slender girl. She felt Remington's eyes on her, twin smoldering, dark orbs, searching her out, sending a cold shiver down her spine.

When they finished the band's theme song at four in the morning on the last night of Lilly's job with the band, she saw Kirk Remington take Jimmy aside, speak with him briefly, then stride out of the club.

Jimmy gave Lilly her paycheck for the week. He told her, "I have a message for you. Kirk wants you to have dinner with him this evening."

Lilly's mouth dropped open. *"What?"*

"Kirk wants to have dinner with you," Jimmy repeated.

Her eyes reflected disbelief, then suspicion. "What on earth for?"

Jimmy shrugged. "I don't know, Lilly."

"Well, I won't do it!" she retorted stormily.

"Better not be too hasty about turning him down," Jimmy suggested. "I have a hunch he wants to talk to you about a permanent job in the band."

Lilly's anger abated somewhat. "Do you really think so, Jimmy?"

"I can't say for sure. He didn't say why, just told me to tell you to be ready for him to pick you up at seven-thirty tonight. It's hard to know what the guy is thinking."

Lilly's innermost reaction to Remington's imperious order that she be at his beck and call was fresh anger piled on her already fuming dislike of the man. But she was willing to suffer almost any indignation if it would mean she could go on being close to Jimmy. She sighed and nodded, "All right. I'll be ready."

That evening, she selected the best outfit she owned

from her meager wardrobe. It was a rust colored, pleated dress she had found on sale for twenty-four dollars back in her college town. The knit was a pullover style with a self-fabric button closing to the waist. The V-neck stopped short of being revealing. The dress had a shawl collar, shirred drop front shoulderline and long sleeves. The skirt portion was pleated all around and it had a self-fabric sash-belt.

She turned slowly in front of the mirror in her dingy little hotel room. It was a presentable dress, flattering her figure, yet with a modest and conservative effect that afforded her a degree of security. She expected to be polite to Kirk Remington, but cool and distant.

A smile teased her lips when she thought about the irony of going out with the rich, high and mighty Kirk Remington in her twenty-four dollar bargain basement dress. No doubt the women Kirk Remington took to dinner wore designer originals from Paris or Rome. But, what the heck—she wasn't out to impress the man. He knew she was just a poor musician. One look at this third-rate hotel room when he came to pick her up would be evidence enough of her financial status.

The dingy room didn't bother her very much. True, it was not much larger than a walk-in closet. A single bed, a battered dresser and one chair left very little room to move about. The rug was threadbare, the wallpaper streaked and faded. But there was a tiny balcony overlooking a typical French Quarter courtyard filled with banana trees and tropical plants. And for that, Lilly forgave the room all its other shortcomings.

She slipped on her brown trench coat and stepped out on her minuscule balcony. She felt the cold touch of the wrought-iron grillwork under her palms as she leaned against the railing, looking down at the courtyard, then across the rooftops of the Vieux Carré. The sunset filled the sky with blood red streaks. Again a damp mist was in the air, lending a soft aura to the ancient buildings. She felt the chilling touch of the mist on her cheeks.

More than that, she felt the mood of the city, the heartbeat of this ancient setting with its character of fun and wickedness. She was acutely aware of the mingling of time, of past and present. She could hear the clop-clop of a horse-drawn sightseer's carriage down the mist slick cobblestone streets and imagined it was carrying caped and gowned aristocrats of another century past street corner gas lights to the French Opera House. The ghosts of slaves, freebooters, plantation owners, dashing Confederate cavalry officers, and Storyville harlots moved wraith-like in the early fog that swirled in across the levee from the Mississippi. They mingled with twentieth century artists, tourists, merchant seamen, jazz musicians, nightclub strippers and antique-shop owners.

She watched as night fell and the mist created soft halos around the street lights. She had the eerie feeling that a single incantation from a voodoo queen could evaporate the present, and she would find herself back in the wicked days of the Storyville red light district. She could almost hear Jelly Roll Morton playing in one of the bordellos and see the beautiful octoroon ladies-of-the-evening in the mahogany paneled rooms of Lulu White's sporting house.

A strange mood possessed her. It was as if she were having an out-of-body experience, leaving the limitations of time and space behind. She saw herself and Jimmy LaCross, walking together down the streets of this romantic city in other times and places. Had they been lovers before, in another lifetime? Was that why she was eager to give her heart to him now, subconsciously remembering the passion they had shared in another existence?

Perhaps she had been a southern Creole belle, and he a dashing Confederate cavalry officer home on leave. Their last hours together had been intense, snatched from a fate that would take him back into battle. They had shared passionate kisses and embraces. They might have known each other intimately in a bed in this very room. Her face warmed with a blush at that fantasy.

Or, maybe he had been a musician playing in the honky-tonks of the old Storyville red light district and she had been his woman.

But the face of her lover in the fantasies became confused with another. The image of Kirk Remington began to intrude, to take over her daydream. He became a Rhett Butler, a blockade runner and freebooter, striding through the streets on a mission of international intrigue. They met secretly, and he rode with her over the cobblestone streets in a carriage that took them to a secret meeting place . . .

Her face became scarlet at the erotic fantasies filling her mind. Why had Kirk taken over her dreams? She felt a stab of guilt that she had been unfaithful to Jimmy even in her fantasy. But Kirk had such an overpowering personality that he could not easily be dismissed.

She was taken from her reverie by a knock at her door. She stood there a moment longer, reluctant to release the dream. She withdrew from it slowly, then turned with a sigh back to the world of reality, a reality dominated tonight by Kirk Remington.

She closed and locked the balcony door. "Just a

minute," she called. She gave her makeup a quick inspection, removing traces of her tears. Then she unlocked the hotel door.

Kirk Remington stood in the hallway, tall, broad-shouldered, looking elegant in a dark overcoat and white scarf. She felt the impact of his presence with the force of an electric jolt. The man was a walking charge of magnetism. His dark eyes raked over her with a force that electrified the air. His gaze blinded and disconcerted her.

"I've made dinner reservations," he murmured. He named one of the famous and most expensive Vieux Carré restaurants. "Will that be all right?"

"Of course," she murmured, feeling a flicker of amusement. Surely she wouldn't object to being taken to a place where a meal would cost as much as her father used to earn in a month's salary!

The feeling of unreality came over her again. It was as if she were standing aside, a slightly amused spectator, watching Lilly Parker being escorted from the building by the oil and shipping tycoon. The situation was too incongruous to be real. The Lilly Parkers of this world did not go out on dinner dates to famous restaurants with men like Kirk Remington. The Lilly Parkers ate in fast-food joints with guys who drove old Chevrolets.

Kirk had little to say to her on the way to the restaurant, which added to the strained feeling between them. He asked if she minded walking since the restaurant was but a few short blocks from her hotel. She said she didn't mind at all, and that ended any exchange between them until they entered the restaurant.

The maître d' instantly recognized Kirk Remington and they were seated with a flourish, at a choice table.

As was the case with many of the famous, old

restaurants in New Orleans' French Quarter, this room was right out of the nineteenth century. The paneled walls were mellowed with age. The gas lights had been replaced by chandeliers with electric bulbs, but otherwise nothing had changed in a hundred years. There were indentations in the tile floor worn by the shoes of several generations of waiters bearing trays of exquisitely prepared food from the kitchen.

Kirk ordered cocktails for them, then conferred with the waiter in French over the menu.

Lilly thought it was a shame that such sumptuous food would be wasted on her tonight. She was too nervous to do much more than pick at her meal. Questions were racing through her mind, turning her stomach into knots. Why had Kirk chosen such an elaborate way to discuss her future with Jimmy's band? Did he think firing her would be made easy by treating her to an expensive meal? Perhaps it was his way of soothing his conscience.

He broke the awkward silence at last, talking about his interest in music, the research he had done into the history of American jazz, discussing books he had on the subject, famous musicians he had known personally here and abroad, his record library. Despite her feeling of resentment toward the man, Lilly was impressed by his extensive knowledge of jazz and of music in general. Granted, he might be a dilettante, but at least he had a genuine sensitivity and appreciation for music. Her judgment of him softened slightly.

He talked about his plans and ambitions for Jimmy's band, and that further melted her chilled response to him. Then he abruptly switched the conversation to her. By then they had finished the meal.

Lilly's attention became acute. Her fingers clenched the napkin on her lap.

"I've been impressed by your musical ability, Lilly," Kirk began. "I'll admit that at first I was totally negative about keeping you in the band. I didn't think it would be good for Jimmy's group. Besides, I didn't think you were in the same league with them. I changed my mind after hearing the band every night this week. I admit it. I was wrong. You are a remarkably talented young woman."

Lilly's heart leaped. "Then I can stay in the band?"

"As far as I'm concerned, you certainly may."

Her eyes sparkled. Her heart flooded with joy. Suddenly, Jimmy's older brother ceased being a horned ogre. He was, in fact, a strikingly handsome man, poised, confident, self-assured. Yet, he was quite reserved, too. She did not yet feel she knew him very well. But now that he had praised her musical ability so warmly and agreed she could stay in Jimmy's band, she felt much more relaxed with him.

He signed the check with his Diners Club card and then escorted her from the restaurant. "The evening is not over yet," he said mysteriously. "I have something to show you."

They walked together a few blocks to a parking garage where he had left his Mercedes. They drove out of the city's old quarter onto Canal Street. It was like leaving the nineteenth century for today's world of bright lights and honking traffic. He sped across town to an elegant apartment tower. An elevator whisked them to the penthouse floor.

Lilly entered his apartment feeling nervous and on guard.

His living quarters were lavish. Costly paintings decorated the richly paneled walls. The furnishings were starkly modern, the carpets luxurious.

He removed his topcoat and helped her take off her trench coat, hanging them both in a closet.

"You—you live in a beautiful apartment," Lilly murmured, keeping a safe distance from him.

"I keep this place for the times I'm in New Orleans. But this is what I wanted to show you." He led her across the living room. "I just had it installed."

Lilly stared at the sound system. Her eyes grew wide as she read the top-of-the-line brand names on the turntable, amplifier, tuner, tape deck. It was obviously worth a fortune.

"What do you think, Lilly?"

She glanced at him, suddenly realizing that he was looking at her with a concerned expression as if anxiously hoping for her approval. Her nervousness evaporated in a rush of concealed amusement. The aloof, cold, austere Kirk Remington actually had a human side! He wasn't a hundred percent sure of himself after all. For some reason he wanted very much to impress her with his new sound system, not unlike a high school boy showing off his hot rod to an important date.

She decided to take advantage of the situation. "Well," she said doubtfully, suppressing a wicked grin, "it looks impressive. But I'd have to hear how it sounds."

"Of course."

He carefully placed a record on the turntable. The rich harmonies of Duke Ellington's band flooded the room with a river of sound pouring from the stereophonic speakers.

Lilly sat on a couch, curling her feet under her, letting her senses become drenched with the experience of pure sound. She closed her eyes, and the band was in the room with them.

When the record ended, she looked up at Kirk, who was waiting expectantly for her reaction. She was tempted to pay him back for the suspense he'd caused her over her job with Jimmy's band. But she couldn't restrain her enthusiasm. "It's fabulous. The best I've ever heard!"

He looked extremely pleased. He mixed drinks at a bar, handed her one of the glasses and sat beside her. "It sounded good to me, but I'm not all that sure of my ear." He gazed at her for a moment, then added, "I really envy your musical talent and perfect ear, Lilly."

"You do?" She glanced around at the richly furnished apartment. "I wouldn't think you'd have to envy anybody anything."

"There are things money won't buy. Jimmy is really the rich one in the family. To be able to play a horn like that—" His voice faltered. A wistful emotion filled his eyes and he looked away.

"I—I had the impression you two don't get along so well," Lilly said.

"Don't pay too much attention to our squabbling," he said, bringing his attention back to her. "I do lose patience with Jimmy. He can be scatterbrained about business at times. And he resents my suggestions about how the band should be run. But we're still brothers, and I love Jimmy. I feel guilty about leaving home when he was so young, although it appears he did all right on his own." He gazed at her in a way that gave his words a double meaning and made her blush.

"I—I think Jimmy is really fond of you, too, Kirk," she said.

She stole a glance at him, increasingly aware of his physical appeal. He kept his body lean and hard. His dark skin glowed with health. He had a clean, firm jaw.

There was a slight touch of premature gray in the temples of his otherwise coal black hair. He moved with the lithe ease of a cat. When he rose and walked over to the sound system to put on a new record, she noticed the compact lines of his hips. His posterior had the firm, rounded contours of that of a high school boy. She blushed at her unexpected physical response to what she saw.

"Do you like classical music, Lilly?"

"I certainly do. Every bit as much as I like jazz."

"Do you? So do I, depending on the mood I'm in. I thought I might like to hear a bit of Tchaikovsky, if that's all right."

"Yes," she nodded, aware that he had chosen one of the romantic composers.

He mixed fresh drinks as the poignant strains of the music enveloped them.

"Tell me about yourself, Lilly," he said as he rejoined her on the couch, handing her one of the drinks. "I can't seem to place your family back home. Did you have any older brothers or sisters I might have gone to school with?"

"No. I was an only child. There wasn't much about our family you would have remembered. My poor Dad wasn't the kind of man to make much of an impression on a town. He was one of life's failures, I'm sorry to say. My mother just numbly accepted the situation fate had given her."

"Then how did you manage to get such a good education in music?" he asked with surprise.

"It started when I was quite young. Do you remember the evangelist back home, Daniel Webster LeDeaux?"

"Brother LeDeaux!" he laughed fondly. "Indeed I

do remember him. He was a marvelous backwoods orator. Used to scare the pants off me with his hellfire and brimstone sermons."

"Yes. That was his style. He was my uncle. He introduced me to music. He taught me what he knew about notes and the keyboard. When I went to school, the choir director took a special interest in me. With their help, I eventually got a scholarship and earned my degree in music."

"And Jimmy? You were high school sweethearts?" There was suddenly a brittle quality in his voice.

Lilly blushed. "I guess I had a crush on Jimmy from the first time I saw him."

Kirk's eyes darkened and his jaw knotted. Then he changed the subject abruptly. "Lilly, I have a lot of plans for you."

She looked at him questioningly. "I don't understand."

"I'd like to build you up as a musical personality. I think you have tremendous potential if given the right kind of promotion. I could arrange some Las Vegas engagements for you, TV spots. . . ."

Lilly was stunned. She'd never had any ambitions for herself other than to become good enough one day to play in Jimmy's band. She shook her head in bewilderment. "I don't understand. Why would you go to all that trouble over me? It's Jimmy and his band that needs the publicity. I'm just the piano player."

"Oh, I intend to see that Jimmy gets his breaks. But you are in another league, Lilly. You have an incredible musical talent and, without realizing it, an unaffected manner of projecting your sweet, loving nature." Then he chuckled, "And when you belt out those old blues songs, you become a dynamite charge of female allure.

I think you could go a long way in the entertainment field."

His hand closed over hers. The warmth of his fingers flooded up her arm. In a daze, she looked down at his strong, deeply tanned masculine hand with its clean, neatly trimmed nails and curling dark hairs. She sensed the strength in his fingers and shivered.

They chatted for another half hour, Kirk talking about his ambitions for Jimmy's band and his plans for Lilly. She felt dazed by the interest he was taking in her and wasn't sure how to respond.

When it was time to go, he brought her coat from the closet and helped her into it, standing behind her. As her arms slipped into the sleeves, she felt him move closer and draw her against him in a light embrace. His cheek was touching her head. His breath stirred her hair. "Lilly, I have something to ask you."

Lilly felt confused, unsure of her own emotions at this point.

"It's rather personal," he murmured. "I hope you won't be offended."

"What—what do you mean?"

"It's about Jimmy. I gather from what you told me that you were childhood sweethearts. . . ."

"It . . . was pretty one-sided," she admitted. "I said I had a crush on Jimmy, but he was three grades ahead of me and popular with the senior girls. I was just a kid who played piano for him."

"That sounds like Jimmy. But you've grown up into a very sexy young lady. He must feel differently about you now."

"I—I don't know—"

"What I guess I'm really asking," he said bluntly, "is, are you Jimmy's girl?"

"Why do you want to know?" she stammered.

"I have a very good reason. Lilly, I'm very attracted to you. So much so that it's hard to keep my hands off you. But I'm not the kind to make advances to another man's girl, especially if she's involved with my own brother."

Again he had succeeded in stunning and confusing her. This was the last thing she had expected from Kirk Remington. She tried to assay her emotions. She couldn't help being flattered. Any woman would sense a deep stirring of her femininity at hearing that she had aroused the interest of such a handsome and fascinating man as Kirk Remington.

But she wasn't prepared for this. Until tonight, Jimmy LaCross had been the only man to fill her romantic ideal. She had never considered the possibility that she could be drawn to anyone else. And yet, Kirk's closeness sent quivering shocks through her body that she couldn't deny.

His low voice near her ear murmured, "I apologize if I've made you uncomfortable. But you can understand my position. I had to speak bluntly."

She felt her cheeks flush. "I respect you for being such a gentleman. I—I am very fond of Jimmy and have been for a long time. But we're not involved in any kind of intimate relationship, if that's what you mean."

She heard a soft release of his breath, like a sigh of relief. Gently, he turned her to face him. For a long moment, his dark eyes drank deeply from her wide-eyed gaze. She felt herself become weak from the power of his look. She swayed against him.

With a murmur of her name, his lips touched hers. He drew her closer. His kiss became warm.

Then, breathlessly, she pulled away from him. Nervously, avoiding his dangerous gaze, she managed a shaky laugh as she said, "Thank you for a lovely evening, Kirk. But now you'd better take me back to my place."

"Of course," he said. "But I expect to be seeing more of you, Lilly . . . a lot more."

Later that night, in her bed in the shabby hotel room, Lilly stared wide-eyed at the ceiling. Her lips still burned from Kirk's kiss. Her body throbbed from his touch. She was both aroused and dismayed. When she thought about Jimmy, tears filled her eyes. She felt that her runaway emotions were making her unfaithful to him. And yet, except for a friendly kiss or two, Jimmy had not shown any serious interest in her.

"Jimmy, please save me from this mess," she whispered, her tears trickling down to the pillow. "Just fall in love with me and I'll know what to do."

Kirk was serious about intending to see a lot more of her. During the following week they had several dates. Because of her evening engagements with the band, they were together only during the day. They had lunches in romantic French Quarter patios surrounded by banana trees and ancient stone walls. Kirk took her for a ride around the bayou countryside and they toured magnificent antebellum plantation mansions. Another day they went for a trip on a Mississippi sightseeing riverboat.

Kirk was treating her with gentlemanly courtesy. He was a sophisticated, urban man who could be devastatingly charming. At times he was witty. He flattered her with gifts of flowers. He had the dangerous ability to make a woman feel as if she were the complete center of his universe. He made no further attempt to kiss her, but the touch of his hand and the expression in his eyes sent her a clear message of his desire for her.

The attention Kirk was giving her did not go unnoticed by Jimmy. When the band finished playing in the early hours one morning, he packed up his horn and walked out of the club holding Lilly's arm. "Okay if I walk you home?"

"Sure," she smiled.

"Band sounded great tonight," Jimmy said as they walked the few blocks to her hotel.

"Better all the time!"

"Thanks to the great little piano player we now have."

"I'll bet you say that to all the piano players," she teased.

"Only the pretty, sexy ones," he grinned.

She glanced up at him, trying to judge the look he was giving her. Jimmy kidded so much that it wasn't easy to dig under the banter to understand his true feelings. Was he looking at her in a special way tonight?

They walked through the dimly lit lobby and up the dark stairway of the side street hotel.

"What a dump," Jimmy muttered. "I hate to think of you living here."

"I don't mind. Really. My room has a little balcony that looks out over a courtyard and the rooftops of the Vieux Carré. I love the view."

"Just the same, I'll be glad when we can afford to pay you more so you can find a better pad."

"Listen, if you're going to live down here in the quarter, you can't be all that choosy," she reminded him. "Rents are astronomical, even for dumps like this."

"Yeah, I guess so."

They had reached her door. She put her key in the lock and turned to tell Jimmy good night.

He was looking at her with a strange expression. "Got a goodnight kiss for an old buddy?" he asked softly.

Her heart suddenly quickened. "You'll never know until you try, will you?"

He slipped his arms around her waist, looked down at her for a moment, then kissed her. This time it wasn't a light friendly brush of her lips. His mouth lingered on hers as he drew her closer, pressing her body against his.

Lilly's arms went around his neck. She held nothing back from her kiss. Her lips parted. She welcomed the seeking quiver of his tongue. The dreams of many years were wrapped up in this moment. A golden haze enveloped her thoughts and emotions.

Finally Jimmy stepped back. "Well, you sure aren't a little kid any more, are you?"

She smiled, her heart giving a tripping beat. "So you've begun to notice?"

He nodded. Then he suddenly scowled. "Apparently my big brother has noticed, too."

She gave him a puzzled, questioning look.

"I know you've been out with him a lot this week."

"Yes I have." A sudden, light frown crossed her brow. "Are you jealous, Jimmy? Is that what this is all about?"

"Maybe a little. But more worried than jealous."

"What do you mean."

"I mean my big brother is bad news for you, babe."

"Oh?"

"Yes. In case you hadn't noticed, he's a smooth operator. With the bucks he can toss around and all that charm he oozes, a girl doesn't stand much of a chance if he levels his sights on her."

"Is that so? Well, I kind of get that impression about the younger brother, too. I'm not blind, Jimmy. I see all the women hanging around the bandstand panting up at the trumpet player!"

Jimmy grinned. "I didn't mean to hold myself up as any model. I just say watch out for Kirk."

"Exactly why?"

"In case you forgot, let me remind you that he's just getting over a busted heart. In fact, I'm not all that sure he's over it."

"Oh. You mean the opera singer, Marie Algretto."

"Exactly. Lilly, I think he's chasing you on the rebound. He's lonesome and he needs a woman's reassurance to rebuild his busted ego. I'm afraid you're letting yourself in for a big heartache. I don't like to see it happen to a sweet kid like you. You haven't been around enough yet to know how to cope with a guy like Kirk."

Lilly nodded slowly. "I've thought about that—"

"You better think about it a whole lot," Jimmy warned. Then he kissed her again.

This time the kiss lingered even longer. His hands moved over her body, seeking her bosom. He cupped her breasts, caressing and fondling, sending waves of heat through her body.

Finally, breathlessly, she drew back. Her lips felt bruised and swollen. She looked at him, wide-eyed with a kind of desperation to see below the surface of the joking, happy-go-lucky Jimmy LaCross.

"How about you, Jimmy?" she whispered huskily. "Do I have to be afraid of you, too?"

His eyes clouded. He avoided her gaze. "Maybe . . ."

She clasped his hands in hers, pressing them against

her throbbing breasts. "Jimmy, darling, I've cared a lot about you for a long, long time. If you asked to come into my room with me now, I wouldn't say no."

"Lilly—"

"But hear me out, Jimmy. I have to know if it's because you really care about me or if it's because you've suddenly become jealous of Kirk. I'm beginning to understand you two. You have something Kirk covets dearly—your musical talent. Now suddenly, Kirk is about to take something that makes you jealous —me. I think there's some kind of deadly rivalry going on between you two, and I don't want to be the prize you're fighting over, no matter how much I care about you."

Jimmy scowled, his handsome young face becoming sullen. "I don't know what you're talking about. What is it you want me to say, Lilly? That I love you?"

"Maybe. I don't know. Maybe that's asking too much right now. But I don't think I can just hop in bed with you on a whim, Jimmy, or because you don't like Kirk beating your time with me. I have to have some kind of commitment . . . to know that you really care about me, that I'm not just another cheerleader riding around in your convertible."

There was a long moment of heavy silence. Lilly felt tears burning her eyes. She looked through them at Jimmy. "I—I don't guess you do . . . what you said . . . love me?" she asked hopefully.

Jimmy scowled again. Making a fist, he pounded softly at her hotel door as if battling with some kind of unseen opponent. "Lilly, I don't know. I do care about you, but I'm kind of mixed up about it. For a long time, I thought of you as the little, long-legged, freckle-faced kid back home. You know, sort of my kid sister. Then you showed up here, all grown up. A woman. But I still had a kind of big-brother, protective feeling toward you. That's all mixed up with how I feel about you running around with Kirk. I don't like to see you get hurt. Maybe I am jealous, too. I don't know. . . ."

She looked at him thoughtfully, sadly. "I wonder if you will ever love anyone but your horn. She's your real mistress, isn't she, Jimmy?"

He gave a helpless shrug. "Lilly, I don't know much about love, or being totally committed to one woman. Up to now, I've gone breezing through life, playing my music, not thinking a heck of a lot about tomorrow or getting too serious about anyone or anything."

She nodded slowly. "I understand. And I guess I've scared you with what I said, like I expect you to change your whole life for me. Maybe that's a mistake. Maybe I have to make up my mind that if I want you, I'll have to take my chances." She smiled ruefully. "Looks like I'm in for a heartache no matter which brother I choose."

Jimmy nodded, giving her a troubled look. "You might be better off to forget both of us."

She slowly shook her head. "I'm afraid it's too late for that, Jimmy," she sighed.

When he was gone, she moved wearily into her room. She felt physically drained. Her emotions were in tatters. She had dreamed for so many years of Jimmy taking her in his arms and kissing her. But now that it had happened, it was for all the wrong reasons. Instead of being filled with joy, she was sad and confused.

The next time she had a night off from the band, Kirk took her to dinner. Again, he was a charming, attentive escort, greeting her with an armful of lush, red roses.

Over their meal, she thought about the magnetic

power of his gaze. *His eyes,* she thought. *I've never seen such probing, penetrating eyes.*

Later, they went to his apartment again to listen to selections from his vast record collection. Kirk drew her close to him. His dark eyes framed with thick, curved lashes gazed deeply into hers, draining her strength.

It isn't fair . . . a weak voice within her protested.

His lips touched hers, sending a shudder through her body. The pressure of his lips grew stronger, seeking . . . eager . . . hungry. Her heart began pounding.

This is all wrong! the voice within her cried out. It was Kirk's brother Jimmy who had filled her dreams all the years she was growing into womanhood. But the dreams had become confused. She could no longer deny the attraction she felt for Kirk.

Jimmy, it's your fault, her heart cried angrily. *If you truly loved me, if you were willing to make a commitment to that love, then I wouldn't be so tempted by Kirk's arms.* . . .

She protested when Kirk gently moved her dress down from her shoulders, but she couldn't find the strength to push him away.

He murmured her name, his voice thick with passion as he pushed her dress down to her waist. His strong fingers touched the satin straps of her bra that crossed her shoulders. He slipped them down. She felt a cool draft of air touch her bared bosom. She gasped a deep breath through her teeth.

"You're exquisite, Lilly," he murmured huskily, drinking in the sight of her.

He buried his face in the soft pillows of her bosom. She writhed as his kisses tasted the delicate white and pink secrets. She felt the stubble of shaved masculine cheeks brush her tender flesh. His masculine scent of shaving lotion, wool, leather, and faint cigar smoke touched her senses.

His caresses moved below her dress, exploring her thighs, bringing fresh waves of heat to her body. But when his hands explored further, she realized with a cold dash of fright that she had arrived at the point of no return. With a sudden chill, a measure of sanity returned.

Her body was crying out for fulfillment. She had responded passionately to this masculine, sensuous man. He had awakened desire that burned in her with a deep, throbbing flame. Her emotions cried out to forget everything, to feel her body molded to his, to let his kisses and caresses fill her with ecstasy.

But sanity reminded her of Jimmy's warning about his brother. Jimmy might have spoken partly out of jealousy of his older brother, but she knew he spoke the truth. Kirk had been desperately in love with Marie Algretto, one of the world's most beautiful women. He was a man who moved in international circles, who could have his pick of gorgeous, stylish women from two continents. It would be insane to think he had suddenly gotten over his broken love affair and had really fallen in love with a small town nobody like Lilly Parker!

"Kirk, I'm sorry," she said, drawing away from him.

His dark eyes smoldered. "What is it?"

She avoided his gaze. "I'm afraid to go any further with you."

"Afraid? Why?" he demanded.

"Afraid of what I'm in store for. You're an experienced man of the world. I'm sure you could handle a casual affair with a certain detachment. I can't. I'm a small town girl who hasn't had much experience with men. I don't think I want to get my heart broken."

He gazed at her with beautiful, luminous black eyes that could search to the very core of her being. "Do you think I'm out to break your heart?"

"Oh, not deliberately. It would just be the fallout from an explosion between us. Explosions can be exciting, but they don't last very long."

"Is that what you think it would be like?"

"Yes. You see, I know about Marie Algretto."

There was a moment of silence. Kirk rose from the couch and poured himself a drink. With his back to her, he asked, "Has my brother, Jimmy, been talking to you?"

"Jimmy told me about your love affair with Miss Algretto. I'm sure he wasn't divulging any family secrets. Every celebrity gossip column in Europe and America has carried the story."

Kirk turned to look at her, shadows of anger in his eyes. "But brother Jimmy felt it was his duty to personally warn you."

Lilly's eyes flashed back at him. "I'm glad he did. It might have saved me from a broken heart, too!"

Sullenly, Kirk said, "You make me sound like a third-rate villain in a melodrama. I'm not out to break your heart!"

"But you were in love with Miss Algretto."

He took a swallow of his drink. "Yes."

"And the affair ended tragically for you."

Kirk shrugged, not replying.

"And," she concluded, "you haven't gotten over her."

"I don't see that it's any concern of yours," he said, his eyes turning to cold steel.

"It is when it involves my going to bed with you! If I'm going to have a relationship with a man I'd like to think it means more than my being a band-aid for his broken heart!"

"That sounds very noble," he said, the anger continuing to flare in his eyes. "Are you sure your schoolgirl crush on brother Jimmy isn't really what stands between us?"

Now her anger matched his. Coldly, she replied, "Perhaps it is. And so I think you'd better take me home, Kirk."

Chapter Six

Lilly resumed her place in Jimmy's band the following night with a feeling of apprehension. She suspected that Kirk Remington was not a man easily thwarted. Would he be so angry with her he'd have Jimmy fire her from the band? Or, would he somehow take out his jealousy on Jimmy and the band?

Having a woman say no to him was probably a new and infuriating experience for a man so accustomed to taking life on his own terms. And he was furious at his brother. Jimmy had two things that Kirk wanted and couldn't buy with all his money—musical talent and Lilly's love.

Or had she judged Kirk too harshly? Was his air of supreme self-confidence a coverup for an element of insecurity? She remembered his almost boyish eagerness for her approval of his sound system.

The first night she was nervous and jumpy. But if

Kirk planned some kind of black revenge, he did not act on it.

She was both relieved and uneasy. Perhaps he hadn't given up on her. If so, he wouldn't try to get Jimmy to fire her. He would want to keep her in the band and in town so he could try again.

She braced herself each time she glanced out at the club's patrons, fully expecting to meet the dark-eyed gaze of Kirk Remington. But the evening wore on and he did not put in an appearance. Nor did he show up at the club the following night or the night after that.

She found the courage to ask Jimmy about Kirk. "Haven't seen your brother around the club this week," she said casually.

Jimmy looked surprised. "Didn't he tell you? He's out of town on one of his business trips. Somewhere in the Mideast on a big oil deal. When he left he told me he didn't know when he'd be back."

He gave her a look of scrutiny, judging her reaction. She felt a flurry of confusion, hoping Jimmy didn't see the emotions that raced through her. Kirk's leaving so abruptly, with no word to her about it, seemed a clear enough signal that he considered his interest in her to be over. That was what her good sense told her she wanted. But another part of her heart had a sinking sensation of disappointment. She had never met a man like Kirk. He had affected her in an entirely different way from Jimmy. But there had been no escaping the powerful attraction she had for him. Perhaps it had only been a physical, biological response, but she had come alive at his touch.

Continuing to see Kirk would have been asking for a broken heart. So part of her felt relief. But it was a bittersweet feeling with a certain amount of regret.

In the cold light of dawn, Kirk had probably decided

that a nobody like Lilly Parker was not worth losing any sleep over. A man like him could have his pick of women all over the world. And that was no doubt what he was doing right now—squiring around a sophisticated European fashion model or a lovely countess. He had probably already forgotten he ever knew a naïve little pianist by the name of Lilly Parker.

Lilly brushed aside a tear and threw herself into her music. Nothing more was said about Kirk. He had absented himself from New Orleans and had apparently cut off all contact with the band. Jimmy appeared happy that he had total control of the band and the club.

One night when they finished playing, he walked Lilly to her hotel room. "I see you took my advice about Kirk," he said.

She shot a glance at him. "What makes you so sure I did?"

"The way he took off without telling you anything about it makes it pretty clear, doesn't it? If there was anything going on between you two, he wouldn't have left town without telling you all about it. In fact, he'd probably have taken you with him."

Lilly shrugged. "Maybe he did and I just didn't want to go," she teased.

Jimmy grinned. "Nope. I know better."

Lilly sighed. "Well, you're right. He is still carrying a torch for the opera singer. It was written all over him. I guess I just happened to be handy when he needed someone to hold his hand. I would just have been letting myself in for a lot of grief."

They had reached her doorway. For a moment there was silence between them. Lilly reached up and brushed back the lock of rebellious hair that persisted in tumbling over Jimmy's forehead. Her eyes met his.

He gave her a contemplative look. "I'd ask if I could come in with you tonight, but I know how you feel about that sort of thing."

She searched his eyes. "How do you feel about it, Jimmy?" she asked softly.

"Well, I don't think I'm ready to get that involved," he said.

"I know." She sighed. "I just don't have much luck with my men, do I?"

He slipped his arms around her waist lightly. "It's not that you don't turn me on, kid. I'd like nothing better than a tumble in the hay with you—"

"But that's all it would be, wouldn't it? A tumble in the hay?"

"I don't know. Maybe I don't want to find out. If that's all it turned out to be, you'd get hurt, and you're too sweet a kid for that. I guess I still have something of a big-brother protective feeling about you. On the other hand, if it turned out to be more, things would get all complicated and sticky. I'm not ready for that, either."

She smiled sadly. "Well, if you change your mind— Remember that wonderful line Lauren Bacall gave Bogey in the movie? Something like, 'If you decide you want me, just whistle?' You do know how to whistle, don't you?"

"Yeah. Just pucker and blow. I saw the movie, too."

"But this isn't a movie, is it, Jimmy?"

She tiptoed and kissed him lightly, then turned the key and went into her room. She tossed her purse on the bed and walked to her balcony door. She opened it and leaned against the doorway, gazing at the scene below. After a bit, she saw Jimmy walking away from the hotel, a corner street lamp briefly touching his tousled blond hair. His broadshouldered form dissolved into the early morning mist.

She raised her vision to the rooftops of the ancient buildings, seeing Jackson Square in the distance, and beyond that the river. She sighed. "One of the world's most romantic cities, and I'm alone again."

A month passed. Then one night Jimmy made an announcement to the band: "Pack your duds. I had a long-distance phone call from my brother just before I came to the job tonight. He's booked a two-week engagement for us in Las Vegas. We're taking the early flight out of here Sunday morning."

The band was galvanized. They were on the way to the big things Kirk had been promising them! As for Lilly, she felt her heart give a hop and a thud. Would she see Kirk in Las Vegas? How would she react? What would he say to her?

But Jimmy's older brother didn't meet the band when they arrived in Nevada. They went straight to the hotel where reservations had been made for them.

Their engagement was at a cabaret on Las Vegas' famous "Strip." It was a place that catered to a jazz-loving crowd. Lilly wrote a number of new arrangements for the event.

The band had never played better. The musicians had become welded into a single, driving force with a common mind. They anticipated one another's ideas, inspiring one another. Lilly found herself on a musical "high." Each evening was more thrilling than the one before.

Jimmy looked handsome and dashing, fronting the band. He charmed the audience with his personality. When he raised his golden trumpet to his lips he filled the night with music that tore at Lilly's heart. Then she glanced from the stage and met the gaze of Kirk Remington.

She felt a jolt run through her body. The tingling of an electric shock raced from her toes to her fingertips, leaving her weak. She stumbled over a chord, bringing a surprised frown from Jimmy. Red faced, she formed the word "Sorry," with her lips as she desperately tried to regain her concentration.

She played miserably the remainder of the evening. She had wondered how she would react if she saw Kirk Remington again. Now she knew. Her emotions were in disarray. A vital force sprang alive in her, coursing through her veins.

When the band left the stage, Kirk met her. Without a word, he took her arm. His touch made her nerves quiver. She saw Jimmy watching them with sullen disapproval.

Then they were out on the street. It was three A.M. A million flashing lights had turned the desert night into day. The names of superstars sprang out from a dozen glittering marquees. Traffic swirled and honked on the busy thoroughfare.

Remington guided her across the street to one of the Strip's great hotels. They walked through the gambling casino in the lobby to a cocktail lounge. Lilly sank into a plush chair in the secluded corner Kirk had chosen for them. A waitress brought two drinks.

"Jimmy said you've been in the Mideast," she said nervously.

"Yes. I just got back. Did you miss me?"

The full power of his penetrating gaze was turned on her.

She shuddered and concentrated her attention on the

drink in her hand. She made an attempt to change the subject. "How does the band sound to you?"

"Very good."

"We're all thrilled at getting to play here. Jimmy and everyone in the band is grateful that you were able to arrange this engagement. It's giving us a lot of new exposure and publicity—"

"You're wasting your time with Jimmy's band," Kirk said shortly. "Remember what I told you? You could go a lot farther on your own, and I could help you if you'd let me. It wouldn't take much to have your name as a headliner on one of those big marquees outside."

"I—I don't know if I want to be a superstar, assuming that were possible. I'm happy playing in Jimmy's band."

She felt his searching gaze measure her. "Are you?" he murmured, a dark flush staining his cheeks, "or do you like being near Jimmy that much?"

An angry retort sprang to her lips. But before she could utter it, he said, "You never did answer my question: Did you miss me?"

She raised her eyes to his, remembering with a rush of warmth the electrifying response to his caresses. "Was I supposed to miss you? When you left without even telling me you were going, I got the message that our last good-bye was final."

"I did leave in something of a huff," he admitted. "But since then I haven't been able to get you out of my mind. How has it been for you, Lilly?"

She refused to reply verbally, but her heart silently answered for her. Had absence made the heart grow fonder? Or was she finally being honest with her true feelings?

There were two men in her life. She knew how she felt about Jimmy. Or, at least she thought she did. Jimmy had been her first love, her teen-age idol. But she was no longer a teen-ager. She was a woman now. Was it the woman who had responded to Kirk with so much passion while the child in her still clung to her high school crush on Jimmy, not wanting to give up the dream?

How did she truly feel about Kirk? Perhaps she had known all along, but lacked the courage to face it. All it took was seeing him again to make her heart see the truth. She was in love with Kirk. And it was no high school girl's infatuation.

She could face the truth about her feelings now and not feel disloyal to Jimmy. It was possible, she knew, to have different feelings about different people. It was even possible to love differently.

Understanding her own feelings was one thing. Deciphering a complex man like Kirk Remington was another. He had made it clear enough that he wanted her. But he had never told her he loved her. Was it because of the shadow of the beautiful woman who still possessed his heart?

"Did you have a chance to see Marie Algretto while you were abroad?" she asked impulsively, surprised at her own boldness.

Again the dark flush spread over his cheeks. He shot her a black-eyed glare. "I told you once not to bring up my personal life."

"You seem to have no hesitation about bringing up my relationship with your brother."

"That's another matter. My relationship with Miss Algretto doesn't concern you."

Lilly flushed. "I think it concerns me very much. The fact that you avoid a direct answer every time I bring up the subject tells me that it's still a very painful subject for you."

He sighed, "Lilly, let's not sit here and quarrel. I brought you over here to tell you that I missed you and that I'm glad to see you again."

The sincerity in his words and expression softened the anger she had felt a moment before.

Kirk reached over and took her hand in his. He was looking at her directly, his gaze holding hers. "Friends?" he asked softly.

Her heart melted. "Yes," she murmured, her weakness for him responding against her will.

He squeezed her hand and sat back. "That's better."

Lilly toyed with her drink. "Will you be in Las Vegas for a while?"

His eyes clouded. "I'm afraid not, Lilly. I just flew down here for a few hours to see how Jimmy and the band were getting along and to see you. I have to catch a plane out of here in a few hours for New York. But I'll be back in New Orleans when Jimmy finishes this engagement here and returns to Bourbon Street. I want to know if I can see you again when that time comes."

Lilly nodded slowly, wondering if she was letting herself in for the heartbreak she had been trying to avoid. But she no longer had the will to say no to him.

But the following night she had second thoughts about ever going out with Kirk Remington again. Jimmy said, "I see you and my big brother are on friendly terms again."

"Yes," Lilly admitted.

"I guess you know why he didn't stick around here very long."

"Yes. He told me. He had to fly to New York on business."

"Oh? Did he also remember to mention that Marie Algretto is in New York this week singing at the Metropolitan?"

Lilly felt the blood drain from her cheeks.

"Wise up, Lilly," Jimmy said. "Kirk wants you for a playmate. But for the rest of his life, any time that redheaded opera singer crooks her little finger, brother Kirk is going to drop whatever he's doing and go running to her side. . . ."

Chapter Seven

Lilly resolved to have nothing more to do with Kirk Remington. Jimmy was right; Kirk only wanted her for a temporary playmate. His heart belonged to Marie Algretto. If the time came that she wanted him back, he'd discard any other woman he was involved with in an instant.

Lilly's realization that she loved Kirk changed nothing except to make her more vulnerable. So, she concluded, there was only one course she could take. That was to refuse to go out with him ever again.

She stuck to that resolve when the band returned to New Orleans. She offered no explanation. She didn't want to let Kirk work his persuasive ways on her. It would be too tempting to give in to him. She simply refused to go out with him. Kirk appeared baffled, then angry. But after several futile attempts, he left her strictly alone.

That might have forever ended her involvement with

him. But fate intervened in the form of a violent falling out between Jimmy and Kirk. Lilly heard the bitter argument between the two brothers through the closed door of the Sho-Time Bar's office one night when the band finished playing.

The next night Jimmy came to work wearing a strained, angry expression. He called the group into the club's small office. "Bad news, fellows and Lilly. We're losing our steady gig at this joint."

There was a moment of stunned silence.

"I don't dig this, man," Cemetery Wilson exclaimed. "I thought you had half interest in the joint."

"Not exactly. Kirk has the lease. I fronted the band for him and oversaw the managing of the club. But the lease belongs to him. The lease is up and he's refusing to renew it. He's closing the operation down."

Skinny Lang had a coughing seizure. When he recovered he said, "Hey, I don't get it. Isn't the club making money?"

"I guess not," Jimmy shrugged. "Kirk doesn't think so. He blames it on the way I've been running things when he's out of town."

"What a drag!" Charlie Neal groaned, rubbing his stomach. "I thought we were on our way after that Las Vegas gig."

"So did I," Jimmy agreed. "Well, that's what I get for teaming up with a square businessman. Kirk may be my brother, but the guy knows nothing when it comes to music and running a band. All he knows is the bottom line in a financial report."

A pall of gloom settled over the musicians. Lilly gazed with stricken eyes at Jimmy. She wondered with a sinking feeling if she were somehow to blame. She knew there was a smoldering jealousy between the two brothers. Kirk was angry because she refused to see him anymore. Was he blaming her attitude on her feeling for Jimmy and had he chosen this way to get back at both of them?

She found it hard to believe that Kirk could be that petty. Still, when two men fought over a woman, no holds were barred.

"How about you leasing the joint, Jimmy?" Cemetery suggested.

Jimmy made a hopeless gesture. "I don't have that kind of bread. Maybe if we could have stayed on here another year or two. But the way it is now—" He shook his head. "No way."

"So what happens to the band?"

"We go back to booking one-night gigs until something steady turns up again." Jimmy made an effort to put on a cheerful front. "Hey, don't let this get you down. There's plenty of work to keep us going. And sooner or later we'll get steady booking again."

But his words had a hollow ring. Lilly knew the odds were against his holding the band together under these circumstances. She felt a cloud of despair settle over all of them.

The band was restrained and somber that night. Their usual *joie de vivre* evaporated into a pall of gloom. Jimmy drank more than usual. Lilly had often seen him drink with customers and friends in the course of an evening at the club, but he held his liquor well and never showed the effects of alcohol. Tonight was the first time she saw it get the best of him. By the end of the evening, he was less than sober and it affected his playing. He didn't seem to care.

The band ended their steady engagement at the Sho-Time Bar on Bourbon Street. From that night on, it was a downhill trip for Jimmy LaCross's Jazz Band. And most of all, for Jimmy LaCross. He was able to find one night engagements for the group here and there, but no steady work. He was hitting the bottle regularly; Lilly seldom saw him completely sober. She was sick with worry over him. He had been so certain that they were headed for stardom. The bottom had fallen out of his dreams and he couldn't take it.

Finances for Lilly became desperate. She had to find other work to pay the rent and eat. One week she had a temporary engagement substituting for a regular pianist at a cocktail lounge in a motel on the outskirts of the city. During the evening, she heard a familiar voice speak her name and looked up, surprised to see the drummer, Cemetery Wilson.

"Hi, babe," Cemetery said, taking a seat at the piano bar.

"Cemetery! What are you doing out here?"

"Not much else to do," he said somberly.

Lilly finished her number and signed off for a break. She took a seat beside the drummer.

"Buy you a drink?" Cemetery offered.

"I'll have a cup of coffee. Are you all right, Cemetery? You look down."

He shrugged. "You know how it is, babe. Looks like the band is breaking up. Skinny is starting with a new group next week. Riley is going back to St. Louis. Jimmy just can't book enough work to keep us together."

Lilly nodded, close to tears. She was afraid if she tried to talk about it, she'd break down completely.

"Jimmy is a great guy," Cemetery said, "and I love him like a brother. But he never was much good at managing his money. I guess blowing that horn is all the good Lord meant him to do well. If Jimmy'd had any sense, he would have saved his bread while we were at the Sho-Time Bar, then he could have leased a place of his own. But with Jimmy, it's easy come, easy go. He likes to show his friends a good time. And he's got a weakness for the horses. That's where his money went."

"But that's Jimmy," Lilly defended. "That's part of him—laughing, making people like him, not worrying about tomorrow. He just blows that pretty horn. That's why we love him."

"Yeah," Cemetery muttered. "I'd like to break his fool neck except he's such a great guy." The drummer scowled darkly down at his glass. "He needs you tonight, Lilly. I can't do anything with him. Maybe you can. He has a special feeling for you, like you're his kid sister. Maybe you can do something with him, talk some sense into him."

Concern rushed through her. "What do you mean? What's wrong with him?"

"He's been down at the Red Lady on Bourbon Street all evening. You know the joint, where Maxie Jones and his band is playing. Jimmy's been drinking since noon. Somebody needs to get him to go home. I tried, but he won't listen to me. Maybe he'll listen to you."

Lilly's torment pained her. "I'll finish here in a half hour. Can you give me a lift down there?"

Cemetery nodded.

When they left the motel lounge, Cemetery took the freeway downtown in his delapidated Toyota. He got as close to Bourbon Street as he could with the nighttime traffic restrictions and let her off on a street corner. "No use in me going along," he said. "Jimmy's sore at me for trying to get him to leave earlier."

"I'll see what I can do," Lilly promised.

The Red Lady was one of the flourishing night spots in the heart of the area. Maxie Jones had one of the popular Dixie bands on the street. Like Jimmy, he played trumpet. The two of them had more than once gotten into "carving" contests when one tried to out-play the other. Jimmy usually won, blowing his horn higher and wilder than Maxie, a situation that created some bad blood between them.

Lilly was upset at the thought of Jimmy being at Maxie's place in his frame of mind, especially if he was drinking heavily. She found him, as Cemetery had described, sitting at one of the front tables, obviously drunk. His trumpet was in his lap. He was holding a half-empty glass in one hand, staring up at the band-stand where Maxie's band was romping through a frantic rendition of *That's-a-Plenty*.

Lilly slid into the seat beside him and put her hand on his arm. Jimmy turned his gaze toward her, focusing his eyes with some effort. "Hi, kid. What'cha doin' down here?"

"I just happened to drop by."

He grinned crookedly. "You shoulda gone some-place else. The band here stinks. Maxie oughta throw his horn in th' river and take up bricklaying."

"Jimmy . . ."

The band finished its number. The patrons, who were crowding the popular place, applauded. But Jimmy called loudly, "That was really lousy, Maxie."

Maxie Jones was a dark, wiry Creole who wore his hair slicked back. Lilly could picture him as one of Jean Lafitte's pirates in another age. His flashing black eyes gave Jimmy a scathing look. "You're drunk, Jimmy," he said, looking down from the bandstand. "Go home before I have you thrown out."

"What'sa matter? 'Fraid I'll take my horn up there and blow you down?"

A hush settled over the crowd followed by a ripple of excited murmurs. The prospect of a musical carving contest between two of the hottest trumpet men in New Orleans electrified the spectators. But it drove a fresh chill into Lilly's heart. Jimmy was in no shape to play against Maxie Jones tonight. He'd make a fool of himself.

Lilly tugged at his arm. "Jimmy . . . let me take you home—"

But he brushed her aside. "How about it, Maxie?" he challenged again, getting unsteadily to his feet.

Maxie bowed with a sweeping gesture. "Be my guest, punk." To his audience he said loudly, "Folks, you are about to hear the great has-been, Jimmy LaCross."

Tears spilled from Lilly's eyes. "Please, Jimmy," she begged. But again he pushed her away and staggered a weaving path up to the bandstand.

Jones called a tune and set the tempo with a tap of his foot. His band swung into a full chorus of *South*. Jones played a solo, then turned to Jimmy. Lilly's heart was in her throat as Jimmy stood unsteadily in front of the crowd, raised his horn, and tried to outshine the other band leader. But his playing was pathetic. He fumbled for notes. His tone cracked. Perspiration ran down his face.

"Oh, Jimmy—" Lilly wept, her heart breaking.

Maxie Jones stopped the band. "Hey, Eddie," he called to the burly bartender. "Throw this bum out of here before he falls off the bandstand and hurts somebody!"

There were hoots and jeers from the crowd as the bouncer struggled with Jimmy, forcibly pulling him between the tables and finally giving him a booting shove out the door.

Only a few weeks ago, Lilly remembered, the fickle public was idolizing Jimmy LaCross. Now he was a joke to them.

She ran outside and found Jimmy slumped against a lamp post. "Come on, honey," she whispered, putting her arm around him. "I'm taking you home."

He hardly seemed aware of her leading him down the street. He was in a daze, stumbling against the buildings along the sidewalk, still clutching his trumpet. He would have fallen in the gutter if she hadn't held him up.

Somehow she managed to get him up to her drab little hotel room. In the room, he slumped on the bed, the trumpet dangling from his fingers as he stared at the floor.

"I'll make some coffee," Lilly said, plugging in a small, portable coffeemaker she kept in a bureau drawer. "You'll feel better in a little while, Jimmy," she promised.

But he suddenly stood up, opened the balcony door and stared at the gaudy lights of Bourbon Street. Tears were streaming down his face. "This is the end of Jimmy LaCross," he choked, and hurled his trumpet into the black night. Lilly heard it strike the pavement of the courtyard with a metallic clatter. She gasped, her heart shattering with the broken instrument.

Jimmy stumbled back into the room, collapsed on the bed and immediately fell into a sodden sleep. Lilly gently loosened his tie, removed his shoes and drew a cover over him. Then she sat in a chair beside the bed. A montage of poignant memories crowded her mind; Jimmy, racing through their home town in his convertible, laughing and waving to all his friends; Jimmy playing his horn in the high school auditorium as she accompanied him; and the grown-up Jimmy, handsome, dynamic, leading his own band.

She fingered the golden locket he had given her many years ago. She always wore the locket. It was part of

Jimmy, part of her, part of the dream that had never come true.

"Jimmy, I can't let it end like this for you," she whispered.

It was obvious that Jimmy could no longer communicate with his brother. Whether the break between them was Jimmy's fault or Kirk's, she didn't know. Nor did she know what part she might have played in their quarrel.

But Lilly knew that it was within Kirk's power to save Jimmy from total self-destruction. Someone had to talk with Kirk. Someone had to mediate to settle the quarrel that had made the two brothers enemies.

Lilly knew it was up to her to go to Kirk. She had to make Kirk realize what was happening to his kid brother.

All that night she sat in the dark room beside Jimmy, dozing fitfully in her chair. When morning came, she quietly left while Jimmy was still asleep and went to see Kirk.

Chapter Eight

Lilly took a taxi to Kirk's New Orleans office building. She gave her name to his receptionist. After the woman spoke into an intercom, Kirk immediately gave instructions to bring Lilly to his office.

When she was ushered into the room, Lilly felt at once the impact of his presence. Seeing him again, being in the same room with him, was unnerving.

He rose from his swivel chair behind his massive executive desk. His dark gaze gripped her, sending a familiar shiver through her body. For a moment she was aware of nothing else. Then other elements of his appearance intruded on her senses. He was wearing a dark gray business suit, white monogrammed shirt and wine-red necktie. She had never seen him in casual dress. The fashionably tailored suit emphasized the lean, hard lines of his body. A shaft of light from a window brought highlights and shadows to his features.

It revealed the olive tint in his dark complexion. Again she was reminded of an old movie in which she had seen the actor Tyrone Power, and recognized the resemblance in the lines of Remington's face—the dark brows above intense, slightly almond shaped eyes and the strong, arrogant jawline. He would have been well cast in the role of a Spanish matador.

"Lilly . . . I'm surprised to see you," he murmured.

"Are you?" she whispered.

She moved closer to his desk on legs that felt weak. Behind Kirk, an expansive window afforded a panoramic view of the Mississippi busy with barges and freighters. A sightseeing steamboat of Mark Twain's day was gliding by, its stern paddle churning the water, and Lilly remembered the excursion she had taken with Kirk on the steamboat. Other than that, she was as oblivious to the view as she was blind to the mahogany paneling, the rich office furnishings, the thick, rust-colored carpet, padded chairs and soft hum of an air filtering unit. She *was* aware of Kirk's strong hands with their heavy, tapered fingers resting on the desk and the faint aroma of shaving lotion, cigar smoke and man-smell of polished shoe leather that emanated from him.

"Yes, I am surprised," he repeated. "How have you been?"

"All right. And you?"

"Busy as usual." He waved his hand toward a pile of papers on his desk but kept his gaze on her.

The perfunctory small talk had gotten them this far. Now an awkward silence ensued.

Lilly struggled for words. "I suppose you're wondering why I came here."

"I certainly am. Especially since you made it excruciatingly clear you wanted to have nothing more to do with me after I got back to New Orleans. Perhaps you've come to explain the mystery of why you suddenly turned so cold toward me."

Lilly avoided the question. "Is it all right if I sit down?"

"Certainly. Please forgive me for being so rude, but you have thrown me for something of a loop. I've been back in the city for several weeks and you've treated me like a case of the plague. Now you suddenly show up on my doorstep."

He quickly escorted her to a plush office chair. He turned to a wall, touched a button and a section of the mahogany paneling slid away to reveal a well-stocked bar. "Can I offer you something to drink?"

"Just a soft drink."

"Ginger ale?"

"Yes . . . fine."

He brought her a glass tinkling with ice. Then he took a chair facing her. He crossed his legs. She was aware of the fabric of his suit pulling tightly over his muscular thighs. With a rush of warmth to her cheeks, she forced her gaze away.

"I—I have a reason for coming here."

"I hope it's to say you've relented and will let me start seeing you again."

She shook her head, nervously clutching the glass. "No, Kirk. It's about your brother."

His eyes narrowed. "What about Jimmy?"

She looked at him appealingly. "He's in trouble, Kirk."

He raised an eyebrow. "Oh? What's he done—got a loan shark threatening to break his arm?"

"Kirk! How can you be so cold hearted about your own brother?"

"I'm sorry, Lilly, but Jimmy tries my patience. Is it anything serious?"

"Yes. Very serious."

Kirk's stern expression softened to a look of concern. "Tell me, Lilly."

"He's hit rock bottom. Ever since you pulled the rug out from under him, he's been going downhill. He's lost his band. He's drinking. His playing has disintegrated. Kirk, he's going to pieces. He's headed for skid row or a sanitarium."

Kirk's gaze darkened. "I didn't pull the rug out from under Jimmy. He pulled it out himself."

"You closed the Sho-Time Bar, took away his steady job."

"I had a good reason."

"You did? What was the good reason, Kirk? Me?"

"You?" he exclaimed, his eyes widening.

"Yes, Kirk, me," she challenged. "I know you're jealous of my affection for Jimmy. Your male ego got bruised because I wouldn't have an affair with you. You probably blame Jimmy for that, thought it was because I cared more for Jimmy. So you took it out on him and struck back at me by closing the bar and throwing the band out on the street!"

Lilly was trembling when she finished her little tirade. She bit her lip, regretting the outburst. She had come here on a peace-making mission, trying to patch things up between Kirk and Jimmy. This was no way to go about it.

The dark flush of anger on Kirk's face confirmed her misgivings that she'd made a dreadful mistake with that kind of approach. "That's a real soap opera scenerio you've dreamed up," he said coldly. "But there happens not to be a word of truth in it. I had other reasons for closing the Sho-Time Bar. You say I was angry at you? Perhaps I was. But 'hurt' would be a better definition. I think you owed me an explanation about why you suddenly refused to go out with me anymore."

"I—I guess you're right," she admitted weakly. "I'm sorry, Kirk. I suppose it was so painful to me that I couldn't talk to you about it. And I was afraid if we talked at all, I'd weaken. You—you can be very persuasive. I thought it safer just to not see you or talk to you at all—"

He frowned. "You know you're not making a whole lot of sense."

"No, I'm not." She laughed shakily. "Women seldom do in matters of the heart."

"You can say that again!" Kirk grunted. "At any rate, I deny emphatically that my firing Jimmy had anything to do with you and me."

"Are you sure?"

"Certainly. It was simply a matter of business. Jimmy needed to be taught a lesson. Lilly, I don't expect you to understand this. Your schoolgirl infatuation with Jimmy has colored your vision of him. You idolize him, put him on a pedestal. You refuse to see his shortcomings. The fact is, Jimmy can be totally irresponsible where matters of business are concerned. When I left the country on the business trip, I put the club's operation completely in his hands. It's what he's been wanting. It was against my better judgment, but I hoped it might turn out all right, that Jimmy would learn some responsibility. I came back to find my worst fears confirmed. Jimmy had made a total mess of everything. Instead of paying attention to business, he spent his time at the racetrack losing what little profit the club had made. I can't go on supporting a losing proposition. Jimmy and I had a violent quarrel. Some bitter things were said that I don't take from any man. The upshot was that I closed the club. If Jimmy thinks he's such a hotshot, let him make it on his own!"

Tears welled up in Lilly's eyes. "He's not making it on his own, Kirk."

There was a brittle silence. Kirk's face was flushed, his jaw knotted stubbornly.

Lilly put her untouched drink on a side table. She looked down at her fingers, clenching them nervously. She struggled for the right words. "Kirk, you may be right, that Jimmy is irresponsible, can't cope with practical matters, has weaknesses like throwing his money away on the horses. But he's a giant where musical talent is concerned. That should make up for some of his shortcomings. And—Kirk, he's your brother. He's told me how you played with him when he was a little kid, how he worshipped you."

Again the hardness melted from Kirk's face. He sighed. "What do you expect me to do?"

"Make up with Jimmy. Help him get back on his feet. Help him get his band together. You love music, Kirk. You know it would be a tragedy to lose a group like that. They have every potential of becoming one of the most exciting jazz bands in the country."

Kirk was silent, wrestling with his thoughts. His brooding gaze fell on her. "If I consider helping Jimmy, will you give me an explanation of why you have slammed the door on me?"

"It—it was for selfish reasons. I can't explain. . . ."

How could she tell him it was because she'd fallen in love with him? Her pride wouldn't let her make that admission.

"Kirk," she said earnestly, "Don't let your anger at me stand in the way of helping your brother—"

"I told you I wasn't angry at you, merely frustrated."

He turned away from her and stood at the picture window behind his desk, staring down at the river traffic on the Mississippi. He was silent for several moments, deep in thought. Then he said, "Lilly, I'm moving my office out to San Francisco. I recently concluded a deal to lease a nightclub out there. It would be an ideal location for Jimmy's band. Traditional jazz has a large following on the West Coast. Jimmy's band would do well."

Lilly's heart leaped with joy. "That would be wonderful, Kirk. Jimmy will be so happy!"

"Wait a minute! I didn't say for certain I would offer him the job. There's a condition."

Her momentary joy chilled. "A—a condition?"

"Yes. I'll offer Jimmy and his band a steady job at the San Francisco club if you'll marry me."

For a frozen second there was a stunned silence. Lilly stared at him, unable to believe her ears. *"Marry* you?" she gasped.

"Yes," he said cooly, giving her a steady look.

"But why in heaven's name would you want to marry me? You don't love me."

"My reasons are my own. What do you say?"

"I—I don't know what to say," she stammered.

Her thoughts were chaotic. Under other circumstances, if Kirk were in love with her, his proposal would bring a joyous response. But Lilly struggled to find a reason for his startling announcement, knowing that he was in love with another woman.

She could think of several causes that motivated him. The most obvious were his jealousy directed at his brother combined with his frustrated male ego. He probably was not accustomed to having women say no to him. Her stubborn refusal to have an affair with him had only made him more determined to have her.

"It's because of the way I feel about Jimmy, isn't it?" she demanded. "You're willing to go to the extreme of marrying me to get me away from him."

His face registered no emotion. "I told you, my reasons are my own."

"Then I have to guess what they are! I think you're partly jealous over Jimmy and partly mad because I keep turning you down, so you've decided this is the perfect opportunity to get what you want from me. You know I'll do almost anything to help Jimmy."

His eyes darkened. "*Would* you do almost anything to help Jimmy?" he asked, a cutting edge in his voice.

She met his gaze with a haughty tilt of her chin. "Yes, I would."

His eyes gazed at her furiously. He said coldly, "Well, then, this is your opportunity."

Lilly had no immediate answer for that. She struggled to gain control of her tumultuous thoughts. Being married to Kirk Remington would be heaven if he were asking her out of love. But under these circumstances, it could turn into hell.

"You're being heartless!"

"Why? That isn't my intention."

"You're trying to bargain with me, aren't you? You'll exchange helping Jimmy for my sharing your bed!"

"I'm merely taking advantage of an opportunity. All's fair in love and war," he reminded her with a triumphant smile.

"It's like a deadly card game and you're dealing from the bottom of the deck!" she cried. "It's not fair!"

"Just good old American enterprise," he said, beginning to gloat because he had her backed into a corner.

"That's how I got where I am in the business world. I'm trained to see an opportunity and seize it."

"Ruthlessly!" she said tearfully.

He shrugged. "Nothing succeeds like success."

"Is that the credo you live by? It's pretty heartless!"

"Not at all. Life is made up of winners and losers. I try to be a winner. If Jimmy doesn't mend his ways he's going to be a loser."

Lilly shook her head. "He's the real winner. He's the one with the talent."

A flash of pain registered in Kirk's eyes, and she knew she had struck a vital spot.

He looked away, regaining his composure. Then his gaze swung back to her. "Well, Lilly, what's your answer? Do we get married and start Jimmy back on the road to success? We can fly out to Las Vegas tomorrow and have our wedding night there. Later, I'll take you to San Francisco with me. You'll have everything a woman could wish for. Better think twice before turning me down."

Everything a woman could wish for . . . except love, she thought sadly. Loving Kirk as she did, marrying him would demand no sacrifice on her part. He was an attractive, vital man. Sharing his life and his bed would be a thrilling experience. The sacrifice would be in marrying a man who did not love her in return, knowing that whenever he took her in his arms, he would be thinking about another woman . . . grieving for her. . . .

"You ought to be willing to help your own brother without getting something in return," she said bitterly.

"Well, perhaps I would help Jimmy anyway. But you have no way of knowing, do you? Then again, I might not. Do you want to take that chance?"

"No," she whispered. She was silent for a moment, blinking back tears. Then her shoulders slumped. "You win. I'll marry you—if you promise to help Jimmy."

Kirk's face was radiant. He caught her shoulders in the strong grip of his hands. "I'll have my secretary take you around town to buy a wardrobe for the honeymoon. You won't be sorry, Lilly."

She raised her eyes to his, thinking about the beautiful opera star, Marie Algretto, whom he loved. *Are you sure about that, Kirk?* she wondered.

Then he stepped back. "There's another condition, Lilly."

She frowned. "What is it?"

"I want you to resign from Jimmy's band. I want you to put your career in my hands. I promise I'll promote you to the stardom in the entertainment world that you deserve."

Disappointment crushed her. "I knew your jealousy was partly behind this. You don't want me around Jimmy every night!"

"That's not it. I simply think you're wasting your time buried in his band. You can go much farther on your own. Trust me."

"I don't trust you," she retorted.

"Suit yourself. But you'll see—six months from now when your name is on everyone's lips."

Lilly thought tearfully, *I only want my name on your lips, Kirk, when you tell me you love me.* But she knew that time would not come.

"Jimmy is going to need help right away," she said. "he's flat broke. He doesn't have the money to buy plane tickets for his band to get to San Francisco. And they'll need some kind of advance to live on until the job starts. Jimmy doesn't even have a horn any more."

Kirk dismissed those problems with an impatient wave of his hand. "I'll see that he has all the money up front that he needs."

"It's not going to be easy. Jimmy has a lot of pride and he's pretty bitter toward you, Kirk. He may get stubborn and not want your help."

"Then we'll just have to talk some sense into him. But you haven't given me your answer, Lilly. Do you accept my conditions?"

"To marry you and resign from Jimmy's band." Lilly nodded tearfully. "Yes," she sighed. "You win, Kirk."

His eyes flashed a look of triumph. He drew her into his arms, the look of a conquerer flashing in his gaze. She was unresisting, all the fight drained from her.

For a long, vibrant moment, he drank in the sight of her as their lips drew closer. She sensed a curious mixture of unrelenting strength and tenderness in his embrace.

His hands moved down her back, molding her to him. She quivered as his lips touched hers. His mouth felt warm and inviting. Was there a spark of true caring in his kiss? Could she dare grasp a fragile optimism that Kirk would come to love her, that their marriage might turn out all right?

He pulled back. Lilly searched his face for some clue to his true feelings. But the enigma of Kirk Remington was unfathomable. He remained a total mystery to her. Why would he go to such lengths to possess her when his heart belonged to another woman?

Perhaps his true feelings were as much a riddle to himself as they were to her. He was being driven into this marriage by emotional forces that for the present neither of them understood. She could only wait . . . and hope.

He suddenly became businesslike. "All right. I'll

keep my end of the agreement. We'll have a talk with Jimmy. Do you know where we can find him?"

"Yes. I took him to my room last night. When I left this morning he was still sleeping. I'm sure he's still there."

The look of glowing triumph faded from Kirk's eyes. His jaw became rigid. Dark anger flashed in his eyes.

Jealousy was clearly written across his coutenance. For a moment, Lilly enjoyed a kind of perverse triumph. Then she said, "Don't fly into a jealous rage. It's not what you're thinking. Jimmy was dead drunk last night. I had to put him to bed somewhere. I didn't sleep with him. I slept in a chair."

But she knew Kirk didn't believe her. Nothing she could say was going to eliminate the jealousy that tormented Kirk.

When they arrived at her hotel room, they found Jimmy awake, looking haggard and unsteady. He had plugged in her little coffeemaker and was smoking a cigarette as he sipped the black liquid. His hand holding the cup was shaking.

Jimmy's eyes blazed when he beheld Kirk walking into the room beside Lilly. "What are you doing here?" he snarled at his brother.

"You look awful," Kirk said with a note of disgust.

"Who asked you?"

Lilly quickly stepped between the warring brothers. "Jimmy, we're here to patch things up. Kirk wants to make you a very generous offer."

"I don't need his lousy money," Jimmy said sullenly.

"Sure, you do just fine on your own," Kirk retorted.

"Jimmy, calm down!" Lilly exclaimed. "And Kirk, you don't need to be so sarcastic. Can't we try to be civilized?"

Jimmy scowled.

Kirk said, "She's right. Look, I'm willing to let bygones be bygones. We both blew our tops and said things we shouldn't have. I guess I expected too much from you. I ought to be willing to accept you the way you are. As mad as I get at you, I still love you. You're my kid brother."

Jimmy frowned, looking down at his trembling fingers. "You try to push people around too much, Kirk," he murmured.

"I guess I do. I had a tough time getting where I am. I had to be tough to survive as a roughneck in the oil fields and to make something out of myself. I suppose it made me a little ruthless. But I don't like to see you like this and I don't want you to lose your band. You guys have too much on the ball. Let's shake hands and make a fresh start, okay, Jimmy?"

The younger brother nodded slowly. He sighed, looked up to meet his brother's gaze and held out his hand.

"Good!" Kirk said, shaking his hand warmly. "Now, I want you to call your guys and tell them to pack up. I'm opening a new club in San Francisco. I want you to be ready to start there next week."

The dull look of defeat faded from Jimmy's eyes. In its place came a glint of excitement. "Do you mean it?"

"Of course I mean it. If you'll stop by my office I'll have some advance money for you. My secretary will take care of plane reservations for you and the band. How long will it take you to get your men together?"

"A day or two."

"Fine. Get up there as soon as you can so the band can do some rehearsing before opening night. I suspect it's rusty after the layoff. Oh, and you'll need to find another piano player. Lilly has decided to resign from your group. I'm going to promote her as a single act."

Jimmy looked shocked. He swung a questioning gaze toward Lilly. She blushed, her eyes sliding away from his look. "It's true, Jimmy."

Jimmy was frowning, some of the excitement melting out of him. "I don't get it. Lilly is important to the band."

Kirk said, "Jimmy, let's face it. Lilly shouldn't bury herself in a band. You know how much talent she has. There's no limit to how far she can go on her own. You want what's best for her, don't you?"

"Sure I do," Jimmy said slowly. "If it's really what she wants to do." He was beginning to look at Kirk with a questioning expression.

"I'm going to see that she has every break," Kirk said. Then, looking directly at Jimmy, he said, "Lilly and I are leaving for Las Vegas tomorrow. We're getting married."

Lilly felt a flash of anger at Kirk for being so blunt. She had wanted to explain the situation to Jimmy herself. But obviously Kirk wanted the satisfaction of telling his brother that he had won and from now on Lilly was his property.

Some of the anger toward his brother filled Jimmy's eyes again. He turned his gaze to Lilly. "I'd like to be able to wish you happiness, Lilly, but I'm afraid marrying Kirk is going to mean nothing but a broken heart for you. . . ."

Chapter Nine

The day that followed was a whirlwind of confused activity. There were conferences with lawyers in Remington's office. Lilly signed papers she didn't completely understand, following Kirk Remington's directions numbly.

Then he sent her on a quick shopping trip in the custody of his secretary. She was whisked from shop to shop in a chauffeured limousine. There was a parade of salespersons, fitting rooms and style shows.

She stared wide-eyed at her reflection in mirrors, seeing herself in the kinds of designer garments she had seen before only in fashion magazines. She was fitted with exquisite lingerie, footwear, and finally a beautiful fur coat ideal for the chilly San Francisco climate.

The secretary never asked the price of any item. She merely signed the sales slips.

Finally, she was driven back to Remington's office building. He stepped into the car beside her, and they were driven to the airport. He gave her a critical examination, ranging from her new hair style to the costly lavender pumps on her feet. He nodded approvingly. "You are lovely, Lilly. A man would be proud to introduce you as his wife."

She drew another meaning from his words. She was now the possession of Kirk Remington, a prized possession like his racehorses or his yacht, one he wished to display proudly to the world.

He drew a velvet box from his pocket. "I noticed you don't have a wristwatch. I want you to have this as a wedding present."

Before her astonished eyes, he opened the box and took out a diamond encrusted wristwatch worth a small fortune. She stared, wide-eyed, as he placed it on her wrist and secured the clasp.

"Do you like it?" he asked.

She could only nod. Reality eluded her. It didn't seem possible that such a dazzling piece of jewelry could grace the wrist of Lilly Parker, the small town girl whose daddy had been too poor to buy her a second-hand piano. The money this watch cost would not only have paid for the piano, it would have bought the small house they lived in as well!

Lilly's heart flooded with emotion and she looked at Kirk with tear-filled eyes. The watch could mean more—a symbol of the extent of Kirk's love for her. How she would treasure its value far beyond its price in dollars! For a moment she was so pleased, she couldn't speak.

But then she sensed that Kirk seemed cold and preoccupied as he put the watch on her wrist. He looked at it with a measuring gaze as if he were only aware of the appearance it made.

The watch was beautiful beyond any woman's

dreams. But suddenly it brought a chill to Lilly's arm. The momentary rush of happiness at the exquisite gift faded and turned to sadness. With a sinking heart, Lilly recognized that the true symbol of the gift was the kind of relationship she was to have with this man.

They arrived at the airport. There, another surprise awaited her. They didn't board a commercial airliner to Las Vegas. Instead, they were taken to a private twin-engine airplane waiting on a runway.

She was even more surprised when they boarded the craft and Kirk took a seat at the controls and indicated she was to sit next to him. "You're a pilot?" she asked in astonishment.

"Yes. I enjoy flying. Don't have the time to do it as much as I'd like."

"How did you learn?"

He smiled. "The government taught me."

"You were in the Air Force?" For some reason that bit of information surprised her.

"Yes. I flew a chopper in Viet Nam."

She gazed at him curiously. He had more unexpected facets than a gemstone. How many other sides were there to Kirk Remington that she didn't know about?

He checked out the plane with experienced skill, switched on the radio and spoke to the control tower. He instructed Lilly to fasten her seat belt. Within minutes they were rolling down the runway. Then she felt the exhilaration of the plane growing lighter, the wheels lifting from the ground, the sudden, sweeping turn up as they were airborne.

They circled the area. An exclamation of pleasure escaped her lips as she gazed at the world of clouds around them, and the scenery far below.

He smiled at her excitement. "You like flying?"

"Oh, yes!" For the time being, she forgot about the

cloud under which she was marrying Kirk. She was inspired by the thrill of the moment.

Kirk laughed. "I find your youthful enthusiasm delightful, Lilly. But I agree; there's no other experience quite like being up here with the world and all its cares far below. You feel closer to the angels." Then he said, "If you think you'd be interested, I could arrange for you to have flying lessons. Perhaps after a while you'd like to have a little plane of your own."

Her gaze moved from the clouds around them to his face. She tried to divine his motives. Apparently, he was ready to give her anything she desired. Was it generosity or his curious need to show off before her, to impress her?

Or, was it more than that? Was it possible that in some way she didn't fully understand and perhaps Kirk didn't understand himself, he did love her? Could she believe that, knowing his heart belonged also to another woman? Men were a total mystery to her when it came to their view on love. And Kirk was the greatest mystery of them all. But she was going to let herself believe that Kirk loved her in his own way. Perhaps it was a fairy story she was making up, but she was going to pretend for now, at least, that it was true.

Holding to that thought, she settled into a strange but happy mood. With a feeling of anticipation, she included Jimmy in her thoughts. He would be flying to San Francisco with the other fellows. Next week he would open at Kirk's new club. Perhaps she would get to see him then.

When the plane took off, Lilly had gazed down at the city of New Orleans, seeing the freeways, the Superdome, the waterfront and finally the cluster of ancient buildings and narrow streets of the old French Quarter. A lump filled her throat. Only a few weeks ago she had come here, filled with young, romantic dreams. Then Kirk had stepped into her life and scattered the dreams, substituting his own kind of romantic reality.

She thought about Jimmy and asked herself if she had any regrets. Some, she admitted. Jimmy had a very special place in her heart. But she couldn't go on living on dreams. Jimmy wasn't going to marry her. She had been forced to make a choice. Was she going to regret the choice? Only the future could decide that. Jimmy had warned that she was asking for heartbreak, marrying Kirk. Was his warning a prophecy?

She was glad for Jimmy's sake that things had turned out this way. He was going to have a brilliant future. She was sure of it. Knowing she had played a part in helping him gave her a warm feeling. She knew she would always love Jimmy in a special way in a secret corner of her heart.

Yes, Jimmy was going to be all right. He would be up there again, blowing his golden horn, in front of his band, happy and smiling. She knew she'd been right when she had said his horn was his mistress.

But what did the future hold for Lilly Parker?

She sat beside the window, watching the panorama of western scenery passing below—the various mountain ranges, the Grand Canyon, the vast stretches of desert, and finally Las Vegas.

The Las Vegas wedding progressed as smoothly as a ticking clock. Kirk's staff had arranged everything. When they landed, a limousine was waiting for them. They were driven to the Cluster of Roses Wedding Chapel. A brief ceremony was performed. Kirk placed a wedding band on Lilly's finger next to a large diamond ring he had also given her.

It was over; she was Mrs. Kirk Remington. It was all so unreal. Could she be dreaming?

By then, night had blanketed the desert. The Strip had sprung to life with blazing lights. The limousine took them to a luxury hotel where more elaborate arrangements had been made.

Lilly was surprised when Kirk insisted on carrying her across the threshold. She didn't think the reserved man was capable of such old-fashioned sentimentality.

When they entered the room, Lilly gasped in amazement. The spacious suite had been transformed into a garden of flowers. Huge blankets of giant red roses banked the walls and covered the tables. Through a doorway, she glimpsed a great, round bed. It, too, was covered with roses. Then her wide-eyed gaze encountered another unexpected sight—a white baby grand piano almost hidden under a basket of flowers.

The rooms of the suite were decorated in white and gold. All the furnishings were in those colors. The deep, soft carpet was white, the walls were white with gold trim. The red roses exploded with brilliant hues.

Lilly became aware of Kirk's gaze regarding her eagerly. "Do you like it?" he asked.

Again she remembered that night in his New Orleans apartment when he had shown her his sound system. She detected the same eagerness and uncertainty, the need to impress her. It was a curious side to this man she had married.

"It's breathtaking," she admitted.

"This is the bridal suite," he explained.

Lilly Parker in the bridal suite of the most luxurious hotel in Las Vegas! She felt a hysterical impulse to giggle. A week ago she was struggling to pay the weekly rent on a third-rate hotel room with stained wallpaper!

"But why the piano?" she asked.

thought you might enjoy playing a little. I haven't heard you play for a while."

She looked at him curiously. Why would he want to hear her play? She moved to the piano and touched the keys. The tone was magnificent.

"I told my staff to rent the piano and have it tuned when it was delivered. Is it in tune?"

She nodded. "Yes. Perfect."

"Well," he said then, "I have ordered a dinner for us to be served here in our room. In the meantime, if you'd like to freshen up and change, there should be something waiting for you in the bathroom."

"More arrangements by your staff?"

The slight edge of irony in her voice seemed to escape him. He merely answered, "Yes," and went over to the white princess telephone to check with room service on the dinner.

Lilly walked to the bathroom. Again, the sight that greeted her took her breath away. The splendor of the room would have done justice to a Roman Emperor's bath. It was decorated in the white and gold motif of the other rooms. The walls were paneled with mirrors. The white carpet was ankle deep. Dominating the room was a heart-shaped whirlpool bath. Dozens of white and gold orchids floated in the swirling water.

Hanging near the door was an exquisite white negligee and gown, her wedding night garments ordered by Kirk Remington's staff. Lilly disrobed. She touched the swirling water of the bath experimentally with her toe. The temperature was perfect, just warm enough to be relaxing.

She sank into the moving, foaming water, losing herself among the orchids. A thousand gentle fingers massaged her sensuously. She closed her eyes, losing herself in the luxurious sensation. It was delightful. She was floating on a magic carpet of feeling that transported her to another realm of existance.

Suddenly, through the steam and vapor that rose from the bath, she saw the outline of a man standing over her. Her eyes flew open. She gasped as she saw Kirk's naked body. The sinewy muscles in his shoulders and chest bulged in smooth symmetry under the golden tan flesh. Her eyes moved down his body. His thighs and calves rippled like those of a stalking jungle cat as he moved to the heart-shaped pool and stepped into the water.

"It will be a little while before dinner arrives," he murmured. "I thought I would join you."

His intense gaze searched out the contours of her figure under the water. The way he drank in the sight of her nakedness embarrassed and disturbed her. Instinctively, she drew away from him.

But he moved closer, pushing aside the floating blanket of orchids. Under the water, she felt their bare legs touch. A shiver ran through her body. Quickfire flashed through her nerve ends.

He was close now. She felt helpless in the grip of his dark eyes holding hers with hypnotic force. For long, throbbing moments, they were motionless, reclining in the water, lost in the gaze that joined their eyes with deep, searching intensity.

She felt herself being drawn closer to him as he began to caress her under the water. The gentle massage of the swirling water was intensified by his hands roving over her arms and back, sending tingling, electrical shocks through her entire being. His palms moved down her spine to the curves below, gently holding the yielding flesh.

Slowly, tantalizingly, he pulled her closer. She felt her soft curves touching and moving against his hard,

...sculine skin. Their wet bodies, gleaming under the water, sent a thousand sensations exploding through her.

It was impossible to think, to remember how hopelessly she had tried to struggle against loving a man who did not love her in return.

Vapor from the warm water billowed around her. Through its soft haze, she saw the reflection in the mirrored walls of the man and woman in the heart-shaped pool like a dream sequence. The bodies were joined in a love embrace, legs entwined, arms locked about one another. Their movements followed the rhythm of the swirling waters. The orchids floated around them. Their murmured cries of ecstasy mingled with the bubbling of the water. Conscious thought was swept away and she only felt and saw and heard and rose to a molten height of gasping fulfillment that gradually fell away to a temporary sense of drowsy peace in his arms.

I love you, Kirk, she whispered in her heart. How she longed to speak the words aloud! But pride stilled them on her lips. What thoughts were going through Kirk's mind, she wondered? Was he filled with a sense of tenderness toward her? But sadness engulfed her as she realized that he must be thinking of Marie Algretto at this very moment, regretting that she was not the woman in his arms.

Remington kissed her. "Forgive me for deserting you, Lilly. I'd like to prolong this moment, but I think it's about time for the catering service to deliver our dinner."

He stepped out of the pool with a shower of wet drops. He toweled himself dry vigorously, then slipped into a robe and left.

Lilly suddenly felt very alone. Her tears mingled with the water, dropping on an orchid that floated near her cheek. If she could be sure Kirk truly loved her, she would have been happier in a third-rate hotel room with stained wallpaper!

Finally there were no tears left. She dried and dressed in the gown and negligee. She caught a sight of her flushed face and her damp, towel-dried hair. A sudden, mischievous mood came over her. Perhaps it was a reaction to the depression she had been feeling. Looking at herself in the mirror, she giggled, "Lilly Parker, you look like a woman who has just been thoroughly slept with!" Kirk Remington might be an egotistical, ruthless man, but he was definitely a master at lovemaking. She almost wished that they were not so good together. It would be easier to deny her love for him.

Suddenly, she remembered, "It's not Lilly Parker anymore, is it?" She held up her left hand with the massive diamond and the gold wedding band. "You're a married woman now. You are Mrs. Kirk Remington."

Again a sense of unreality gripped her. Lilly sighed, fastened the negligee around her slim waist, and rejoined Kirk in the main room of the suite. While she had been dressing, the catering service had delivered their dinner. It was waiting for her, a lavish spread of gourmet meats and sauces, steaming vegetables and crisp salads. Kirk was opening a bottle of wine.

The food was as delicious as it looked. Succulent Maine lobster melted in her mouth. Tender asparagus in hollandaise sauce brought an ecstatic response from her taste buds. The excellent wine spread its warmth through her.

Kirk was watching her with an amused expression. "You have quite an appetite, Mrs. Remington."

Lilly stopped eating. She averted her gaze, looking down at her plate. She felt painfully self-conscious.

"I would say," Kirk observed with a teasing note in his voice, "that lovemaking agrees with you."

She felt a hot flush spread from her throat up her cheeks to her hair line.

"Am I embarrassing you?"

"You certainly are!"

"Nothing to be embarrassed about," he smiled, raising his glass of wine. "We're married. It's quite legal . . . and moral now."

"Legal, perhaps," she murmured. "I think there may be a good question about how moral it is."

"But I didn't hear many protests from you. Be honest, Lilly. Admit it. You liked making love with me. You reveled in it."

Angrily, she looked at him. "Don't rub it in! All right, yes, sex between us is good. I'm not a frigid woman. I suppose you've found that out to your satisfaction. Is that what you want to hear?"

He gazed at her with a questioning expression. "Then why sound so angry about it?"

"I think you know the answer to that. It's the situation. All of this has been forced on me. You certainly didn't marry me because you loved me! I don't know why you did. Probably to satisfy your swollen ego. Sex doesn't add up to love. You may be able to arouse a physical response in me. You're quite good at that. I suppose you've had enough practice! But you'll never own my heart."

He flushed angrily. "Then I'll settle for what I do own!"

They lapsed into a cold, remote silence. Lilly no longer enjoyed the food. She left the table, went to a window, pushed the drapes aside and gazed out at the scene below.

Kirk remained at the table, moodily drinking. After a while he rose, moved to where she was standing and said, "Suppose we declare a truce. We might as well make the best of the evening. Why don't you try the piano?"

Lilly shrugged, not wanting to speak to him. She moved away from the window to the baby grand. She touched the keys and found the response irresistible. Here, at least was a friend, a lover she could trust. Taking a seat on the bench, she began to play, limbering her hands first with arpeggios, then allowing melodies to flow from her heart to the keyboard. She found herself playing Beethoven's *Moonlight Sonata*.

As she played, she caught a glimpse of Kirk. He had settled into a chair nearby, watching her intently. He seemed transfixed, his attention heightened and centered on her. Strong emotions played over his face as he listened.

She played for half an hour, during which time Kirk did not move from the chair. When she paused for a moment to rest, he suddenly rose and moved to her side. "That was superb," he whispered huskily. His eyes were aflame with a passion she couldn't define.

He caught her arms and lifted her from the piano bench until they were standing close together. He kissed her, a lingering kiss, different from his other kisses. She was at a loss to describe the feeling he put into the embrace. She sensed that her playing aroused some kind of emotion in him that she did not yet understand.

He touched the ribbons on her robe and gown, whispering against her lips, "Please don't stop, Lilly. Play for me again."

With a feeling of being half dazed, she again took her seat at the piano. He stood nearby, hungrily drinking in the sight of her as she played. She felt his gaze like a hot mantel over her trembling flesh. It was a moment of unreality. Incredible as it seemed, it was as if her music had become an intimate link between them, a joining of something deeper in both of them than a mere physical union.

She sensed that his passion was fueled by the music that sprang from her fingertips. She heard his breath, deep and strained as he drank in the sight of her swaying and moving on the piano bench to the rhythm of the melody she was playing. She was gripped in the spell of the moment, compelled to play harder. Was this the secret key that would unlock his heart? Had she temporarily wiped the image of Marie Algretto from his mind? Was he in love with Lilly Parker in this moment?

Her left hand moved in a sensuous eight-to-the-bar rhythmic bass while her right hand sought out rich melodic chords, all of it building in tempo and intensity into a heated jazz improvisation.

Suddenly, as if his storm of emotions had become too violent to control, Kirk swept her up from the piano bench in his strong arms. He carried her into the bedroom, covering the distance in long, powerful strides. He placed her on the round bed, flung his robe aside and joined her. He seized her with a primitive kind of passion more demanding than anything she had experienced in him before. At first she recoiled from his rough approach, but then the yearning nature of his desire communicated itself to her and a primitive force of her own responded. She was overcome by the moment, controlled by passion, swept into a furious storm of emotion, sensation, elation.

Long afterward, when the passion they'd shared had been drained, she lay still and spent in the quiet, darkened room, gazing at the ceiling. Now in the coldness of returned sanity, she pondered the incredible sequel of events that had aroused Kirk. She was beginning to understand that Kirk had married her for her musical ability as much as for herself. But more than that, perhaps the two were somehow linked. He had expressed more than once his fascination and envy of persons with her talent. Was his own frustration so great that he was driven to possess her and thereby seek to become part of her music? The concept was so confusing and so new, that as yet she couldn't get a grip on it. But she was certain that her playing was somehow mixed up with his physical desire for her. There were sexually related overtones involved with her musical ability. If she could understand that, perhaps she could understand the baffling mystery of the man she had married.

Chapter Ten

The next day they left on the final lap of their flight to San Francisco.

"I've bought a house for us to live in," Kirk told her. "But it needs some work. We'll be staying at the Hyatt Regency for a short while until the house is ready."

Lilly saw the blue Pacific and then the bay area of San Francisco below them. When they left the airport, she was greeted by a gust of chilly, damp air off the Pacific. She snuggled into her new fur coat, glad of its protection.

They were met by a limousine ordered by Kirk's San Francisco office. The sleek automobile transported them up and down the steep grades of the San Francisco streets. Then Kirk escorted Lilly into the incredibly luxurious Hyatt Regency hotel. She gazed in wonder at the great lobby, the vast open spaces, the fountains, the stringed orchestra, the caged doves, and up at the eighteen-story tiers of rooms rising in terraces above the huge lobby. She saw the lighted glass gondolas that sped up and down open shafts, whisking guests to their floors.

She felt like pinching herself. Could Lilly Parker really be in a place like this?

In the luxurious, pink-tiled bathroom of their suite, Lilly had a few moments of privacy. She stared at her image reflected in the expanse of mirrors above the long counter. "Is this really you, Lilly, in this place? Is all this actually happening?" She felt a hysterical impulse to giggle. She remembered the bare little frame house that had been her family's home back in Miller-dale. In winter they had battled with an open space heater the cold drafts that came around the windows. Summers without air-conditioning had been stifling. There had been no closets in the house. Her few garments had been hung behind a door on an im-provised rack. When she went off to college she had shared a small, furnished room with a girlfriend and when she went to New Orleans, the shabby third-rate hotel room had been her home. Now she suddenly found herself in one of the most glamorous hotels in America, the wife of a wealthy, sophisticated man of the world. It was small wonder that there was an aura of unreality about the situation.

When she undressed, she saw the gold locket she had worn for so many years dangling between her breasts. She unfastened the clasp and opened the locket, seeing Jimmy's high school picture. She put the locket in her purse. If Kirk discovered she carried a locket given to her by Jimmy, it would only start another jealous argument.

She soaked in a warm, scented bath, allowing her tense muscles to relax, her nerves to grow more calm. Surrounded by the soapy liquid that gently caressed her body, her thoughts languidly drifted. She closed her eyes, experiencing in her memory Kirk's caresses, his murmured endearments, his kisses. A fresh thrill raced through her and her flesh tingled. She hugged herself, aware of her anticipation and attraction for Kirk.

Then her daydreams turned to more practical matters—her own career. By accepting Kirk's bargain she had saved Jimmy's future. But what would the future hold for her? Kirk had promised her big things. Obviously he had important connections in the entertainment world. Would she become a star as he promised? She felt a surge of excitement. Was she headed for some kind of thrilling appointment with destiny?

She stepped from the tub and rubbed her body until it turned a glowing pink with a great, thick bath towel. She ran a comb through her hair and applied makeup lightly. Then she slipped into a filmy nightgown and fastened the sash of a robe tightly about her slim waist.

Kirk was standing at a window, gazing down at the city. He was wearing a wine-red robe and smoking an expensive cigar. Hearing her, he put out the cigar in an ashtray and turned to gaze at her. He drank in the sight of her with a look that made her blush to the roots of her hair. But at the same time, it brought a quickening response of her heartbeat. Kirk had a way of looking at a woman as if she were the center of the universe. He seemed oblivious of their surroundings, only aware of her.

"You're beautiful, Lilly," he murmured. "The sight of you takes my breath away."

She swallowed hard, not knowing what to say, but feeling a magnetic attraction drawing her to his side.

"I've been looking out at the city," he said, putting his arm around her.

The lights of the city spread before her, a twinkling

blanket of rolling hills, streets that swept up at steep angles, then dropped swiftly to the sea. A light fog formed halos around the lights, creating a scene of soft, transparent beauty.

"It's lovely," she murmured.

"Yes. San Francisco is my favorite city. I'm going to enjoy showing it to you—Chinatown, Fisherman's Wharf, the Japanese Gardens, the art museums, the theaters. It's a picturesque and cosmopolitan city."

Then he moved to a nearby table where a bottle of champagne was cooling. The loud pop of the cork caused Lilly to start. Kirk poured two glasses and handed one to Lilly.

She sipped the bubbly liquid, feeling it tickle her nose. It gave her a light-headed, giddy feeling, a reckless feeling of daring.

Kirk downed his glass, refilled it, but left it on the table. He moved to her side and suddenly swept her up in his powerful arms. He carried her lightly and sat in a chair, holding her on his lap.

"You're very tense, Lilly. You feel stiff."

"I'm sorry. I'm trying to relax."

"Perhaps some more champagne?"

"No . . . just talk to me. Tell me about yourself, Kirk. I—I feel shy with you because I don't know you very well. You're not an easy person to know. Do you realize that?"

He laughed. "Yes, so I've been told. I've been accused of being cold and distant."

She was silent for a moment, mulling over his words. "I'm not sure if I'd describe you that way," she said slowly, "though you certainly are reserved and a private person, not all that easy to get to know. But why do you think you give some people the impression that you're cold and distant?"

"Why? I'm not sure. Perhaps because life made me that way. Don't you think we're the kind of people we are because of the experiences we have in life?"

"I'm not sure if I agree," she said thoughtfully. "I always had the notion that we are born with certain personality traits. You can see that in babies. They are little individuals from the moment of birth."

"But surely what happens to them as they grow up can change them. If they are loved or not loved, if they are given opportunities or denied them, if they are sickly or robust—all of those things must have a lot to do with how they behave as adults."

"Did it in your case, Kirk?"

"I think so. I might be a different person today if my real father had lived. He was a great guy, Lilly. He played with me, took me fishing, told wonderful stories—" His voice suddenly caught in his throat.

Lilly felt a rush of sympathy. "I hadn't realized he played such a part in your life. I guess I was under the impression that he died before you were old enough to remember him. I don't know where I got that idea. Perhaps because you never talked about him before."

"It's a painful subject for me. I'm not able to talk about it to many people. I don't think even Jimmy knew how much I missed my real Dad. He died when I was seven. My mother remarried, and she had Jimmy when I was ten. My stepfather and I never got along. He was a stupid, unfeeling, selfish old bastard. I don't know what my mother ever saw in him."

"That's why you left home and went to work in the oil fields?"

"Yes. I had to get away from that situation. You see, that's what I mean by life shaping our personalities and character. It makes me wonder sometimes if we really have much free will. I went to work in the oil fields filled with anger. All the rage I felt toward my stepfather, the bitterness I felt at losing my real Dad, I took out in hard work. I drove myself. If anybody got in my way, I ran over them. I was determined to get back from life some of what life had taken from me."

"You think it would have been different for you if your real father had lived?"

"Yes, I'm certain of it. My real father was a sensitive man. He didn't have much of a formal education but he had a feeling and appreciation for beautiful things in life—nature, music, poetry. Compared to him, my stepfather was a dumb brute. Jimmy got his musical talent from our mother. When she was married to my father, she sang a lot. She had a beautiful soprano voice. My father played guitar. After she married my stepfather, Mother didn't sing anymore. My stepfather thought music was a dumb waste of time. I wanted to learn a musical instrument. I had inherited my father's guitar. It was the only thing he'd been able to leave me. I begged my stepfather to let me take lessons so I could learn to play it. He said it was a waste of time and money. We had a big row about it one night. He snatched up my Dad's guitar and smashed it to pieces. I . . . I think in that moment I could have killed him—"

Kirk's voice had become harsh. Lilly saw beads of perspiration on his forehead. His eyes had become as hard as polished glass.

He passed his hand over his eyes as if to wipe away an ugly picture. With a trembling hand, he reached for his glass of champagne on the nearby table and quickly downed it. When he spoke again, his voice had lost the cutting edge. "Jimmy was the one with the real musical talent. And he was smarter about dealing with his father. He didn't lock horns with the old man head-on the way I did. He kept his music to himself, getting what he needed at school. By the time the old man found out Jimmy was musical, he'd been playing first trumpet in the school band for several years with a horn the band director provided for him."

Now Lilly understood why Kirk was so jealous of Jimmy's musical ability and why he envied people with artistic, creative talent. His story explained his interest in jazz, his activity in the nightclub business, promoting Jimmy's band and wanting to do the same for Lilly's career. Through them he was vicariously experiencing the creative experience life had denied him.

The conversation and the champagne had lulled her tension. The steel muscles in his thighs under her hips radiated his masculinity. She gradually settled more comfortably against his broad chest.

As he talked, his right hand moved gently over her thighs, caressing the delicate flesh under the gossamer fabric of her gown. His touch awakened an electric tingling throughout her body.

He pressed a button on the table near their chair and the lights in the room dimmed. Soft, romantic music filtered from a wall speaker.

With slow, deliberate movements, he undressed her. As the garments slipped from her body, Lilly's heart pounded. Kirk's face grew flushed. Lilly rose from his lap and moved away from him. She trembled with a fresh wave of shyness but part of the trembling grew from a thrill of knowing that the vision of her body was setting him afire.

Then she caught up her robe, put it back on and tied the sash tightly. "Please stop looking at me," she said, red-faced. "I'm embarrassed."

Kirk smiled. "Modesty is appealing in a woman."

"You're probably used to more sophisticated, liberated women. You must think me very childish."

"Hardly childish," he grinned, pulling her back to his lap. "A bit naïve, perhaps, but that adds to your charm."

That night they came together more fiercely than ever before. Her body writhed, her nails raked his back. His demands of her were urgent, and she met them gladly. She gave vent to her passion with choked cries that were smothered by his kisses.

Dawn was sending soft, pink shafts through the window before their storm of passion subsided. She lay exhausted beside him. He lit a cigar. She watched the coal on its tip move above her in the semi-darkness. Her damp hair rested on his shoulder.

He talked about the house he had bought for them, about the things he had planned for them to do, about the future he had in store for her career.

She felt very secure in his arms. She listened to his voice knowing that no harm from the outside world could befall her as long as she was his wife. The harm would only come from loving him. . . .

Chapter Eleven

$\mathcal{T}$he house Kirk had bought for them was ready for their occupancy the following week.

Lilly was not surprised to find the home located at Pacific Heights in a neighborhood of the most affluent residences in the city. That was Kirk Remington's style. It was one of San Francisco's classic Victorian structures with large, comfortable rooms and bay windows designed to capture the fleeting sunshine as well as afford a sweeping view of San Francisco bay. Nor was she surprised to find a music room furnished with a grand piano. She fell in love with the room at once and knew it would be where she would spend most of her time.

"I'm having my record library and sound system shipped from New Orleans," Kirk told her. "We'll have it installed in this room when it arrives."

That first night in the house, they dined at home.

Kirk had hired an excellent cook. He prepared a delicious meal of freshly caught seafood, a crisp salad and French pastries. Lilly ate slowly, savoring every mouth-watering morsel.

After dinner, Kirk asked her to play the piano.

When she took her place at the beautiful instrument, she glanced toward the great bay window. The view it afforded was spectacular. The entire bay was spread before them. The lights of the Golden Gate Bridge twinkled through a soft, drifting fog. The only light inside the room was the shadowy, golden glow from a lighted candelabrum near the piano.

She began to play, lost in the romantic mood of the setting. Kirk sat in the shadows, sipping a brandy and watching. Although she could not see his eyes, she could sense the burning intensity of his gaze.

It was a tender moment of shared intimacy beyond the limitation of verbal communication. She let her music speak what was in her heart, her love for him, this strange, intense man that was still in part a mystery to her. She poured her heart into her melodies, thanking him for the beautiful home, the room where she could enjoy her music and the exquisite instrument that came alive under her touch. As she played, her music became a prayer, too, that somehow God would work a miracle in Kirk's heart, making him love her the way she loved him, letting a love for her so fill him that Marie Algretto would become a ghost from his past.

An electric tension had grown in the room. Suddenly, Kirk uttered an exclamation, swept her up in his arms and carried her into the bedroom. Her heart pounded with anticipation. Were her prayers being answered? Was Kirk's desire flamed by love, or was it merely physical hunger?

Later, as she rested drowsily in his arms, Kirk said, "I wanted to make sure you're comfortably settled here before I leave."

Her glow of happiness chilled. She frowned. "Leave?"

"Yes, I'm going to be out of the country for about a month. I wish I could take you with me, but much of the time I'm going to be in some areas of the Mideast where the climate is brutal and the political situation is dangerous. If you need anything at all while I'm gone, all you need to do is call my office."

Lilly felt a strange cold draft. This past week, she had been lulled into a feeling of security with Kirk. She had begun to hope that perhaps he did love her and her doubts about marrying him would fade away. Now his announcement brought a fresh concern. Why would he leave on such a long trip only a week after they were married? There was something ominous about this development. Was there more to it than he was telling her?

She said nothing, but her body grew tense. She could tell he sensed her reaction.

"I wish I didn't have to leave at this time," he said. "But I have no choice, Lilly. There are some pretty vital issues at stake that could affect the future of my business."

His explanation did not reassure her. Perhaps it was her imagination, but his words seemed to have a hollow ring. Her skepticism about his motives for marrying her returned in a rush, stronger than ever. He'd gotten what he wanted. He had conquered her, had gotten her to share his bed, even if he'd had to resort to marrying her. With his ego satisfied, he was already growing restless. Getting out of a marriage would be an easy matter for a man with Kirk's money and legal staff.

She was in the same cold frame of mind the next morning when she gave him a cold farewell.

Lilly roamed around the silent house feeling deserted and lonely. That afternoon she decided to visit the nightclub where Jimmy's band would be playing. She had not spoken with Jimmy since they left New Orleans. She missed him and the guys in the band. Perhaps they would be rehearsing.

The nightclub, called The Landing, was located in a colorful waterfront section of the city. Lilly took a cab to the place.

When she walked through the front door, she heard a sound that caused her heart to speed up— the rich, mellow tones of a trumpet. Lilly's high heels tapped swiftly between the tables, which were stacked with up-ended chairs. She felt a lightening of her spirits when she saw Jimmy on the bandstand. The lock of hair that he could never quite control had tumbled over his forehead. A smoking cigarette was clamped in the fingers of his left hand, which held the trumpet, while the fingers of his right hand deftly touched the pearl-covered keys of his instrument. He was running through some warm-up scales.

He finished his exercise, laid his trumpet on the piano, turned, and suddenly caught sight of her. "Lilly!" he exclaimed. He sprang down from the bandstand and walked toward her, his face wreathed in a welcoming grin.

Lilly's heart warmed at the transformation that had come over him. Gone was the look of dull defeat from his eyes. His shoulders were no longer slumped. There was a spring in his step. He was on top of the world again.

"Jimmy!" She reached out both hands and he squeezed them warmly.

"Take a look at you!" he exclaimed, his gaze trailing down her stylish designer garments to her shoes and back to her face. "Just dig them threads! You're dressed up like Mrs. Astor. Old brother Kirk doesn't mind spending a few bucks. Have to give him credit for that."

Lilly blushed. "You're looking terrific, Jimmy."

"Yeah. Feeling just great, Lilly. I'm off the sauce and back in the groove. Hey, just look at this joint, would you? Isn't this something else?" He waved his arm around. "This place makes the Sho-Time Bar in New Orleans look like an upholstered sewer."

"I'll bet the band is excited."

"Are they! We've finally arrived. We're playing just fine, Lilly. Of course we miss the heck out of having you in the band. We found a replacement. The guy is okay, but he hasn't got your spark."

Lilly felt a rush of sadness, but quickly changed the subject. "Are you ready to open Friday night?"

"Why don't you come see for yourself?"

"I fully intend to!"

Jimmy was silent for a moment, growing more serious. "How is everything with you, Lilly? You and Kirk getting along all right? Is he treating you okay?"

"Yes. Everything is fine . . . Kirk is very generous," she murmured, trying to cover up her own misgivings.

"Where is he? He hasn't set foot in this place since we got here."

"He's been busy with a house he bought for us. And . . . today he had to leave on a business trip out of the country."

Jimmy frowned. "He didn't take you with him?"

"No. He had to go to the Mideast. He thinks it would be too dangerous for me. . . ."

Jimmy's face took on a peculiar expression. He started to say something, but changed his mind. "Hey, come up here and tell me what you think of this piano."

Lilly returned to the club opening night. She was thrilled at how good the band sounded. Wistfully, she watched the new piano player, wishing she were in his place. The happy jazz beat had her feet tapping. It made her forget her loneliness and apprehensions about her own life.

She returned to the club for several hours each night. Talking with Jimmy and the band members and listening to them play helped fill the lonely hours while Kirk was away.

Then she came down with a cold. She went to a newsstand, gathering up an armful of light reading material, planning to spend a day in bed, pampering herself. She was comfortably settled with cold remedies and a box of tissues on her bedside table, leafing through the publications, when Kirk's face leaped out at her startled eyes. The publication she was looking at was a tabloid, one of the kind that specialized in scandal stories about celebrities. The full-page picture showed Kirk at a table, dining with a group of people in Milan, Italy. Seated beside him at the table was Marie Algretto! The caption read, "The world's most beautiful opera star dines with American oil tycoon, Kirk Remington. Are the embers of an old flame beginning to stir again?"

Lilly's world came crashing down around her. She stared at the picture for several minutes in numb shock. Kirk's face dissolved as tears began to fill her eyes.

So this was Kirk's "dangerous mission" to the Mideast! They had been married barely a week, and he had to dash off to pursue his lost love again. How foolish Lilly had been to entertain delusions that he might be falling in love with her. How naïve she was!

Cold anger swept through her. Since he left on the trip, Kirk had been having flowers delivered to her every day, and making overseas phone calls to her periodically. What a hypocrite he was! she thought furiously. He wanted to have his cake and eat it. All he needed her for was someone to warm his bed during the times he was in San Francisco. She felt no better than a kept woman, a high-priced call girl.

Well, she wouldn't be here the next time he phoned, and she wouldn't be in this house when he returned from his "business" trip!

Ignoring how miserable her cold was making her feel, Lilly crawled out of bed and began throwing clothes into a suitcase. Kirk had paid for them, but she didn't feel the least bit guilty taking what she needed. He owed her that and much more. When they got to the divorce settlement, she was not going to let him push her around. Then she remembered the papers she had signed in his New Orleans office. "The lousy rat probably had me sign some kind of pre-marital agreement," she fumed. "I don't know what those papers were."

Then she thought angrily that it really didn't matter. She didn't want a dime from Kirk Remington. She just wanted out of his life forever.

She took a cab to a hotel and spent the next few days in bed, nursing her cold, having her meals sent to the room. It was the lowest ebb of her life up to that time. She felt dreadfully ill. She alternated between spells of shivering under thick blankets and burning up with fever. Her state of mind was worse than her physical problems. She was filled with anger one minute and grief the next. Her worst fears had been confirmed. What a fool she had been! Jimmy had warned her that involvement with Kirk would only mean heartbreak for her. All of her instincts had warned her. Well, she reminded herself, she had done it for Jimmy's sake. At least she'd accomplished that much. But she hadn't dreamed it was going to wind up hurting so much. . . .

Lilly was so sick physically and spiritually that her time frame became disoriented. She lost track of time. With the shades drawn, she had no sense of day or night. She didn't know how long she had been in the hotel room. She didn't care if she lived or died.

The spells of high fever added to her confusion. She began having vivid dreams and she didn't know if she was asleep or awake when she dreamed.

In one of the dreams, Kirk strode into the room. He sat on the side of the bed, shaking her. His face was contorted with emotion. He was repeating her name, "Lilly . . . Lilly—"

She brushed her hand across her eyes, trying to make the dream go away. "Leave me alone. . . ." she mumbled.

"You're going to be all right, Lilly," he said gruffly. "I'm going to get you to a hospital."

He picked up the phone, dialed, and barked instructions. She began to realize this wasn't a dream. "What're you doing here?" she muttered.

"I think that's the question I should be asking," he stormed. "Lilly, what possessed you to do this? I've been frantic with worry. I've tried to phone you. The maid said you'd packed some things and moved out without saying where you were going. I flew back yesterday. I've had the police looking for you ever since. We've been to all the hospitals, the morgue, and finally began checking the hotels."

"Didn't want you to find me," Lilly mumbled. Her head was splitting. The high fever was making her groggy. She had the feeling that she was slipping in and out of a dream state.

"Why, for God's sake?" Kirk gasped. "What has gotten into you?"

"I just want out of your life, Kirk. Please go away and leave me alone. . . ."

He gave her a look of mingled frustration and concern. "I'm not going to sit here and argue with you now. You're much too sick. I called Dr. Harrison and he'll meet us at the hospital."

The ambulance arrived in a few minutes. Lilly was taken to the hospital where her condition was diagnosed as severe influenza bordering on pneumonia. She responded quickly to proper medical care.

Kirk had florists bringing in deliveries until her hospital room was transformed into a flower garden. The nurses treated Lilly as if she were something of a celebrity. She supposed being the wife of Kirk Remington had that effect.

Kirk came to visit her as soon as she was feeling stronger. "How are you feeling?"

"Much better," Lilly replied, eyeing him coolly. Her head was clear now. Her fever had abated.

Kirk moved a chair closer to the hospital bed. "Then we can have a talk."

"There's nothing to talk about."

"Oh, yes there is. There's a great deal to talk about. I demand to know what possessed you to run away from our home like that."

"I don't know why it would matter that much to

you." Her voice was as brittle as icicles dropping from a tree limb.

"Don't be childish. Of course it matters a great deal."

"Oh, yes. I suppose it would. In the sense of your swollen ego losing a prize possession. Such as one of your racehorses running off."

He frowned. "That's a callous thing to say."

"No more callous than your marrying me when you didn't love me!" She hesitated, then couldn't resist the impulse to blurt out, "By the way, I really would flunk a geography test. I had no idea that Milan, Italy, had been moved to the Mideast."

He looked at her with a puzzled expression. "Milan, Italy? How did you find out I was in Milan? Is that what got you upset?"

"Not exactly. But you do admit to lying about where you were going."

"I don't admit lying about anything. My trip did take me to the Mideast most of the time. I flew to Milan one weekend to confer with some important business associates. We have a branch office there."

"How convenient. And what a romantic coincidence that Marie Algretto happened to be in Milan that same weekend."

He gave her a long, piercing look. "Now I'm beginning to understand. That photograph in the tabloid. You saw it and jumped to conclusions." He scowled darkly. "I had a hunch that picture was going to wind up in a scandal sheet and cause problems. I'd like to break that photographer's neck! Now let me explain—"

"Oh, Kirk," she sighed wearily, "please don't string me along with a bunch of lies. Why don't we just agree this marriage isn't going to work and call it quits."

Anger exploded in his eyes. He leaped to his feet and

paced the room in furious strides. "I wouldn't be so self-righteous if I were you. I'm the one who has every right to be angry, discovering that you've been seeing Jimmy every night since I've been gone!"

An angry response made her eyes glitter. "You've had a private detective spying on me!" she gasped.

"Oh, stop sounding so melodramatic. You insult me to even suggest I'd stoop to anything like that. I just stopped by the club this morning to check on how the operation was going. In the course of the conversation, my club manager mentioned that you had been there nearly every night since the place opened. You just can't stay away from Jimmy, can you?"

"It's a public club. I can go there if I wish. Do you expect me to sit home and watch television every night when you're away having your romantic fling with your girlfriend?"

"Girlfriend?"

"Your mistress. Your paramour. Marie Algretto. Who else? I must say I can't blame you. She's certainly the most gorgeous woman I've ever seen."

Kirk stood menacingly over the bed. Lilly shrank against the pillows with sudden fright. He looked as if he were on the verge of hitting her or giving her a violent shaking. But then in a strangely controlled voice, he said, "Miss Algretto is acquainted with influential people all over Europe. She happens to be friends with the business associates we have in Milan. Yes, it was a coincidence that she was there the same weekend I was. She came to the cafe with mutual acquaintances. You'll remember, if you saw the picture, that a number of people were seated around the table in our dinner party. I certainly was not at the cafe with Miss Algretto alone."

Lilly did not believe him for one moment. Kirk stepped back from the bed. She gazed at him with troubled eyes that were filling with tears. "Kirk, I should never have married you. It was a mistake to marry anyone under those circumstances. You didn't marry me because you loved me. I don't know why you married me. I suppose because you were lonely. You were heartbroken over Miss Algretto. You were impressed by my musical talent. Jimmy said you had a weakness for talented women. Maybe it has something to do with your own frustrated desire to be able to play an instrument. You can't live your music vicariously through a woman who belongs to you. . . ."

Kirk had moved toward a window as she spoke. His back was to her.

There was a long, painful silence. Then in a strained voice, Lilly asked, "Can you look at me right now and tell me you are in love with me, Kirk?"

The silence lengthened. She gazed through her tears at his back. His lack of an answer to her question was all the answer she needed. Her tears trickled down to her pillow.

"Now do you see why I want to end this marriage?" she choked.

He turned. His dark-eyed gaze engulfed her with a strange expression she couldn't define. At the moment she seemed very distant. There was a great space between them. "I don't think that's the real reason you want to leave me," he said slowly. "I think it's Jimmy. It's been Jimmy all along who stands between us. You never have gotten over your high school crush."

"And you've never gotten over being jealous of him," she shot back. "Maybe *that's* the reason you wanted to marry me, why you're so stubborn about letting me go. You're bitter because Jimmy has the thing you want so badly—his musical ability. You couldn't take that away from him, but you could take me away from him."

"It's not easy for me to forget that you cared so much for him that you agreed to marry me just to be sure I'd help him!"

Lilly had no answer to that. Her pride refused to let her tell him that she could not have agreed to Kirk's bargain if she had not been in love with him. She was in love with him now and always would be, but that didn't change this impossible situation.

Then his eyes flamed with an overpowering intensity. "Lilly, I am not ready to give up this easily on our marriage. And I refuse to let you leave."

"Oh? And how do you propose to stop me? This isn't the nineteenth century, you know, when women were mere chattel."

"How do I propose to stop you? The same way I got you. By reminding you that Jimmy's career depends on me. I could end his engagement at The Landing just as I did when he was at the Sho-Time Bar in New Orleans. He'd be out on the street without a band again. Do you want that?"

"You're the most heartless brute I've ever known!" she gasped, the blood draining from her cheeks.

"Lilly, all I want you to do is be reasonable. We've hardly been married a month. That isn't giving marriage a fair chance. I want to make a deal with you. Give the marriage at least six months. I've tied up the loose ends of my business. I'll be free to devote more time to you. I'm eager to help you with your career. I want to start by booking you into one of the top hotels in Las Vegas. How about it? Will you agree to six months?"

Again Kirk had the upper hand. The episode ended with Lilly agreeing reluctantly to the six months' test of their marriage.

When she was released from the hospital, Kirk announced that he had a surprise for her.

Kirk drove her to the airport with an air of mystery. He watched her face as he led her into a hangar. There sat a beautiful little Beechcraft Sierra. The monoplane was like a silver eagle, impatient to be airborne. A giant red bow had been tied around the tail section. "Remember, I promised you an airplane of your own?" he said.

She realized he had chosen this time to present the gift as an effort to patch things up between them. He couldn't have chosen a better gift.

Lilly was beside herself with excitement. Kirk was obviously happy that the gift pleased her so.

It turned out to be one of the better days of their stormy marriage. Kirk offered to take her up in the plane for her first lesson, an offer she eagerly accepted. The event signalled a temporary truce between them.

Attendants wheeled the plane out to the runway. Its fuel tanks were full and it was checked out and ready to fly. Lilly sat in the left seat. Her gaze trailed over the array of instruments on the panel. Would she ever be able to figure out what they all meant?

Kirk took his place in the pilot's seat beside her. As usual, he brought with him an air of strength and confidence. His strong, suntanned hands tested the controls with practiced skill. He was a man who knew what he was doing.

"Don't worry about all the dials," Kirk said. He pointed to one of the instruments. "For the time being, just concentrate on that one—the altimeter. It tells you how far above sea level you're flying." It had white numbers and a needle pointing to zero.

"First, let's familiarize you with the controls," Kirk went on. "This yoke that looks like a bent steering wheel is called the 'stick.' In the early days of flying, this control actually was shaped like a stick. Turn the wheel from side to side as you do a steering wheel in a car and you move the ailerons. Those are the hinged flaps on the outer trailing edge of the wings. If you look out there, you can see them move as we turn the wheel. They help you keep the plane level in straight flight or tilt the plane when you bank. Go ahead, try it."

Lilly obeyed, delighted with the feel of the control in her hands.

"Okay," Kirk said. "Next move the stick in and out. That controls the elevators, the horizontal flaps on the tail. They direct the plane up or down."

The plane had dual controls. Lilly kept her hands lightly on her set of controls, feeling the movements Kirk demonstrated.

"Now place your feet on those pedals on the floor," Kirk went on. "When your heels are on the floor, you push the pedals in and out with the balls of your feet. That moves the rudder. That is the vertical flap in the tail section. It controls the direction in which the plane is heading.

"When you move your feet up to the top of those floor pedals you have control of the brakes on the wheels," he said. "You operate those brake pedals back and forth the entire time the plane is rolling on the ground to control the direction you're going in, like steering a car on the ground. But you have to use the brakes gingerly. If you stop too suddenly, you'll toss the plane over on its nose."

Finally, he said, "There's one other control that's perhaps the most important of all. I've always said a good pilot can fly with nothing but the throttle. That's a slight exaggeration, but very close to being true. And here it is." Kirk reached for Lilly's hand and placed it on a round knob on the end of a shaft. A peculiar tingling sensation ran up her arm like an electric current, reminding her that despite the bitterness between them, the touch of his strong hand on hers could still awaken a physical response. She gave an involuntary shiver. All of her senses were alive today, her nerve ends keyed up by the excitment of the moment, her desire vulnerable to Kirk's undeniable masculinity.

She pushed the disturbing thoughts and emotions aside, forcing herself to concentrate on Kirk's voice.

"The throttle controls the airplane's power," he was saying. "Push it in for more power, pull it back for less. But do it gently. In fact, everything you do in an airplane, you do carefully, gently. There's no need, except maybe in case of an emergency, for sudden maneuvers.

"All of this probably sounds complicated," he went on, "but it will become an easy routine once you are familiar with it. We'll take one at a time. Today, you'll just concentrate on flying straight and level."

Kirk opened his side window, called "Clear!" in a loud voice, then started the engine. The roar was almost deafening.

"Keep your hands on your set of controls, your feet on the pedals on the floor and just follow through."

"What does that mean?"

"That means let me do the flying. You can feel through your controls what I'm doing over here. They are dual controls, so whatever I move on my side moves on your side, too. That will give you a feeling for the movements I'm going through."

Kirk picked up a microphone from the dash, turned some dials, and spoke into the radio transmitter, asking for permission to taxi. The radio loudspeaker crackled and a voice from the control tower cleared the Beech-craft to go ahead.

The ride was slightly more bumpy than being in a car. Lilly tightened her seat belt as the plane moved to the taxi way. The craft seemed very light and flimsy. The metal covering the frame was thin. The doors were not heavy like car doors.

Kirk stayed to the left of a stripe on the pavement. He steered the plane down several hundred yards of a ribbon-like stretch of blacktop and stopped short of a wide expanse of concrete than ran perpendicular to them.

Lilly kept her hands on the stick, trying to relax her muscles so she could follow through on Kirk's movements without interfering.

His feet moved to the top of the floor pedals, mashing against them hard to set the brakes. He pushed in the throttle and kept his eye on the needle of one of the instruments.

The engine roared. The propeller became a shining circle. The plane vibrated. It seemed suddenly tense and alive, as if eager to be on its way.

"Why are you doing that?" Lilly wanted to know.

"It's a customary check to be sure we have enough power to get us off the ground."

Kirk pulled back on the throttle. The roar of the engine died down. He spoke over the microphone again, asking for permission to take off.

When his request was granted, he eased in the throttle. The plane rumbled merrily onto the runway.

Kirk pushed in the right brake, and the plane swung around and headed down the long strip of pavement.

He shot her a challenging look. "Ready?"

She nodded, every nerve in her body suddenly alive with anticipation.

"Here we go!" He pushed in the throttle, worked the foot pedals back and forth to keep the plane going straight down the runway and called over the sound of the engine, "You'll feel when she's ready to take off. When she lets us know she's ready to leap into the air, I'll pull back gently on the stick. I want you to try and sense that moment, Lilly. Flying is done mostly by feel. The best pilots rely more on themselves than on instruments."

The engine whined, the plane vibrated harder. Lilly felt sure the forward thrust exceeded the pull of gravity. She wasn't sure how she knew, but she could feel the little plane just begging to leap from the ground.

"Now!" she cried.

Kirk pulled back on the stick. Lilly felt the control on her side draw closer to her belly. When the plane jumped into the air, Lilly felt a jolt of exhilaration. Suddenly, they were free of the constraints of the earth. The runway dropped away below them. The landscape around the airport began to appear minuscule. It didn't seem to her that they were pulling away from the earth, but rather that the earth was falling away from them. Gravity clutched at them, mashing them into their seats.

"Pull back on the stick to climb," Kirk said, "but also give it more throttle. Power is the key, remember."

As the plane circled higher and higher, Lilly's spirits soared with it. She adored this little machine. It already had a personality. The engine was singing with joy as the craft flew happily through the sky. She was so entranced by the excitement of the moment and the beauty of the landscape below, that she forgot to keep her hands on the controls.

"Plane heading right at us!" Kirk shouted.

Lilly tore her gaze from the earth, looking frantically ahead of them, cold fright tearing through her. But she saw nothing. "Where?" she gasped.

"Nowhere," Kirk said calmly, ". . . this time. But next time you might not be so lucky. Keep your eyes on the skies ahead of you," he warned. "Flying is not exactly like driving a car. If you have a wreck here, it's a long way to fall. A collision is a disaster. Look in front of you, above, and below you, especially near the airfield. Never rely solely on the air traffic controllers. If you start daydreaming or sightseeing, it could be fatal. A mistake in the air can cost your life, so always depend first on yourself. Understand?"

Lilly nodded.

"Now are you ready to take over the controls for a little straight and level flying?"

"I think so," she replied, with a fresh wave of anticipation.

"Okay. Watch the altimeter. Remember, that's the instrument I said shows your altitude above sea level. We want to stay about 3,000 feet above the ground. Now it's all yours!" He took his hands and feet off the controls, placed Lilly's right hand on the throttle and leaned back in his seat.

Lilly awkwardly fiddled with the stick and the rudder pedals. The needle in the altimeter moved back and forth. First she climbed, then she descended. Try as she might, she could not maintain a consistent altitude.

"Remember, the throttle is the key," Kirk advised. "More power means more altitude. Less power and you lose altitude. Control your flight with a little bit of elevation, but mostly with power. In a car, the more you push in the accelerator, the faster you go. But in an airplane, the faster you go, the more altitude you'll gain, unless you compensate with the controls."

Lilly gently pushed the throttle in a bit and the altimeter began to climb. She pulled back and they descended. She spent several minutes adjusting the throttle before she was able to maintain her altitude for more than a few seconds.

"You're doing fine," Kirk encouraged.

When they were back on the ground, Lilly turned to Kirk. Her eyes were sparkling, her face flushed. "Kirk, how can I thank you for this wonderful gift? I just love this little plane!"

He smiled. "The joy is your eyes is all the thanks I need, Lilly. I'm glad the airplane pleases you."

"It must have cost a lot. You—you have been very generous with me."

He looked at her thoughtfully, appearing pleased by her approval.

True to his promise, Kirk began energetically promoting her musical career. He arranged a booking for her at a prominent Las Vegas hotel where she was an immediate success. One of his companies funded a half hour musical show for public television. The show was built around Lilly. She recorded a song that hit the top charts around the country and was on her way to becoming a star in the entertainment world.

It was an exciting period in her life.

Kirk hired a good instructor to complete her flying lessons. She had a natural feel for flying as she did for music. By the end of the first week she had progressed enough at the controls to solo. Then there were ground school classes to attend, navigation to study, and more flying hours to be logged. Somehow she worked it all into her busy schedule and at the end of two months she had her license. Then she could fly to Las Vegas when she was performing there or simply spend hours in the clouds by herself, escaping the tensions and cares of the world.

Lilly sometimes puzzled over Kirk's interest in her career. Why was he so eager to see her talent recognized? One day she made a discovery that she thought gave her an answer and at the same time a fresh insight into the complex man she had married.

She was spending a week in their San Francisco home between musical engagements when she took some of her things to a storage room in the house where a large cardboard box caught her eyes. Curiosity prompted her to open it. In the box were a number of oil paintings. She took one out, wondering why they had not been hung in the mansion. It was a coastal scene of waves breaking on great rocks. Although she was no expert in such matters, she thought it looked as if it had been painted by an amateur. Then her gaze fell on the signature in a lower corner—"Kirk Remington."

She stared at the name, her eyes widening with shock. Kirk had never mentioned having an interest in painting. She tried to envision Kirk as an artist, but failed. It was more natural to picture him controlling a board of directors' meeting.

She looked over the other paintings in the box. The subject matter was varied, including landscapes, still lifes and portraits.

Then, at the bottom of the stack of paintings, she saw one that drove a stabbing jolt through her heart. It was a figure study, a woman gracefully posed in a garden setting. It was probably the best he had done. Like the others, it had an amateurish quality. But despite the flaws it had obviously been painted with a loving hand. Lilly recognized at once the beautiful woman in the painting. It was Marie Algretto. She was nude.

Lilly stared at the painting. Emotions boiled through her, ranging from anger to heartbreak. This was just one more piece of evidence of how much Kirk had passionately loved the opera singer—and how much he still loved her. If she no longer meant anything to him, he wouldn't keep this painting, would he?

Theirs must have been an intimate relationship for her to have posed nude for the painting. Lilly tortured herself with fantasies about the circumstances of the painting. Had they taken a break from her posing to make love? Had passion shaken his hand as he drank in the sight of the gorgeous woman as he transferred her flawless beauty to the canvass? Hot images burned through Lilly's imagination, sending waves of bitter emotion churning through her.

She sat there for several minutes, engulfed in bitterness and aching jealousy. Then she spent the rest of the afternoon hanging all of the paintings in her bedroom. Angrily, she was planning a surprise for Kirk.

During their evening meal, she forced herself to act in a normal manner toward Kirk. She could tell by the way he was looking at her that he was in a mood for making love that evening.

After dinner, he swept her up in his arms and carried her into her bedroom. He crossed the threshold and suddenly froze. He stared about the room, seeing his canvasses on every wall. Lilly had deliberately highlighted the painting of Marie Algretto with a lamp.

"Where did you get these?" he demanded.

"I found them in the attic by accident."

His expression was dark, angry. "I should have thrown them away long ago."

"I wonder why you didn't?" Lilly murmured, looking pointedly at the nude painting of the opera singer. "Perhaps you couldn't bear to part with them for sentimental reasons."

He crossed the room in quick strides and ripped the paintings from the walls. "They're silly, childish dabblings."

"I'd hardly call them childish. A child wouldn't do a figure study of a nude woman!"

He shot her a dangerous glare.

"When did you paint them?"

"A long time ago. It was a silly whim. As you can plainly see, I have no talent whatsoever as a painter."

"You seemed to have no difficulty getting a model."

The look he gave her was cutting. "I was spending a year in Paris. Marie encouraged me to take painting lessons. After a year, I saw it was a waste of time." Suddenly his voice was bleak with bitterness. "I am simply devoid of talent."

She gave him a narrowed look. "You feel that keenly, don't you, not being able to express yourself creatively through music or painting. . . ."

"Of course. It's like having something vital locked up inside, clamoring for release, but damned forever to be imprisoned. I even tried to write a novel once and failed dismally. So I took my frustrations out on my business enterprises. At least there I am successful."

"It does make some things clear to me," Lilly mused thoughtfully. "I have not been able to understand why you went to such lengths to marry a nobody like me when you could have your pick of beautiful women, and why you have worked so energetically to push my musical career. By possessing me, you came as close as you could to possessing my talent. You want to own me so you can own my music. Through me you realize your frustrated creative desire. Perhaps your money can't buy you talent, but it bought you me, the next best thing!"

"That's ridiculous!" Kirk exclaimed angrily.

"I don't think it's ridiculous at all. By marrying me, trying to possess me body and soul, you are trying to reach through me the thing you crave most in life and are denied. You have everything else a man could want—power, money, position. But deep down under that cold, defensive armor of yours, Kirk Remington, is a frustrated artist. You're like a blind person wanting to use me as your eyes. You've never gotten over the childhood trauma of your stepfather refusing to give you music lessons, then smashing your father's guitar. Now through my fingers you play the piano. Through my voice you sing. Physical desire is a way of making me more a part of you. But love certainly does not enter into it."

Tears were blinding her. She said, "But what a comedown it must be to have me after your relationship with someone like Marie Algretto! She's a world renowned artist, not only more beautiful than I'll ever be, but far above me in the music world. She's a great opera star, a genius, and I'm merely an entertainer, a jazz pianist and a blues singer. You must compare us every time you make love to me!"

Lilly was trembling. Kirk's face was black with anger. The battle of emotions he was trying to contain exploded in his eyes. He quivered with a superhuman effort to gain control of himself. Then, as if not trusting himself to speak, he simply turned and stalked from the room.

Lilly had the ominous premonition that the conflict between them was moving to a climax. Finding this nude painting of Marie Algretto among his possessions was a warning of what was to come.

It was two weeks later that she glanced through a newspaper and saw an item that seized her attention. A dark cloud of despondency settled over her as she read that a traveling opera company was coming to San Francisco to perform *La Traviata*. The tragic role of Violetta Valery would be sung by Marie Algretto.

Chapter Twelve

$\mathcal{A}$s the date drew closer for Marie Algretto's performance in San Francisco, Lilly's feeling of nervous apprehension increased. Surely Kirk and the opera singer would meet while she was in this city. Kirk would find her as irresistible as always.

Lilly couldn't shake the sad conclusion that her marriage to Kirk was approaching an end.

These past weeks, she had felt more hopelessly in love with Kirk than ever. In spite of their quarrels and Kirk's jealousy over Jimmy, Lilly had found a vitality and excitement in sharing life with Kirk that she had never known before. Their lovemaking became more thrilling each time he took her in his arms. His touch never failed to set off a volley of sparks through her nerve endings. One of his dark-eyed looks could reach to the depths of her being and bring a quiver to her entire body.

How she wished he had let her leave him after that

first week when she fled to the hotel. It would have been so much easier then!

She watched Kirk for signs of restlessness and anticipation as the date for Miss Algretto's performance drew near. But he kept his feelings so well under wraps that she couldn't detect anything. Then there was a development that confused and surprised Lilly. A few days before the Algretto performance, Kirk announced that a buisness trip was going to take him to Chicago for a week. He wouldn't be in town for the performance of *La Traviata!*

What did it mean? Lilly's thoughts were scrambled. Was he going out of town because he couldn't trust himself to be in the same city with Marie Algretto? Was he actually going to try that hard to preserve his marriage to Lilly? It awakened a glimmer of hope in her.

That week, Lilly was concluding a dinner club performance in Las Vegas. She slept late the morning following her final performance, spent the day doing some shopping, and late that afternoon flew her little plane back to San Francisco. It was nighttime when she arrived in the city. With Kirk out of town, the house would be empty. She decided to stop off at The Landing to visit Jimmy and the band for a while.

She sat at a small table near the stage, thrilled at how good the band was sounding these days. Every time she heard them they were better. While her own career was doing well, she remembered how exciting it had been to play with Jimmy's jazz band. A part of her wished she could still be a part of the group.

The lights on the band dimmed. The spotlight faded to a single beam focused on Jimmy's golden trumpet. Everything else was in darkness. And then Jimmy played the blues, soft and mellow, summing up in an expression of wry emotion all the misery life could deal to an individual. Lilly forgot everything except the shimmering beauty of Jimmy's music. The real world faded away. The universe became centered on the golden horn in the spot of light surrounded by darkness.

Suddenly, Lilly found herself being drawn magnetically to the stage. She moved beside Jimmy. The spotlight left Jimmy's horn and touched her and she sang one of Bessie Smith's unforgettable blues songs. It welled up mellow and husky, throbbing with emotion from deep in her throat.

When the number ended, there was a moment of hushed silence. Then the audience exploded into wild applause. Lilly heard the band applauding her. She was gazing at Jimmy and he was looking at her with a peculiar expression. Her eyes filled with tears. They were both overwhelmed by the emotion they had generated with the spontaneous performance. It was one of those rare moments that come to artists when they have tapped some deep wellspring of inspiration that puts them close to the source of all creation.

Lilly's feelings became too intense to bear. She fled from the stage and left the club. She took a taxi home, glad that Kirk was out of town. She wanted to spend the rest of the night alone, savoring the afterglow of the evening's musical experience. No matter how much she loved Kirk, tonight's artistic event could only have been shared with Jimmy.

She was lost in reverie as the cab drew near their home. Then she looked up with surprise when she saw a black Mercedes pulling out of their driveway.

It was Kirk's automobile. But he was in Chicago!

Lilly stared with wide-eyed disbelief as the black car sped by the cab.

She caught sight of the driver. There was no mistaking his identity. It was Kirk! He was so engrossed in conversation with his passenger that he didn't even notice Lilly's cab.

Then Lilly's startled gaze swung to Kirk's passenger. She recognized the beautiful woman at once. Lilly had seen her often enough in the tabloid photograph with Kirk, in the painting he had done of her, on television and once in person at a performance in her college town. It was Marie Algretto.

When the cab stopped at her door, Lilly sat frozen, her mind in a turmoil. Obviously, Kirk had either made up the story about going to Chicago or had rushed back several days early. In either case, he had lied to her! He knew she would be performing in Las Vegas this week and didn't expect her back so soon. He had brought the opera star to their home for a secret rendezvous!

Lilly couldn't remember paying the cab driver and stumbling into the house. Through scalding tears, she saw the evidence of Kirk's tête-à-tête with his mistress. Two wine glasses were on the coffee table, one bearing lipstick stains.

Kirk hadn't even bothered to hide the evidence of his infidelity. It was a brutal emotional slap across Lilly's face!

The fragrance of the opera singer's expensive perfume still lingered in the air. It was strongest in the bedroom. Lilly stared at the rumpled bed, the lipstick smears on the pillow case. They had made love in this room, in the bed Lilly had shared with Kirk!

A broken sob tore from her throat. Something ended forever in Lilly's heart. A curtain closed for the final time.

Blindly, she threw some belongings in a small suitcase. This time she was leaving Kirk for good.

She returned to the airport, had her little plane refueled. She filed a flight plan for Las Vegas. At the moment she was too distraught to know what she was going to do.

Without thinking, she had automatically started back to Las Vegas. But once in the air, her mind cleared. Las Vegas would be the first place Kirk would go to look for her. She did not want him to find her, to pressure her into going back to him the way he had the first time she'd left him.

The pattern of Kirk's continuing involvement with Marie Algretto was now agonizingly clear to Lilly. The singer probably had no desire to commit herself to Kirk in any conventional arrangement like marriage. She wanted the freedom to pursue her career wherever it took her. Still, she remained attracted to Kirk. Perhaps he was one of several lovers she had. Whatever the situation, Kirk couldn't get her out of his system. From time to time, they renewed their affair. Between the times they met in various cities of the world, Kirk wanted to keep Lilly on his string to fill the lonely weeks.

She knew she was facing a crossroads in her life. She had done a whole lot to help Jimmy. But she'd reached the end of her rope. It was simply no longer possible to keep up this farce of a marriage. For everyone's sake, and the sake of her own sanity, she wished she could simply disappear.

Suddenly, she faced the fact that she was a fugitive. She was running away from Kirk, from an impossible situation, from her own life. She had no destination in mind. She wished she could stay here in the endless blue sky forever.

She flew over Las Vegas and kept going. The engine hummed smoothly. The tanks were full. The little plane was eager to keep flying.

It was foolhardy to take off blindly across the country, ignoring the flight plan she had filed. But she was controlled by a reckless impulse just to keep running. She had a vague notion of flying back to Louisiana where her life had begun, an instinctive desire to flee to the safety of her childhood. She wanted to go where she could hide forever from Jimmy LaCross, Kirk Remington and the general mess she had made of her young life.

She was over a wild and desolate stretch of desert near the Arizona-New Mexico border when disaster struck. She found herself lost in the dark clouds of an unexpected thunderstorm. Her radio went out. The light plane was tossed around by violent wind gusts. Blinding streaks of lightning flashed around her and played along the wings. Frightened out of her wits, she fought to regain control of the plane. The engine whined. The craft vibrated and shuddered. Suddenly, she was in a deadly stall. Then the nose dropped and the airplane plummeted toward the desert. Panic clamped its icy chill around her heart.

Seconds before the crash, she got control of the airplane enough to bring the nose up. It was all that saved her life. The crash landing destroyed the plane and threw her around like a rag doll. But the wreck could have been worse. She was conscious enough to unbuckle her safety belt and stagger away from the plane which was starting to burn. Bruised, burned, in a state of shock, she collapsed on the sand a hundred yards from the plane. There was a billowing flash as the plane exploded. By nightfall, the remains of the airplane had been reduced to a few smoking metal parts. Already the desert sands were blowing around them, covering them. In a few days, the broken skeleton would be almost totally lost to sight.

The chill of night stirred a glimmer of consciousness in Lilly. An instinct of survival dragged her to her feet and sent her staggering on a long, tortured trek across the barren desert. She had no conscious knowledge of who she was or where she was or how far she walked. Her legs would carry her for a while, then she would lose consciousness again and collapse. Her body was a mass of pain. Her tongue became swollen from thirst, her lips cracked. The next day, the sun scorched her flesh.

It was in that pitiful condition that Henry Brownfeather discovered her not far from the Indian pueblo. She had awakened, not knowing who she was. Her memory lost, she had become Lilly Smith—the woman without a past. There had been the convalescence, when she had been nursed back to health by her new friend, Raven Brownfeather. Dr. Glenn Marshall had come into her life, had taken a personal interest in her. There had been the plastic surgery that gave her a new face, and, finally, the painful, partial return of her memory that had sent her on this trip to Millerdale, Louisiana, in search of her past. Now she was standing before the little frame house where she had been born, coming to grips with the reality of who she was and all that had happened to her up to the moment Henry Brownfeather found her in the desert.

Now she knew why she had been wandering injured and out of her mind on the desert. She had been the victim of a plane crash. The remains of her airplane had never been found because she had crashed in such a remote area. The plane had burned, and what was left had no doubt been largely obscured by the shifting sands.

Now her past had taken its place in her identity. The important people in her past, Jimmy LaCross, Kirk Remington, assumed again their roles in the drama of her life. She knew the story behind the gold locket she wore, and who had given it to her and why it meant so much to her.

The afternoon shadows lengthened as she stood there, reliving the bittersweet memories that added up to everything she was now. She had to become reacquainted with Lilly Parker.

When at last she moved back to her rented car, she felt emotionally exhausted.

That night in a motel room she sat before a vanity, staring at her reflection. She was no longer Lilly Smith, the lady without a past. Now she had a past. She could no longer escape it or who she was.

But as she gazed at her face in the mirror, a shocking realization came to her. The face that gazed back at her was no longer the face of Lilly Parker or the wife of Kirk Remington. The plastic surgery had given her a new face, a new identity. Even her voice was altogether different. The trauma to her vocal chords had left her with a deeper, huskier voice.

As far as the world was concerned, she was a different person. No one from the past could recognize her. Had the fates, regretting the heartbreak she had endured, arranged this accident to give her a fresh, new start?

She was stunned by all the implications. If she wished, she could return to her former life, a different person! No one would know her. As far as Kirk

Remington was concerned, she was dead. If she went back to Jimmy LaCross, he wouldn't know her either. She felt a wave of loneliness for Jimmy. She had no other family. Marriage to Kirk had been a disaster. Would it be possible to rediscover her childhood dream with Jimmy?

It was not often that life gave one a second chance. But did she really want that chance?

The questions pounded through her mind feverishly. She felt both excited and frightened by the options suddenly opening to her.

Before she could make any decision about her future, she knew she must return to Albuquerque. Raven and Glenn Marshall would be worried about her. She must hurry back and break the news of her discovery of her past identity.

With trembling fingers, she reached for the telephone, called the airport and made a reservation for the earliest flight back.

Chapter Thirteen

When Lilly's plane landed in Albuquerque, Dr. Glenn Marshall was at the airport to meet her. She saw his familiar, tall, ungainly figure towering a head above the crowd. A wave of warmth and fondness brought a rush of tears to her eyes.

Catching sight of her, he rushed through the crowd. He was wearing a trench coat that flapped wildly as he walked. As usual, his coat sleeves were too short for his long arms. His tie didn't match his suit. But she was aware only of the way his eyes engulfed her with love and concern. His doctor's worry over a patient was struggling with a more personal involvement.

Lilly had phoned Raven Brownfeather before leaving Louisiana, telling her briefly what had happened. She'd asked Raven to relay the message to Glenn Marshall.

Now as her hands were swallowed by his big grasp,

she blurted out, "Glenn, I got my memory back. Just the way you promised. It's a miracle!"

He studied her face and eyes. "Are you all right, Lilly? How do you feel?"

"Wonderful! A little dazed, but—yes . . . wonderful! Oh, Glenn, you can't imagine what it's like. It's as if a terrible, dull cloud has lifted from my brain and I can think clearly again."

He took her arm. "Let's have some coffee. I want you to tell me everything."

He led her through the crowded airport to a coffee shop where he sought the privacy of a booth. He gave a waitress their order. When steaming cups of coffee were placed before them, Lilly clasped hers, warming her hands that were cold from excitement.

She said, "As soon as I got to Millerdale, memories started coming back to me. Glenn, I drove straight to the house where I was born. I don't know how I knew, I just *knew*. I stood there and I felt as if a door that had been closed in my mind suddenly burst open. I knew who I was and everything that had happened to me before in my life."

He nodded gravely. "It happens that way sometimes. No doubt going back to your hometown, being surrounded by so many familiar sights, was the jolt you had been needing to break the mental block."

He hesitated. There was a moment's silence. He laughed unsteadily. "There are so many questions I want to ask you, I don't know where to begin. I feel as if I were meeting you again for the first time."

"Yes," she nodded thoughtfully. "It's true. I'm not the same person who left here to go back to Louisiana. I was Lilly Smith, then, the woman without a past. Now I am Lilly Parker Remington, and I very definitely have a past."

Glenn Marshall's face grew solemn. "Lilly Parker Remington," he repeated.

"Yes. Mrs. Kirk Remington, Glenn."

A shadow crossed his eyes. "Then you are married. You remember your husband."

She nodded. She had suspected for some time that his interest in her had gone beyond a doctor-patient relationship. Now, she could see the evidence in his eyes. She felt a rush of emotion. She was filled with gratitude and tenderness for this kind man who had restored her health. The last thing she ever wanted was for him to be hurt because of her.

He looked down at his cup. His jaws knotted. He raised the cup for a sip, then put it back down. She saw that his fingers were trembling. "And you know how you came to be lost in the desert?"

"Yes. I was flying a small, private plane. I crashed during a thunderstorm."

"A plane crash!" he exclaimed. "That clears up the mystery. No wonder you were so bruised and burned. It's a miracle you weren't killed."

"A lot of miracles have been happening to me," she nodded.

The doctor consulted his watch. "I have to get back to the hospital. I'll drop you off at Raven's apartment. We have to talk some more. Will it be all right if I come by to see you tonight?"

"Of course, Glenn," she replied

"It's an incredible story," Raven Brownfeather exclaimed, wide-eyed. She was beside Lilly on the couch of her Albuquerque apartment. For the past hour, Lilly had talked without stopping.

"What a shock it must have been to suddenly know who you were—to remember all those painful things about your past." Raven's eyes filled with tears. She clasped Lilly's hand. "I should have been there with you."

"I'm still kind of numb," Lilly admitted. "But I think it was for the best that I went back there alone, Raven. No one can really go with a person when she makes a trip like that back through her past."

The beautiful dark-haired Indian girl said, "All those mysteries about you—who you were, what you were doing out in the desert where my father found you— now they're all cleared up. We imagined all kinds of wild possibilities, that someone might have beaten you up and left you out on the desert to die. I don't think it occurred to any of us that you had been flying your own plane."

Lilly shrugged. "I hadn't dreamed I could fly a plane. But I hadn't known I was a musician either until I happened to sit down at the piano that night I was out with you and Glenn." Then she frowned. "But I wonder why someone didn't find the wreckage of my plane?"

Raven shook her head. "Lilly, that's a totally wild part of the countryside, filled with ravines, arroyos, outcroppings of rocks. It would be like hunting a needle in a haystack. Probably most of the wreckage was covered by the sandstorms that sweep across there regularly. I doubt if it will ever be found. There's no telling how far you strayed from the wreck."

Lilly drew a deep breath. "It really doesn't matter now anyway."

"That's true," Raven agreed. "What does matter is what your plans are now that you know who you are. Are you going to notify your husband?"

A cold shadow darkened Lilly's mind. "I—I don't think I'm ready to deal with that, Raven. It's still too painful. I'm going to have to be a lot stronger before I can face Kirk. Every time I think about that situation, I sense all those bad feelings coming back. My head starts throbbing." She shook her head. "No, I don't want to talk to Kirk yet. When I do, it will be through a lawyer, anyway."

"There's no rush, I suppose—"

"I don't see why there should be. It would be a different matter if Kirk loved me, if we'd had a happy marriage. The first thing I'd want to do would be to rush to a telephone. But Kirk never loved me. By now he's convinced I'm dead. I'd just as soon leave it that way for the time being. Eventually, I'll talk with a lawyer about the situation. He can notify Kirk I'm alive and that I'm filing for a divorce."

"Then you plan to stay here in Albuquerque?"

Lilly hesitated. "No . . . I want to go back to the West Coast and pick up the threads of my life there again, Raven. I think I'd really like to go back and see Jimmy again."

"Jimmy? He's the trumpet player you fell in love with when you were in high school, your husband's brother. . . ."

Lilly nodded.

"Raven, I'm not exactly sure how I feel about Jimmy. You see, for so many years, Jimmy was the only man in my heart. I wore his locket and dreamed that I'd grow up and he'd fall in love with me. Then I went to New Orleans and Kirk, his brother, came into my life and swept me off my feet. I still cared a lot for Jimmy, but Kirk convinced me that what I'd felt for Jimmy was a carry-over from an adolescent crush. Perhaps it was. I guess it wouldn't have mattered one way or another because Jimmy just wasn't the type to commit himself to a serious relationship. He only wanted to blow his horn and have a good time. Jimmy lives for today and to heck with tomorrow. I guess that's one of the things that makes him so lovable."

"Anyway," Lilly continued, "I fell so desperately in love with Kirk that I no longer thought of Jimmy in those terms. I was still as fond of him as ever. Perhaps a part of me still loved him. But Kirk filled my life. If Kirk had loved me in return, there never would have been another man for as long as I lived. But it wasn't me Kirk was in love with," she said sadly. "Now I'm back where I started. I have a strong urge to see Jimmy again. Maybe, with Kirk out of the way, things between Jimmy and me might be different."

Raven rose and went to the little kitchenette where she brewed a pot of tea. She brought the tea with cups and saucers on a tray to the coffee table beside the couch and took a seat again, curling her legs under her.

Lilly sipped the cup of steaming liquid, lost in thought. Finally she broke the silence. "I've been thinking, Raven. . . . I could go back to San Francisco and nobody would know me. The surgery has changed my face completely. I could dye my hair dark."

Raven stared at her in astonishment. "Why would you want to do that?"

"I'd like to see how Jimmy would react. He always thought of me as a little kid he knew in school. He was fond of me, but more the way a brother would be toward a younger sister. What if he met me and I were a totally different woman? Would he feel differently? I'd be safe from Kirk, too. He wouldn't try to make me go back to him by threatening to fire Jimmy. Nobody would know me."

"Then—you're still in love with Jimmy?"

Lilly's hand instinctively moved to the gold locket. "I—I'm not sure, Raven. I do love Jimmy. I always have. But am I *in* love with him? Maybe I would have been if Kirk hadn't come into my life. It's a question I can't answer. But I have this eerie feeling that fate has taken a hand in all this. I'm being offered another chance with Jimmy . . ."

"You mean you'd go back to San Francisco, arrange to meet Jimmy and let him believe you were a total stranger?"

"Yes."

"You don't think he'd recognize you?"

Lilly opened the locket. "Look at my picture, the way I was before the plastic surgery. Then look at me now. What do you think?"

Raven studied the small photograph thoughtfully. "There's a drastic change, no question about it. And with a different hair color . . ." She nodded. "You're right; I doubt if anyone would know you are really Lilly Remington."

There was a moment's silence as Raven chewed her bottom lip thoughtfully. Then she said, "Lilly, you've been through a dreadful experience. Aside from the wreck, the temporary amnesia and the plastic surgery, you had the shock of discovering your husband was still carrying on a long-standing affair with another woman. You must feel rejected, heartbroken and lonely. Is that why you're turning back to Jimmy?"

Lilly sighed. "Perhaps. I—I really don't know, Raven. Maybe that's one reason I want to go back to Jimmy as a different woman. I can hide behind my new identity. It's a kind of protection. As Lilly Parker, all life gave me was heartbreak. I'd like to start all over as a different woman. That may be part of it. But I'd really like to find out how Jimmy would treat me if I were somebody besides little Lilly Parker, the home-town girl he knew like a kid sister. Who knows, maybe

Jimmy would really fall in love with me and want to marry me. Then I'd have a whole new life with Jimmy. Maybe it would be a way of fate making my childhood dreams come true after all."

"All right! Suppose Jimmy did fall in love with you under these circumstances. Could you marry him knowing you were still married to another man? Would you spend the rest of your life masquerading as another woman?"

"Oh, of course I couldn't do that. Eventually, I'd have to tell Jimmy the truth . . . and deal with all those problems when the time came. But right now all I can think of is that life has given me the opportunity to see Jimmy again as often as I like and Kirk can't do anything to stop me. He couldn't try to get me to go back to him on the threat of putting Jimmy's job and band in jeopardy if I refused, because he wouldn't know who I am."

Raven was slowly shaking her head. "It sounds absolutely wild, but I can see you have your mind made up to do this crazy thing!"

Later that evening, she revealed her plans to Glenn Marshall. "I know all this sounds a bit flaky, Glenn, but I want to give it a try."

"But how will you live out there?" Glenn demanded. "If you're no longer drawing on the resources of Kirk Remington's wife, you won't have any money."

"I have a little money in a private account in a San Francisco bank in my maiden name. It's enough to get me back out there and enough for me to live on for a while. Then I can get a job. A pianist with my experience can always find a job in some restaurant or cocktail lounge."

"Well, I suppose I can't talk you out of it," Glenn sighed. Then he took her hands warmly in his. "Just remember, you always have friends here who love you—"

A few days later, Lilly flew to the West Coast. In San Francisco, she learned that Jimmy and his band had gone to Sacramento for the big spring Dixieland jazz festival held in that city, so she took a bus to Sacramento for the Memorial Day weekend.

Sacramento was in a holiday mood to match the happy music filling the streets. Most of the festivities were taking place in "Old Sacramento," a section covering several blocks that had been preserved in its original state. The cobblestone streets, board sidewalks and false-front buildings were relics from the Old West of the last century, when this frontier village had been headquarters for the pony express.

The old section had been blocked off from vehicular traffic so sightseers and jazz fans could fill the streets. Shuttle busses, running every ten minutes, transported visitors from the main section of the city.

Many of the spectators added their personal touch of color by dressing in costumes suited to the mood of traditional jazz. Lilly, caught up in the excitement of the jazz celebration combined with her own personal anticipation of seeing Jimmy again, fell into an exuberant, uninhibited mood. In a costume shop she found a red, fringed, "roaring twenties" Charleston dress.

Before leaving Albuquerque, she had died her hair chestnut and had had it restyled. When she tried on the red, fringed dress, she stood before a full-length mirror, filled with amazement at the stranger who gazed back at her. She still had not grown accustomed to the astounding change in her appearance, a change that had become even more dramatic by her turning into a brunette. The plastic surgery had changed the shape of her eyes, giving them a slightly exotic, oriental shape. But she was aware of changes that went deeper than the surface; the shock and trauma she had been through in the past months had given her a new maturity and sense of destiny.

But this was a time and place to put aside the dark thoughts of the past weeks. The jaunty Charleston dress put her in a daring mood. She held onto the feeling as she caught a shuttle bus and joined a crowd of happy jazz fans wearing their Sacramento Jazz Jubilee emblems.

The musical carnival began with a parade down the main street of Old Sacramento. Afterward, the jazz bands would perform on mobile stages in the streets as well as at the Delta Queen Courtyard, Freeway Gardens, the Firehouse Courtyard, and dozens of other restaurants, bars, clubs and outdoor stages. There would be a flood of music from early morning until long past midnight.

Lilly stood on the curb, joy bubbling up in her at the beat of the happy music coming down the street. A high-spirited jazz aficionado in a derby hat, holding a pink parasol, cavorted in front of the first truckload of musicians who rolled along the street playing *Muskrat Ramble*. Some groups like the Resurrection Jazz Band came marching along in traditional New Orleans style. Another group was perched on a fire truck.

Suddenly, Lilly's attention funneled to a flatbed truck in the parade. Everything else was shut out. Across the truck was a red, fringed banner with foot-high gold letters spelling out "The Jimmy LaCross Jazz Band." And there was Jimmy himself, standing high and proud, playing as he'd never played before. He tilted his horn toward the blue sky. The sun glinted on the golden bell of his trumpet as he blew his notes right up to the angels.

Around her, Lilly heard the crowd go wild, applauding furiously as Jimmy passed them. Her heart filled to the bursting point with pride and love. It was obvious that Jimmy was making a big name for himself in West Coast jazz circles. Everyone seemed to know him. According to the program, his band was one of the headliners at the Jubilee.

Suddenly the sacrifices she had made for Jimmy became worthwhile. He wouldn't be enjoying this success if it were not for her. Even if no one else knew that, she knew it, and it filled her with a sense of worth.

More than thirty jazz bands, some as far away as Germany, England and Japan, would be playing for the throngs of Dixieland jazz fans during the festival weekend. But Lilly was concerned with only one. She consulted her Jazz Jubilee program, marking the locations where Jimmy's band would perform.

His first performance was on a stage at an outdoor restaurant patio that afternoon. Lilly was there early, securing a seat at a table directly in front of the bandstand. She felt a singing thrill of excitement inside. When Jimmy arrived, her heart gave a thump.

Once, as the band was assembling on the stage, Jimmy glanced in her direction. He looked again, staring straight at her. Lilly's heart pounded. Had he seen through her masquerade?

But he turned to the band, and she breathed more easily.

His group started with a rollicking performance of *The Dixieland One-Step.* The crowd responded with unrestrained enthusiasm. It was a time to discard inhibitions and hang loose. People were clapping to the beat, dancing between the tables.

Lilly was swept up in the joy of the moment. For the first time since the crash of her small plane, she was able to shake off the dark cloud of worry and depression. Happiness bubbled through her veins. She felt reckless and daring. The happy, infectious rhythm of the Dixieland jazz was a tonic for the soul. Impulsively, she jumped to her feet. Her "roaring twenties" dress was made for dancing. When she did an impromptu Charleston step, she heard laughter and applause around her, urging her on.

The jazz number came to a rousing climax and ended. She realized the band, too, was applauding her dance. Suddenly red-faced with mortification, she sat down. What had possessed her to suddenly become such an exhibitionist?

But the band quickly romped into another happy tune, and Lilly's wave of self-consciousness evaporated. Her heart filled and tears blurred her eyes as she watched the sidemen on the band that she'd grown so fond of: Skinny Lang strumming his banjo, Cemetery Wilson playing his driving style drums, lifting and carrying the band, Charlie Neal's fingers racing over the keys of his clarinet, and short, tubby Ted Riley, bouncing around the stage as the slide of his trombone pumped out vigorous tailgate glissandos.

In front of them all stood her childhood hero, Jimmy LaCross, searing the air with the cutting edge of his brilliant, high notes.

When the group concluded their performance, Jimmy stepped down from the stage and walked directly over to Lilly's table. Again she froze.

"Hi," Jimmy grinned with the easy warmth he had with people.

Lilly touched her tongue to her lips. "Hello," she murmured.

"That was neat Charleston. You're quite a dancer."

She swallowed hard. Her cheeks felt warm. "I got carried away by the music. You're—you're very good."

He smiled again. "You're a jazz fan?"

She nodded.

"We have some record albums on sale over at the record shop if you're interested."

"Yes—I am. I'll—I'll buy one and get you to autograph it for me."

"Sure." He was staring at her again in a way that made her uneasy. "Have I seen you before somewhere?"

"N—no. I don't think so."

"Funny. There's something kind of familiar about you . . . but I can't put my finger on it. Guess I'm mistaken. Are you going to be here for the weekend?"

"Yes."

"Maybe you'll hear us again. We're playing tonight at the Firehouse Courtyard. Bring that record album around and I'll autograph it for you."

"I will," she promised.

He smiled, winked and walked off into the crowd, whistling. He was instantly surrounded by fans, cut off from her view.

She let her breath out, feeling her tense body relax. Jimmy hadn't recognized her! The masquerade was working. But he was interested in her . . . in the new version of Lilly Parker!

She went straight to the record shop. She was delighted to find that Jimmy's dreams were coming true. He was becoming recognized. His band was being invited to jazz festivals. They were starting to record.

214

He was becoming well known on the West Coast. Obviously, his career had flourished during the time she'd been gone.

She bought the albums. That night she was again seated in the front row at his second concert. Afterward, she took the albums backstage. "Remember me?" she asked, when she found him.

"Sure," he chuckled. "The lady Charleston dancer. Hey, I see you bought our albums."

"Yes." She held them out, her gaze lingering on his face, growing soft and tender. Her love for Jimmy swept over her in a shimmering, golden wave of emotion. It was a reprise of the exact feeling she'd had when she was a tongue-tied little school girl, and he had fastened the gold locket around her neck. How stunned he would be if he knew that same locket was hiding under her clothing at this very minute!

He took out a pen. "How do you want me to autograph these? What's your name?"

She was prepared for this moment. She gave him the name she planned to use as part of her masquerade, "Billie Smith."

"Billie Smith," he repeated, and signed the albums, "To Billie Smith With Love, Jimmy LaCross."

When he handed them back, he asked, "Where do you live, Billie?"

"San Francisco."

He grinned. "That's cool. We have a steady gig at The Landing. Maybe that's where I've seen you."

"No," she murmured. "But maybe I'll come hear you there sometime."

"You do that, for sure. Promise?"

"You can count on it," she assured him.

Her plan was working, she thought with heart-quickening excitement. Jimmy hadn't recognized her. And he was looking at her with definite male interest. She didn't think her new face was as pretty as the one belonging to Lilly Parker before the accident. But evidently it was attractive enough to catch his attention. Would he fall in love with her new face—with "Billie Smith?"

After the exciting weekend in Sacramento, she returned to San Francisco. She had rented a room there. It was a modest place, a far cry from the luxurious Victorian mansion she had shared with Kirk Remington. But she was satisfied and comfortable enough. The ceilings were high, the closet spacious. And the bay window looked down on the trolley car track. All during the day, she could hear the cheerful jangle of bells as the cable cars rumbled past under her window.

After she was settled, she wrote long letters to Raven and Glenn Marshall. To Raven, she confided her feelings about seeing Jimmy again. She described the Sacramento jazz concerts, and the thrill of coming face to face with Jimmy LaCross. "My masquerade is working!" she wrote. "Jimmy didn't recognize me. Now I plan to visit The Landing, where he's playing. I plan to do a little subtle flirting! Pray for me, Raven. . . ."

To Glenn Marshall, she wrote, "I'm happy and comfortable in my new quarters here. I have enough reserve so money is not an immediate problem. But I plan to start looking for work before it gets to be a problem!"

She had success almost immediately in that area. Before the first week was over, she had auditioned for a job at a piano bar at a businessmen's dinner club that had recently opened. She would play from seven-thirty to eleven-thirty in the evening with Sunday and Monday nights off. Since Jimmy's band played until one A.M., she could hurry over to The Landing any night when she got off work to catch the last hour of his performance.

She used her new name, Billie Smith, at her job. The name was on a placard at the entrance to the cocktail lounge. "Billie Smith at the Piano."

When the matter of supporting herself was taken care of, she made plans to see Jimmy again. Her strategy required a suitable dress. She spent a day shopping and decided on a red knit that was ideal for a brunette in the chilly San Francisco climate. The fabric was soft and lustrous. The design was classic and could be dressed up or down depending upon the occasion. It was a pullover dress with a ruffled edge around a "V" neckline and surplice front. The shirred, drop-front shoulders joined long sleeves with ruffled, elasticized wrists.

The dress made her feel utterly feminine. She stared at her reflection in the fitting room mirror with a sense of unreality. As difficult as it had been for her to adjust to the new appearance of her face, living as a brunette after being a blonde all her life was equally difficult. However, she had to admit that the darker hair went well with the new, slightly oriental slant of her eyes.

That night she caught a cab to The Landing when she finished her stint at the piano. It happened to be a slow night and she was able to find a table not far from the band. But it soon became obvious that Jimmy was not going to see her. She had to make herself more obvious. The chance didn't come until the band played its closing theme for the evening. Jimmy left the stand and stopped at the bar for a nightcap.

Lilly gathered her courage and moved to where he was sitting. "Good evening, Mr. LaCross," she murmured.

He turned. "Hi." For a moment his face was blank. Then he exclaimed, "Hey, you're the Charleston dancer." He grinned.

As usual, when she was near him, warmth stole through her heart. "So you remembered me."

"Sure. Are you kidding? A neat-looking chick like you? Why wouldn't I remember? How did you like the records?"

"Fine."

He glanced over her shoulder. "You, ah—here with a date?"

"No," she said, looking directly at him.

He grinned again. "What's the matter with the guys in this city? How did they overlook you?"

She smiled, growing warmer at the obvious interest he was showing.

Jimmy said, "Well, under the circumstances, how about having a drink with me, then?"

"All right."

She took a seat beside him.

He ordered a drink, then turned to her, giving her a thoughtful look again. "I've been trying to think where I saw you before. It's been bugging me ever since I met you in Sacramento. Are you certain we never met before?"

She looked down at her drink. "Certain," she murmured. "You're mistaken, Mr. LaCross."

"Hey. All my friends call me Jimmy."

"All right—Jimmy."

"Let me see, you're—"

"Billie Smith."

"Sure. I remember now."

They chatted over the drinks. Lilly was amused at the obvious line Jimmy was handing her. He hadn't changed since high school. He still radiated charm, as irresistible as ever. The Irish would say he had kissed the Blarney Stone.

Of course, it was the way he charmed all the girls. When she had been Lilly Parker, Jimmy had treated her with a kind of amused, protective air. Now, she was like one of the pep squad leaders who rode around their home town in his convertible. He found her attractive. She was a target for his appeal.

Jimmy . . . Jimmy, her heart smiled, *you don't have to work overtime to charm me. I succumbed to you a long time ago. All you have to do is ask and I'll say yes.*

Yes to what? Once before, in New Orleans, she had been ready to invite him into her room. But she had been more cautious then. She had been afraid to trust herself to him. She had wanted something more permanent than she thought Jimmy could give her. Kirk had offered her that—marriage. And look what it had gotten her!

Now she was bitter and disillusioned. Nothing was permanent. If Jimmy wanted her, she was in a reckless mood to live only for the moment. Perhaps in Jimmy's arms, she would forget the heartbreak Kirk had brought to her life.

When the club closed, Jimmy took her to her rooming house in a cab. On her doorstep, he kissed her.

She slipped her arm around his neck. "Don't rush me, please, Jimmy? I have fallen for you in a big way. But give me just a little more time. Okay?"

For a moment he looked frustrated, but then fell back on his easygoing, cheerful manner. "Okay. So I'll play it cool." He kissed her again.

She closed her eyes, enjoying the warmth of his kiss,

being held. . . . When the kiss ended, she reached up and brushed back the unruly lock of hair from his forehead. "I've been wanting to do that for a long time," she whispered.

He gave her a puzzled look. "What do you mean, a 'long time'?"

"Never mind. You wouldn't understand."

He continued to look puzzled. "You're a strange little chick. But you've sure got me turned on."

He kissed her again and his hand moved up to cup her breast. She put her fingers over his hand. She let him caress her for a moment and felt a poignant sweetness, being close to him. She closed her eyes, swaying closer, feeling the warmth of his body.

But then, something intruded. A pair of dark, probing eyes flashed into her mind. Suddenly, Kirk's face was there, as clear as if he were standing between them.

A shiver ran through her body. She pulled away from Jimmy. "Good night, Jimmy," she whispered and fled up the stairs to her room.

Long after she had gone to bed, she stared up at the dark ceiling, her emotions in confused disarray. She was furious at herself for allowing the memory of Kirk to intrude that way. She owed no loyalty to Kirk. She hated him!

She had made the decision when Jimmy asked to drive her home, to sleep with him tonight. This was to have been the start of a new Lilly Parker. Her face was different. Her voice was different. She had a new name. And there was going to be a different man in her life. She intended to erase the memory of Kirk Remington from her existence.

Was he going to continue to haunt her forever?

She rolled over and pounded her fist into her pillow with mingled frustration and anger.

The following night, she went to work at the usual time. This was a club that catered to business executives. Often they came here to relax after a board meeting or to sit in a corner and discuss a business deal. For the most part, they ignored her. She was just part of the setting. She didn't have to contend with the kinds of drunks who often hung around piano bars.

Tonight, as she played, she became conscious of one of the men in a group seated at a table. He was staring at her. When she glanced in his direction, her fingers turned to ice. She saw an olive complexion, heavy eyebrows, a pair of jet black eyes that drove searing rays into the depths of her being.

The man staring at her was Kirk Remington.

Chapter Fourteen

*H*e suddenly rose and headed straight for the piano bar. Lilly became stiff with consternation. Had he recognized her? What would she say? She was not emotionally prepared for a confrontation with Kirk. Where he was concerned her emotions were still too raw.

He took a seat at the bar, placing his drink before him. She felt his gaze fixed on her.

She fought a terrified impulse to leap up and run out of the room. What had possessed her to take a job at a club frequented by business executives? She should have considered the possibility that Kirk would come here. The anonymity afforded by a big city had made her too complacent.

She used all of her willpower to continue playing. She tried to convince herself, *Jimmy didn't recognize you. There is no reason why Kirk should unless you panic and give yourself away.*

She glanced up, catching sight of her reflection in a

mirror behind the room's main bar. She tried to gain reassurance from the face that stared back at her. It was not the face of Kirk's wife, she assured herself. He couldn't possibly see through her masquerade, and yet he continued to stare at her.

She finished the melody she was playing. Kirk spoke to her. "Miss, may I make a request?"

"Y—yes."

"Do you know the Moonlight Sonata?"

Of course she did, but she dared not play it. It had been Kirk's favorite, those nights she had played for him when they were living together. The association would be too strong, the risk too great. It might be the clue that would make him see through her masquerade and recognize her identity.

"No," she murmured. "I'm sorry. I don't know it. Is there anything else you'd like to hear?" She avoided looking at him, gazing instead at her fingers that roamed nervously over the keyboard.

"No. Whatever you want to play is fine. You're very good."

"Thank you," she mumbled.

He sat at the bar for the next two hours. He didn't make any more requests or speak to her again. He just sat there listening, lost in his own thoughts.

It was the worst two hours of her lifetime. She went home that night a nervous wreck. She had wondered how she would react if she ever saw Kirk again. Now she knew. All the emotions she had buried awoke in a raging storm—hurt, anger, jealousy . . . and bitter heartbreak.

She prayed he would not return the next night, but he did. This time he made no effort to speak to her. He just sat there in brooding silence, listening to her play, drinking steadily.

Before the evening was over, she had made up her mind that she would have to give the club owner her notice and try to find a job someplace else. But Kirk did not come back the following night.

Lilly regained an uneasy peace of mind. But she couldn't feel totally secure. Kirk often had to fly out of town on business. Was that the reason he hadn't returned to the club on the third night? Would he come back again when his business was completed and he returned to San Francisco?

Jimmy called, asking her to meet him again one night when his band finished playing for the evening. She was so unnerved, she put him off until the weekend. By then Kirk had not come back. She relaxed enough to meet Jimmy again.

On Sunday, Lilly experienced a spell of loneliness. She needed to talk with a friend, and her best friend was hundreds of miles away in Albuquerque. She decided to phone Raven.

"Lilly!" Raven cried when she heard her voice. "Gee, it's good to hear you. I got your letter, but it didn't tell me a whole lot. I've been hoping every day to get a longer letter from you."

"I really feel guilty about that," Lilly apologized humbly. "Raven, I've been selfish, I know. But so much has been happening, I couldn't seem to get my thoughts organized to write a letter. I guess I'm not very good at letter writing anyway. That's why I decided to phone instead."

"I'm so glad you did! How are you? I guess you know Glenn Marshall has called me every day wanting to know if I've heard from you again."

"Please tell him I'm fine. My health is entirely back to normal. I have plenty of energy to walk up these San

Francisco hills. And the cool temperature out here is invigorating."

"He'll be glad to hear that. Be sure and keep on taking your vitamins. You don't have any more of those headaches do you?"

"I haven't had a single one since my memory returned."

Lilly spent a few minutes telling her friend about her new living quarters and the job she'd found.

Then she said, "Raven, I told you in my letter I'd seen Jimmy in Sacramento where his band was playing at a big jazz festival."

"Did he suspect who you were?"

"No! My masquerade worked! He told me I reminded him of someone, but he never suspected my identity. As far as Jimmy is concerned, I'm a new person, a woman he has just met."

"It's incredible! Lilly, I can't believe you're pulling something like this off."

"Well, I am. I've seen him again at the nightclub in San Francisco where he's playing, and we're becoming friends. It's a whole new relationship, starting from scratch. His attitude toward me is entirely different now. Before, he seemed to have some kind of hang-up that he should treat me like I was his kid sister. Maybe it was because we knew each other too well, growing up in the same hometown, going to school together—and he was so much older when we were in high school. Or, maybe it wasn't that at all. Maybe I just didn't turn him on when I was Lilly Parker. Maybe I wasn't sexy enough for him or something, or the chemistry between us wasn't right. It's different now that I'm 'Billie Smith.' He's definitely *interested*." Lilly giggled. "Maybe I'm sexier as a brunette."

Raven laughed with her. "Well, I have to hand it to you, Lilly. It's the wildest scheme I've ever heard of, but I guess I have to admit you knew what you were doing. At least it's apparently working out for you."

Lilly grew serious. "Well, yes, and no. . . ."

There was a moment's silence. Then Lilly said, "Raven, I'm going to tell you something shocking. The last thing I'd expected to happen—Kirk showed up at the club where I'm working."

"Oh, Lilly!" Raven exclaimed. "Did he recognize you?"

"I don't think so. He didn't give any indication that he did. But I was frightened out of my wits. And he came back again the following night. He sat at the bar, listening to me play. He just looked at me. He's hardly spoken to me."

"You must be under a terrible strain."

"Well, yes. I was petrified. But Raven, I don't know what I'm afraid of. Kirk isn't a physical threat to me. Even if he discovered who I am, what could he do? Nothing, really. He can't force me to go back to him. And Jimmy's future is secure, now. He has a large following out here on the West Coast. He's making records. He's being invited to play at the big jazz festivals. Even if Kirk found out that I'm back and that I'm seeing Jimmy, he can't hurt Jimmy any more. If he fired Jimmy from the club he owns, Jimmy has become so popular, he'd have no trouble finding another job for his band.

"So why did I come so unglued when Kirk walked back into my life? I can't explain it to you when I don't fully understand myself. My mind goes haywire where Kirk Remington is concerned. My emotions turn into a hurricane. I can't think straight when he's in the same room. Any kind of response to him that I've ever had has been a violent one. I can have plans for my life all neatly lined up, and then Kirk can scatter things in all directions.

"Anyway, I'm probably worried needlessly. Kirk sat right there at the piano bar, not three feet from me, for two nights last week and showed no sign of recognizing me. If I can stay cool and not give myself away, there's no more reason for him to recognize me than anyone else could. After all, Jimmy has known me since school days, and he didn't catch on, so why should Kirk?"

"Still, it's putting a dreadful strain on you, Lilly. And that isn't good for you. After all you've been through, you don't want to risk a relapse, now that you've just gotten your strength and health back."

They chatted a while longer. Before ending the conversation Lilly asked Raven to call Glenn Marshall and assure him that she was fine and would write him a long letter—a promise she kept as soon as she hung up.

Chapter Fifteen

Lilly was beginning to relax at her job, again. Monday, Tuesday and Wednesday nights passed without Kirk putting in an appearance. "He's not coming back," she assured herself. And then on Thursday night, shortly after she began playing, she glanced up and he was there.

She looked away with a sharp intake of her breath as he slid onto a bar stool. A couple was seated on the other side to her left. She concentrated on them, playing several requests for them. Then they left. It was a slow night. A few customers were at the main bar and seated at tables. But Kirk was the only customer seated at the piano bar. Lilly realized it would only arouse his suspicions if she ignored him. She forced herself to look at him with a professional smile. "Hello," she heard herself say in a calm voice that belied her inner turmoil. "Haven't seen you for a while."

"I know. I wasn't going to come back. I tried, but I couldn't stay away. . . ."

She laughed uneasily. "I'm not that good, surely. There are many better piano players in town."

"Oh, you're good all right," he said in a strange voice. "But that's not the only reason I had to come back." He hesitated. "I'm sure an attractive young woman like you, being an entertainer at a piano bar, must hear this line many times. But the truth is, you remind me very much of someone I once knew. Someone very important to me."

A quality in his voice compelled her to look more directly at him. It was the first time she'd allowed her gaze to linger on his face. She realized with a shock that he did not look well. He had lost weight. His face was drawn and lined, his eyes lacked the bright, cold glint that had made her think of black agates. They appeared dulled, vacant. He looked like a man who had suffered a long illness.

Disconcerted, she jerked her gaze away, turning her eyes downward toward the piano keys. "Who—who do I remind you of," she asked, forcing her voice to sound light, "an old girlfriend?"

"No," he said quietly. "My wife. She's dead."

"Oh . . . I—I'm sorry," Lilly stammered. Now she was disoriented with a new wave of emotion. Was this the same man who had ruthlessly blackmailed her into his bed? She couldn't believe he was capable of feeling remorse over losing her. Surely she was mistaken.

But out of the corner of her eye, she saw him raise his glass and his hand was trembling. She had never known Kirk to drink to excess. A glass or two of champagne, perhaps a dinner wine, or an after dinner brandy. But he had been too obsessed with being in control of himself and life to ever allow alcohol to control him. Yet, the nights she'd seen him here, he gave every evidence of a man drinking beyond his capacity.

"What . . . was your wife like?" she asked, her fingers rippling the keys in an automatic improvisation.

"She was a pianist, too. An excellent musician. There is a remarkable resemblance . . . you could be a close relative. I was in a state of shock that first night when I saw you playing here. It's nonsense, I know, but I thought for a moment I was seeing her ghost. She had blonde hair, though, and on closer look, I saw that your features are different, and your voice isn't the same. Perhaps you've heard of her, being a musician yourself. She was becoming pretty well known when—when we lost her. She used her professional name, Lilly Parker, when she performed."

Lilly swallowed hard. She shook her head. "I never heard of her, but I haven't been on the West Coast very long."

"She was a fine jazz pianist. And a singer. She was a little thing, your size, but could she belt out those blues numbers! She had learned all the songs recorded by the great blues singers like Bessie Smith and Billie Holiday."

Lilly had the unnerving sensation that she had lost touch with reality. She couldn't be sitting here with Kirk Remington, discussing herself in the past tense! It must be a dream. Cold chills were starting to creep up her spine. Kirk was actually making her feel like a ghost.

Then she reminded herself that she had no one to blame for this impossible situation but herself. She had put herself in this position with her reckless masquerade!

"It—it sounds as if you know something about music," Lilly murmured.

"Well, I don't know if I could go so far as to call myself a critic," he replied. "But I am acquainted with music, both serious and jazz. I suppose you could call me a student of music, or a serious aficionado. It was my passion for music that attracted me to my wife in the first place."

It sure was, Lilly thought grimly. *And that's why you married me—to possess my musical talent. That's all you cared about, Kirk Remington! Someone to keep you company when you weren't with your mistress, someone to vicariously fulfill your creative hunger.*

Remembering that and remembering his unfaithfulness, his affair with Marie Algretto, rekindled the hatred that had driven Lilly away from him.

But he went on in a quiet, dull voice. "The reason I requested the *Moonlight Sonata* that first night I heard you play was because it was my favorite melody from my wife's repertoire."

Again Lilly felt a peculiar shock. It strained her credulity to believe Kirk could exhibit any kind of sentimentality over her. Yet he sounded like a man genuinely lost in grief. She was growing more confused and unsure of her own emotions.

She was relieved when some other customers moved over to the piano bar. Playing their requests afforded her the opportunity to regain her composure.

But Kirk remained at the piano bar, and when it was time for her break, he spoke to her again. "Would you be so kind as to join me at a table for a drink, Miss Smith?"

The sense of unreality swept over her again. Where was the imperious note of command she was so used to hearing in Kirk's voice? He sounded weary, almost humble.

Her first impulse was to make an excuse and flee to the women's lounge. But this new element in Kirk's personality was intriguing. She was drawn by curiosity to hear him talk some more. And she felt more confident of her disguised identity.

She accepted his invitation. Kirk escorted her to a quiet table in a secluded corner. She ordered a cup of coffee. He had a refill of his double Scotch. The heavy way he was drinking had her puzzled and strangely concerned.

"What part of the country are you from, Miss Smith?" he asked.

"New Mexico—Albuquerque," she said.

"Is Billie Smith your real name, or a professional name?"

"Why do you ask?" she countered, suddenly wary.

"Forgive me. I didn't mean to be giving you the third degree. It's just that you remind me so much of Lilly, my wife, that I wondered if by some freak coincidence you were related to her. She didn't have any immediate relatives that I knew of, but I thought you might be a cousin. She came from a little town in Louisiana, Millerdale. But I'm sure you would have known if you had a relative like Lilly. I realize people don't have to be related to resemble one another. It's quite common to run into 'look-alikes.' I once had a business associate who was a dead ringer for Walter Cronkite. People were always coming up to him on the street and asking for his autograph."

Lilly smiled. "Well, I don't have any relatives in Louisiana."

Kirk nodded. "It's such a coincidence that you also play piano. My wife was exceptionally talented. She had perfect pitch, and was remarkably adept at sight reading as well. She knew many of the classical compositions as well as jazz. She could play Chopin or Debussy, and turn right around and play a Scott Joplin rag. Being a musician, you no doubt are familiar with Bix Beiderbecke, the legendary jazz cornettist. Not everyone knows he also played piano and composed. Not many jazz pianists can play his compositions, *In a Mist* and *Candlelight,* but Lilly knew them well."

Lilly thought she should be flattered, but instead felt the old anger returning. "Apparently," she said dryly, "her musical ability was the thing most important to you."

The irony in her voice seemed to escape him. He stared into his glass with a brooding expression, then downed the drink. "It's odd that you should say that," he sighed heavily. "She accused me of that very thing. I don't think she ever quite understood. For someone as untalented as myself, she was someone extremely special, far closer to the Gods than I could aspire to being. I was almost in reverence of her talent. But to be completely truthful," he nodded sadly, "I know now it's true. That's exactly why I did want her in the first place. She was like a rare jewel that I had to own. Beautiful women are not difficult to find. I could have had my pick. But to find one with her incredible talent as well as her beauty and physical appeal—that comes to a man only once in a lifetime. It wasn't until later—too late, I'm sorry to say—that I realized how much I loved her."

Lilly's fingers holding the cup of coffee suddenly trembled. She quickly put the cup down and hid her hands in her lap. She stared at him. "You—loved her?" she asked in a dazed voice.

"Certainly," he said, frowning angrily. "You don't

think I'd still be grieving if I hadn't loved her, do you? I lost her months ago, but I miss her more every day that passes."

Lilly was unable to speak. Her emotions had suddenly been up-ended. She stared at Kirk Remington, making a supreme effort to marshal her dazed thoughts.

"What do you mean, you realized too late?" she stammered.

"To be honest, I'm not sure I was in love with her when we first married. I was getting over an unhappy love affair. As for Lilly—well, there was another man in her life. My own brother, to be exact. She had known him long before she met me. I doubted that she ever loved me the way she did him. I was quite angry and jealous over their relationship. In any case, the longer we were together, the more precious Lilly became to me. But when I finally realized how much I did love her, I lost her before I could tell her." He laughed ruefully. "And here I am, telling you, a stranger, the things I couldn't tell the woman I loved. But that's human nature, isn't it? Sometimes we can say things to strangers that we can't bring ourselves to say to those closest to ourselves—"

He suddenly broke off. He placed his empty glass on the table with a sharp click. "I hope you'll forgive me for unloading all this personal garbage on you, Miss Smith. You can blame it on the drinks. I'm normally a very private person."

"That's—all right," she said. Never in her wildest imagination had she believed she could feel any compassion for Kirk Remington. But now her bitterness toward him was fading as her heart reacted with sympathy. He was obviously a tortured man. Her mind and emotions were in a tailspin.

"I suppose you've had drunks crying on your shoulder before, Miss Smith," he apologized. "It must go with the territory of being a pianist in a cocktail lounge—kind of like a bartender who listens to everyone's troubles. I apologize for becoming so maudlin, but I do thank you for listening. It helps to talk with someone. I usually keep my feelings to myself. Seeing someone who resembled my wife so much brought it all to the surface, I guess."

"It's all right," she murmured. "But it is time for me to go back to work—"

"Of course!" He pulled himself together with an effort, and again became the polished, restrained gentleman, escorting her back to the piano with smooth, good manners.

That night, Lilly spent sleepless hours replaying the conversation in her mind. *Kirk was in love with her.* It was incredible! She hadn't believed him capable of any emotion.

Her own reaction to his surprising revelation was hard for her to analyze. She felt confused, bewildered. For so long, the only feeling she had had toward Kirk Remington was anger and bitterness. Now, suddenly, her attitude was no longer so clearly defined. Things were no longer simply black and white.

Kirk had become a far more complex man than she had ever suspected. When she was living with him, she believed she had understood what motivated him. She had seen him as a cold, ruthless man driven by the need for power. She had been convinced that he was incapable of feeling any love or tenderness for her.

Had losing her changed him so drastically? Or had she not fully understood him before?

The next night, she found herself almost hoping he would return. She felt a need that she didn't fully understand, to talk with him some more, to hear him express his feelings. For some reason, she needed to have more input. She needed to sort this new development of feelings out. She felt confused and bewildered. He had succeeded in throwing her life off course. He was good at that! She remembered what she had told Raven Brownfeather, "I can have plans for my life all neatly lined up, and then Kirk can scatter things in all directions."

He added to her distraught state by not coming back to the lounge for several nights. Jimmy LaCross called her, but she made an excuse not to go with him. She didn't want to see Jimmy again until she got some things about Kirk straightened out in her mind. Being with Jimmy under these circumstances would only add to her confusion.

On Friday, Kirk appeared in the lounge again. Seeing him, Lilly felt conflicting emotions storm through her. As he approached the piano, something inside her trembled.

He took his usual seat. Lilly glanced up, forcing a smile. He nodded, his brooding eyes engulfing her. For a tense moment, she was unable to tear her gaze away. His look searched deeply, touching deep recesses of her being with a vibrant intensity.

Finally, she brought her gaze back to the keyboard. She felt almost too weak to press the keys. What was this unearthly power the man had over her? After all the grief he had put her through, that black-eyed look of his could still turn her world upside down!

He didn't speak to her until her first break. Then, as she was leaving the piano, he moved to her side. "Miss Smith . . . Billie . . . could I speak to you for just a moment?"

"Y—Yes."

"After the way I carried on the last time, I wouldn't blame you if you'd prefer not to have any more to do with me. But I have found the courage in spite of that, to ask if I could see you sometime when you're not working?"

She stared at him, wide-eyed, playing his words over in her mind. He had spoken in his characteristic, formal manner, each word precisely enunciated. Yet she had difficulty in grasping the full meaning.

She felt a hysterical impulse to giggle. The situation was totally bizarre. Without realizing it, he was asking his "dead wife" for a date! But she was more disturbed than amused.

She did want to see him again! This masquerade of hers was getting out of hand. If he was truly as grief-stricken as he appeared, then she was going to have problems with her own guilt. She needed to spend some time with him, to gain a better measure of his true feelings—and hers—in the light of this new development. She might as well be candid with herself. No matter how bitter she had been toward him, they were married, they had lived together. It wasn't possible to be that intimate with another person and not leave something of yourself behind.

She nodded slowly. "I have this Sunday off. The club will be closed that night. . . ."

For the first time, she saw a flicker of light in his dulled eyes. "Suppose I pick you up Sunday morning and we drive to Muir Woods for a picnic. It should be very pleasant there this time of the year. We could spend the day."

"All right." She gave him her address.

From that time until Sunday morning, her emotions

were a battleground. She spent part of the time berating herself for accepting the invitation, and part of the time being glad she had agreed to go with him.

Sunday morning dawned unusually warm and sunny for San Francisco. Perhaps, she hoped, it was a good omen. It would be a warm drive, so she dressed casually in shorts, a blouse and sandals.

He called for her promptly at ten o'clock. He was wearing tan slacks and a white sport shirt open at the collar. The shimmering white material was a stark contrast against his olive complexion. The open throat of the shirt revealed a glimpse of the tightly curled black hair on his chest.

Her gaze was pulled to the masculine contours of his body outlined by the tight fitting slacks. She remembered the nights their bodies had been clasped in passionate love-making, and a hot flush spread up her cheeks.

"We're going to have a beautiful drive," he commented as he escorted her out to his Mercedes sports coupe parked at the curb with the wheels cut to prevent its rolling down the steep grade. "I'm going to leave the top down if that's all right with you."

"That will be fine. I've brought a scarf for my hair."

He opened her door. When she was in the car, he walked around to the driver's side and slid behind the steering wheel. "I'm glad to see you're prepared for a warm drive," he said, his gaze straying to her bare legs.

She felt a prickling sensation ripple through her body. She remembered, with a sudden quickening of her pulse, those times they had been so good with each other.

The Golden Gate bridge was nestled in a pocket of fog, its cables dissolving in the mist. Lilly shivered with the chill of the damp air. But then they had crossed the bridge and emerged in the sunlight.

From here, past Sausalito and into the hills north of San Francisco, they were bathed in the rays of a bright, warm sun. They exchanged only a few words. Lilly settled against the cushions of the expensive car, enjoying the smooth ride. It was the first time she had gone for a long drive with Kirk. He handled the car with the same sure skill as he flew a plane. Her eyes strayed to his strong, capable hands gripping the wheel. She remembered that she always felt secure from the dangers of the world when she was with him. No matter what might befall them, he was the type who could handle anything or anybody.

The final lap of the journey took them through winding, corkscrew turns, down to the valley where the redwood forest was located, a 550-acre national monument on the southwest corner of Mount Tamalpais. They entered Muir Woods. Lilly gazed up at the breathtaking grandeur of the enormous redwoods whose lofty spires reached for the clouds.

"It's awesome," she gasped. "I feel like I'm in a cathedral built by the hand of God."

"Very well put," he nodded. "This is certainly grander than anything we poor mortals could devise."

He stopped the car in a designated parking area. When he switched off his engine, the silence of the great forest fell upon them, the hush broken only by an occasional bird's call. The noise, pollution and stress of the civilized world became a bad dream in another existence. Sunlight glittered through a canopy of leaves that kept most of the forest floor in deep, cool shade. Clear, cold streams played soft music through the lush undergrowth of these ancient woods.

Picnicking was not allowed in the national park, so they went to a nearby park area where they found a secluded corner. Kirk took a picnic basket from the car and spread the lunch he had brought. Lilly was not surprised to find a gourmet meal that included cold wine, caviar, imported cheeses and French pastries. Kirk had a way of doing these things with style.

"Hungry?" he asked.

"Starved," she nodded.

Kirk ate sparingly, watching her enjoy the lunch.

"I'm afraid I'm being a glutton," she apologized. "But I don't care. It's all so delicious. And these beautiful surroundings are wonderful for the appetite."

"I'm pleased that you're enjoying yourself." He sipped a glass of wine, leaning on his elbow in the grass as he gazed at the wall of trees. He seemed to be looking through them, lost in thought. Then he brought his attention back to her. "Billie, I want to thank you for giving me your company for today. I've been leading something of a reclusive existence since I lost my wife."

"But surely your wife would want you to go on living." She couldn't restrain the edge that crept into her voice. "I'm sure you must have another romantic interest to console you."

He frowned. "Why would you say that?"

She shrugged, realizing she was treading on dangerous ground. Making an effort to stifle her jealous anger, she said, "You're an extremely attractive man. There must be other women in your life." She hesitated, but couldn't resist another probe. "How about the broken romance you mentioned, the one you were getting over when you met your wife?"

Kirk waved his hand impatiently. "That was over a long time ago."

Lilly stared at him, now totally baffled. How could he possibly dismiss his involvement with Marie Algretto so lightly? There would be no reason for him to lie, since he believed Billie to be a total stranger. Lilly was becoming even more confused.

To cover her turmoil, she changed the subject. "What happened to your wife?"

"She disappeared while flying her private plane. She had filed a flight plan to Las Vegas, but she never arrived. We think she went down somewhere in the desert. There's some wild country and mountains in Nevada. A plane could crash in a remote area and never be found. There were search parties, but the wreckage was never located. . . ."

He sighed. A sudden wrenching pain crossed his face. "I bought her that plane, encouraged her interest in flying. I have trouble forgiving myself for that."

"But if she died in a plane crash, it was an accident. It wasn't your fault."

The shadows in his eyes deepened. "Well, there's another factor. Something happened that night that I fear might have caused her to rush away from home and could have played a part in her accident." He hesitated. "I've gone this far. Do you want to hear the rest of it?"

She shrugged. "If you feel like talking about it," she murmured, making a supreme effort to hide her personal involvement in a subject that was wrenching violently at her heart.

"Have you ever heard of Marie Algretto?"

"The opera singer? Yes, of course." Lilly swallowed hard and hid her gaze from him.

"She was the woman in my life before I met Lilly. It was over between Marie and me, but I could never convince my wife of that. I could hardly blame her. A scandal sheet tabloid printed a picture of Marie at a cafe with me in Italy when I was there on a business trip. It was totally innocent. She just happened to arrive with mutual acquaintances. But my wife saw the picture and was convinced I was continuing the affair with Marie.

"Marie was scheduled to appear in an opera in San Francisco. That week, I had to fly to Chicago on business and Lilly was performing in Las Vegas. I finished my business earlier than I'd anticipated and returned to San Francisco. That same day, Marie Algretto had arrived in the city. Even though our romance had ended long before, we were civilized people who remained friends. She was having some difficulty with her hotel accommodations. She was exhausted from her flight and suffering from a migraine headache. Some construction work was going on in her hotel. It was impossible for her to get any rest under those noisy conditions. She was terribly upset, knowing she had a difficult performance ahead of her that night. She knew I was living in San Francisco and phoned me at my office. She explained her plight. I suppose it was not very wise of me, but on an impulse, I invited her to go to our home to rest and freshen up before her performance. After all, Lilly was in Las Vegas and I was at my office downtown. It just seemed like an act of hospitality—almost an act of mercy—for an old friend, and altogether innocent. I called home and instructed the maid to let Marie in when she arrived.

"I was at my office until late that evening. I drove home in time to have a drink with her and chat for a few minutes, then I drove her to her performance.

"As near as I can reconstruct it, Lilly came back from Las Vegas that same evening. The maid said Lilly came home but left again very shortly, taking a suitcase. The maid said my wife appeared to have been crying and was obviously upset. The airport records show she had her plane refueled, filed a flight plan back to Las Vegas and took off close to midnight.

"Now I have to believe that Lilly found out Miss Algretto had been at the house with me and had jumped to entirely the wrong conclusions, thinking I'd had some kind of romantic encounter with an old flame in our home. In that emotional state, she might not have concentrated on her flying. That could have been a factor in her crash. So you can see why I feel so guilty. Why else would Lilly have turned right around and rushed back to Las Vegas in the middle of the night?"

His voice sounded gray with fatigue when he finished talking.

He fell into a brooding silence. Lilly was struggling with thoughts and emotions that cascaded through her being like a thundering waterfall.

Was Kirk telling the truth? Had Lilly been that mistaken all along? Had his affair with Marie Algretto really been over before he married Lilly? Was the opera singer's visit to their San Francisco home completely innocent?

He must be telling the truth, she thought with stunning force. He might lie to Lilly Parker. But there was no reason to lie to Billie Smith, a stranger!

"It—it wasn't very smart of you to invite an old girlfriend into your home," Lilly exclaimed.

"No it wasn't," he admitted. "I really didn't think much about it at the time. I was embroiled in some complex business matters at the office that day Miss Algretto phoned me. She sounded desolate. She was exhausted and had a splitting headache and was facing an important performance that night. She really need-ed a place to relax for a few hours. It seemed the only hospitable thing I could do was offer my home. It was an impulse I later regretted. But you see, if there had been the kind of trust that should exist between a man and wife, the situation wouldn't have caused Lilly to rush off blindly into the night. Our marriage just wasn't on sound footing. She believed I was still carrying on an affair with Miss Algretto. I had reason to believe she was still in love with my younger brother. I suppose the marriage was doomed from the beginning. A marriage without mutual love and trust can't endure."

He suddenly sighed and sat erect, looking at her with a different expression. "Billie, I don't know what to say to you. First I get half drunk at the piano bar where you're playing and cry on your shoulder. Then, after you're gracious enough to go on this picnic with me, I sit here spilling my guts and using up the afternoon talking about my deceased wife. You must think I am the most outrageous boor on the face of the earth."

She touched her tongue to her lips, unable to meet his eyes. She was sitting on the grass, her chin resting on her knees. Fighting back her own tears, she said, "I don't mind. I—I had the feeling you needed to talk with someone."

"I did, very much. It might make you feel better to know that you're the first person I've met in months I've been able to talk with like this. Now, why don't we get off this morbid subject and talk about you for a change. I'd really like to know you better."

"Oh, there isn't anything to tell. I'm a very ordinary person," she said. She made a desperate effort to gather her confused thoughts, to put together some kind of believable story about herself. "I grew up in Albuquerque, went to school, took some music lessons, and started playing professionally. Nothing very exciting."

"Any men in your life?"

Again, she quickly thumbed through her mental files to come up with material for the fictional life she was leading. "Only one," she murmured, thinking of Jimmy.

"Is it serious?"

She shrugged. "I . . . doubt anything will come of it."

He was looking directly at her. "For selfish reasons, I'm glad to hear that. I'll be frank, Billie. And I hope this won't frighten you off. But since meeting you, for the first time since my wife's death, I think I could become involved with a woman again."

Panic flashed red lights in her mind. She suddenly jumped to her feet, brushing leaves from her shorts and legs. "Why don't we take a hike through the woods while there's still light?"

"All right."

There were six miles of trails they could follow to explore the woods. Bridges over Redwood Creek in the heart of the forest provided loops in the paths.

As they walked, Lilly contemplated all Kirk had revealed about his love for her. She held the words close to her heart, reaching out to understand the relationship of her life to this new development.

In this setting of tranquility and quiet dignity, with the stately trees soaring as much as two hundred forty feet into the sky above her, Lilly felt she had been transported to a remote existence. She was aware of the tall, strong man beside her in a totally new context. She sensed a kind of shimmering about her, the pulse of the universe, and she realized with a sense of awe that they were very close to the heartbeat of creation.

Kirk talked about the woods as they explored the paths. It was a community of plants: red alder, western azaleas and tan oak, all dominated by the redwoods. California laurels were bent and curved in graceful forms as they grew from shade to sunlight. Ferns were thick in the rich, humus soil. The most common fern was the evergreen sword fern. The lady fern grew along the banks of the stream while western bracken thrived in the dark shadows of the dense forest. Western gray squirrels and Sonoma chipmunks scurried across clearings. Birds fluttered through the branches.

Lilly became aware of holding hands with Kirk as they strolled along the forest trail.

At one point in the deep and secluded area, Kirk paused. Lilly turned and gazed up at him. Nothing was said. They simply stood looking at one another, seeing the forest reflected in each other's eyes, sensing the depth and awareness of life surrounding them like an aura. Lilly felt no conscious thought, only a deep sense of truth and life flowing through her like a river that spread out into the vast ocean of the universe. The life in her flowed through her fingers to Kirk, and his life's essence flowed back. They were both touched by the pulse of creation deep within them.

The understanding that flowed between them reached beyond the limitation of verbal communication.

Silently, they returned to the car. Night was falling when they crossed the Golden Gate Bridge. The lights of San Francisco sparkled in a gathering mist. A penetrating chill reminded Lilly that she was not dressed for a San Francisco evening. But the strange mood that gripped her separated her sense of identity from her physical being.

She saw the outlines of a familiar structure and realized that Kirk had brought her home to the Victorian mansion where she had lived with him as his wife when she had been Lilly Remington.

In the house, he placed logs in a fireplace. Soon a crackling blaze was sending its dancing glow across the room.

Kirk brought snifters of Napoleon brandy. He touched his glass to hers, his dark eyes searching hers with the smoldering fever she remembered when he was physically aroused.

Lilly sipped the liquid, relishing the warmth it spread through her body.

Idly, she wandered through a doorway into the next room—the music room where she had played the grand piano so often. She gazed through the French doors at the lights of the city, the hazy shape of the Golden Gate Bridge that was rapidly being swallowed by the fog.

She sensed Kirk behind her, felt the warmth of his body.

He suddenly turned her to face him. He uttered a choked exclamation and his mouth found hers.

Flames exploded inside her. Trembling, she responded. Her lips parted. She drank deeply of the kiss, letting herself go with the moment. Life flowed through her veins.

His fingers, trembling with passion, opened her blouse, cupped her quivering breasts. Her flesh burned under his touch.

He opened the buttons on her shorts. His palms slid along soft, yielding curves.

It was a sudden, overwhelming eruption of passion between them. In another moment, she knew she would be on the thick carpet, naked, a willing partner locked in his embrace.

But with the same suddenness that he had kissed her,

he thrust her away from him. He buried his face in his hands and sank into a chair, sobbing.

Lilly closed her blouse, staring at him, more shocked by his emotional breakdown than anything she had before experienced with him. The strong, ruthless, cold Kirk Remington, shedding tears? She must be dreaming!

Then her dazed ears heard him say in a choked voice, "How can you ever forgive me, Billie? I was about to use you. I haven't had a woman since my wife died. I haven't had the desire. To be frank, I doubted if I could function as a man if I were to be with another woman. But I suppose the physical need has been stored up in me even though my mind rejected it. When you came along, resembling my wife so much, I thought I could close my eyes and make love to you, pretending you were Lilly. But I can't do it. It's a rotten thing to do to you. And I am still not capable of being intimate with another woman while the memory of Lilly is so strong. I can't shake the feeling that I'd be unfaithful to her. It's irrational, I know—but it's true. . . ."

Lilly didn't know what to say. She was close to tears, herself.

Then, quietly, she picked up her handbag and turned to the French doors. She opened them and stepped out onto the balcony. She welcomed the damp chill. It cooled her feverish body and cleared her mind.

She opened her handbag and groped in it. Her fingers touched the gold locket Jimmy had given her. She thought that it was not easy to give up a dream that had lived in her heart for so many years. But at last she had outgrown the dream. She knew that she had fallen in love with Jimmy when she was a young girl. There is nothing quite so precious as a first love. She had clung to that first love through the years, refusing to see reality for the dream. A dream is often more beautiful than real life. But one cannot dream forever. The dream had already begun to fade when she came back as a different person and had gone out with Jimmy. She had dreamed so long of the moment when he would kiss her, but when that moment came, something was missing. She had dreamed of giving herself to Jimmy, of sleeping in his arms, but when the opportunity came, she had backed away from it because she was still too much in love with Kirk.

As the dream faded, her vision of Jimmy had cleared, and now she must accept the truth about him. He was a wonderfully talented boy who would never grow up. He would forever be riding down Main Street with a convertible full of pretty girls. He would never make a lasting commitment to anyone. He had been her hero for so long, it hurt to admit the truth—that Jimmy LaCross had no real substance. He was the football hero, the cowboy, the band leader in every girl's dream life. He was born to laugh his way through life, playing his horn. Life would ask no more of him, for the world needed people like Jimmy to remind them of their dreams.

"Play it pretty for the people, Jimmy," Lilly whispered, a tear trickling down her cheek. "Blow your horn for the angels to hear, and love all the pretty girls, for that's what you were meant to do. I'll always keep a special, private place in my heart for you, because you were my first love. But now it's time for me to grow up."

She held the locket clasped tightly in her fingers for a moment, then she thew it into the night.

She groped in her bag again and found the simple gold wedding band that she had kept when she sold her other jewelry in Albuquerque. She slipped it on her ring finger, then she turned and went back into the house.

Kirk was still sitting slumped in the chair. She gazed at him, knowing she loved him as an adult. She knew how very much she had loved him from the very beginning or she could never have surrendered herself to his lovemaking with such passion. Now she knew beyond a doubt that he loved her. There was no longer anything to keep them apart except her masquerade. And she was ready to take off her mask.

"Kirk," she said softly, "please brace yourself. I am about to tell you something astounding. And when you get over the shock, we will love each other forever."

She squeezed his hand and sat at the piano. Her fingers moved over the keys as she began to play the *Moonlight Sonata*.

Silhouette Special Edition

MORE ROMANCE FOR
A SPECIAL WAY TO RELAX

$1.95 each

1 ☐ TERMS OF SURRENDER Dailey
2 ☐ INTIMATE STRANGERS Hastings
3 ☐ MEXICAN RHAPSODY Dixon
4 ☐ VALAQUEZ BRIDE Vitek
5 ☐ PARADISE POSTPONED Converse
6 ☐ SEARCH FOR A NEW DAWN Douglass
7 ☐ SILVER MIST Stanford
8 ☐ KEYS TO DANIEL'S HOUSE Halston
9 ☐ ALL OUR TOMORROWS Baxter
10 ☐ TEXAS ROSE Thiels
11 ☐ LOVE IS SURRENDER Thornton
12 ☐ NEVER GIVE YOUR HEART Sinclair
13 ☐ BITTER VICTORY Beckman
14 ☐ EYE OF THE HURRICANE Keene
15 ☐ DANGEROUS MAGIC James
16 ☐ MAYAN MOON Carr
17 ☐ SO MANY TOMORROWS John
18 ☐ A WOMAN'S PLACE Hamilton
19 ☐ DECEMBER'S WINE Shaw
20 ☐ NORTHERN LIGHTS Musgrave
21 ☐ ROUGH DIAMOND Hastings
22 ☐ ALL THAT GLITTERS Howard
23 ☐ LOVE'S GOLDEN SHADOW Charles
24 ☐ GAMBLE OF DESIRE Dixon
25 ☐ TEARS AND RED ROSES Hardy
26 ☐ A FLIGHT OF SWALLOWS Scott
27 ☐ A MAN WITH DOUBTS Wisdom

28 ☐ THE FLAMING TREE Ripy
29 ☐ YEARNING OF ANGELS Bergen
30 ☐ BRIDE IN BARBADOS Stephens
31 ☐ TEARS OF YESTERDAY Baxter
32 ☐ A TIME TO LOVE Douglass
33 ☐ HEATHER'S SONG Palmer
34 ☐ MIXED BLESSING Sinclair
35 ☐ STORMY CHALLENGE James
36 ☐ FOXFIRE LIGHT Dailey
37 ☐ MAGNOLIA MOON Stanford
38 ☐ WEB OF PASSION John
39 ☐ AUTUMN HARVEST Milan
40 ☐ HEARTSTORM Converse
41 ☐ COLLISION COURSE Halston
42 ☐ PROUD VINTAGE Drummond
43 ☐ ALL SHE EVER WANTED Shaw
44 ☐ SUMMER MAGIC Eden
45 ☐ LOVE'S TENDER TRIAL Charles
46 ☐ AN INDEPENDENT WIFE Howard
47 ☐ PRIDE'S POSSESSION Stephens
48 ☐ LOVE HAS ITS REASONS Ferrell
49 ☐ A MATTER OF TIME Hastings
50 ☐ FINDERS KEEPERS Browning
51 ☐ STORMY AFFAIR Trent
52 ☐ DESIGNED FOR LOVE Sinclair
53 ☐ GODDESS OF THE MOON Thomas
54 ☐ THORNE'S WAY Hohl

Silhouette Special Edition

MORE ROMANCE FOR
A SPECIAL WAY TO RELAX

LOOK FOR *SEASON OF SEDUCTION*
BY ABRA TAYLOR AVAILABLE IN FEBRUARY
AND *AN ACT OF LOVE* BY BROOKE HASTINGS
IN MARCH.

Coming Next Month

After The Rain by Linda Shaw
One man had already hurt Patrice Harrows
and she was not yet ready to trust Madison Brannen. But
there was one thing the lady lawyer couldn't argue away:
her love for him.

Castles In The Air by Tracy Sinclair
Mike Sutherland was determined to buy Morgan
Construction but the owner, Sam Morgan, to his surprise
was a woman—all woman—and equally
determined not to sell!

Sorrel Sunset by Gena Dalton
Dynah Renfro and Reed Harlan struck a bargain
to be co-owners of a race horse . . . but Reed soon had full
ownership of Dynah's heart and her future.

Traces Of Dreams by Jane Clare
Art historian Pia Martell and photographer
Jules d'Archachon seemed made for each other. Would
love be strong enough to hold them together when
jealousy threatened to tear them apart?

Moonstruck by Christine Skillern
Until Caroline Conal set sail with Jake St. Simon she had
never known real work—or real love. Beneath the starry
Pacific sky they lost themselves in a love without regrets.

Night Music by Kathryn Belmont
Carla Santucci tried to remind herself that Harrington
Bates was her boss—but on one special evening she saw a
side of him that refused to leave her memory.

Silhouette Desire
15-Day Trial Offer

A new romance series
that explores
contemporary relationships
in exciting detail

Six Silhouette Desire romances, free for 15 days!
We'll send you six new Silhouette Desire romances
to look over for 15 days, absolutely free! If you decide
not to keep the books, return them and owe nothing.

Six books a month, free home delivery. If you like
Silhouette Desire romances as much as we think you
will, keep them and return your payment with the
invoice. Then we will send you six new books every
month to preview, just as soon as they are published.
You pay only for the books you decide to keep, and
you never pay postage and handling.

READERS' COMMENTS ON SILHOUETTE SPECIAL EDITIONS: